TO SNARE A BARBARIAN . . . !

As he felt the leather thongs coil serpentlike around his ankle, Conan flung himself backward, away from the cliff. With his sword still at his waist, he had both hands free to break his fall.

The Cimmerian landed, rolled, then lashed out with his feet. The savage lunge of powerful legs snapped the thongs like twine before Kalk could draw his steel. The sergeant's blade was still coming clear when Conan's feet lashed out again.

This time one boot drove against Kalk's knee . . .

The Adventures of Conan
Published by Tor Books

Conan the Bold by John Maddox Roberts
Conan the Champion by John Maddox Roberts
Conan the Defender by Robert Jordan
Conan the Defiant by Steve Perry
Conan the Destroyer by Robert Jordan
Conan the Fearless by Steve Perry
Conan the Formidable by Steve Perry
Conan the Free Lance by Steve Perry
Conan the Great by Leonard Carpenter
Conan the Guardian by Roland Green
Conan the Hero by Leonard Carpenter
Conan the Indomitable by Steve Perry
Conan the Invincible by Robert Jordan
Conan the Magnificent by Robert Jordan
Conan the Marauder by John Maddox Roberts
Conan the Outcast by Leonard Carpenter
Conan the Raider by Leonard Carpenter
Conan the Renegade by Leonard Carpenter
Conan the Rogue by John Maddox Roberts
Conan the Triumphant by Robert Jordan
Conan the Unconquered by Robert Jordan
Conan the Valiant by Roland Green
Conan the Valorous by John Maddox Roberts
Conan the Victorious by Robert Jordan
Conan the Warlord by Leonard Carpenter

CONAN
THE RELENTLESS

BY

ROLAND GREEN

A TOM DOHERTY ASSOCIATES BOOK
NEW YORK

CONAN THE RELENTLESS

A Tor Book
Published by Tom Doherty Associates, Inc.
175 Fifth Ave.
New York, N.Y. 10010

Cover art by Ken Kelly

ISBN: 0-812-50962-5

First edition: April 1992

Printed in the United States of America

0 9 8 7 6 5 4 3 2

To the memory of Robert Adams,
who buckled a pretty good swash too.

PROLOGUE

Night in the wilderness of the Border Kingdom was not only the absence of light. Darkness was a presence in itself, which reached out to suck a man in until he could never return to the world of light.

In that darkness, the man who called himself Lord Aybas awoke slowly and reluctantly. In another life, under another name, he had been fit to drink and wench until dawn tinted the sky, then rise to do a day's work.

Now he was older. His name was different. The chief he obeyed was likewise different, and was harsher than any Aybas had served back in Aquilonia. Also, it was more often than not an uneasy sleep Aybas had here in the wilderness, on beds of cut branches or piled reeds, or even of leaves strewn on the sullen rock of the mountains.

Yet the true reason for Aybas's slow awakening lay elsewhere. It was a sound that he heard, riding the night wind as harshly as a troop of cavalry in a stone courtyard. He knew what followed on the heels of this sound. If he could sleep, he would not hear it and memories of what he heard would not trouble his dreams.

The sound grew louder. It was not a roar, or a growl, or a hiss, or a rumble like that of a great grindstone hard at work. It had something of all of these in it, but more that was its own.

It also had much in it that was not of the lawful earth or of any of its gods. Called on to put a name to these unearthly sounds, Aybas might have called them slobberings, or suckings.

He would also have prayed not to be asked to tell more. He could not, without revealing that he knew what those sounds meant. That was knowledge cursed alike by gods and men, neither of whom seemed to care much what happened in this wilderness.

At last Aybas threw off his sheepskin and stood. He would not sleep again tonight, unless the cause of the sounds did. The wizards might send it back to sleep, or at least silence it before dawn. They might also keep it awake and at its work until the sun shone even into the deepest parts of the gorge and the valley.

Even if he could sleep through the grisly uproar, it would not be an untroubled sleep. He had seen too much of what those sounds meant to ever forget any of it. Aybas's memories of what he had seen since he came among the Pougoi tribe would die only with him.

Even if it would cleanse his mind, death was not something he sought. To avoid it, he had fled his native Aquilonia, changed his name, sold sword, honor, and everything else for which he could find a buyer, to end here in the Border Kingdom.

In tales told to Aquilonian children, the Border Kingdom was next to Stygia as a place where anything might happen, little of it clean or lawful. Aybas had long since learned that too much truth lay behind the tales told of Stygia. He was now learning the same about of those told of the Border Kingdom.

Boards creaked as Aybas walked to the door of his hut. Like most of the huts in the village, it was built on a slope so steep that one side had to be braced by entire tree trunks. Otherwise, anything left on the hut floor would roll merrily down to the low side. One fine night the hut itself might even leap wildly down the hill to its ruin.

The door also creaked as it opened on leather hinges, letting Aybas into the main street of the village. The street was actually a flight of steps, some carved from the rock itself, others rough-hewn planks pegged in place. What level ground the tribe called its own lay on the valley floor at the foot of the slope. Such rich bottomland was too precious to use for huts and storehouses.

Aybas had long since decided that if he stayed much longer with the Pougoi, he would find himself growing a tail for the better climbing of hills and trees. Then, if he survived the service of his present master, he could find work as a performing ape such as the Kushite merchants showed at fairs!

The village was lit only by the odd torch burning before a hut here and there. Clouds had veiled the moon since Aybas had retired. The wizards who called themselves Star Brothers did their work in darkness, save when they wanted to sow even more terror by showing what they did.

Aybas's breath caught in his throat as he saw the

3

door open in a hut just downhill. A girl stood there, the shadowy figure of a man behind her. The girl wore nothing above the waist and only a leather skirt from supple waist to dimpled knees. The hut's torch spilled harsh yellow light on coppery hair and firm young breasts, and on muscular legs that Aybas had often imagined locked around him. . . .

As if Aybas's thoughts had been an unwanted touch, the girl turned. Green eyes met his brown ones, and it was the Aquilonian who finally looked down. He was still staring when he heard a gruff voice say, "Come within, Wylla. There is naught to do, standing here to be gawped at."

"It was not that which I came for, Father. I thought—I hoped that if I was out here, the . . . the folk up yonder might know it. Even take comfort from it."

"Hsshht! No gabbling about that where *he* can hear!" The "he" was as plain as a pointing finger in meaning Aybas.

The Aquilonian waited until the door thumped shut behind Wylla, then let his breath out in a long, gusty sigh. So Wylla was losing her fear of the Star Brothers, at least enough to show pity for their victims?

This was more common among the Pougoi than either the wizards or Aybas's master cared to admit. Indeed, if all who had doubted the Star Brothers' virtue—if not their power—had been sacrificed, the Vale of the Pougoi would be very scant of inhabitants.

Perhaps it was time to make another example? If it was Wylla, could Aybas come forward and make a great show of asking for mercy? In return for certain long-craved favors, of course. . . .

The thought made the chill mountain night sud-

4

denly seem warm. Aybas felt sweat on his brow and wiped it away with a greasy hand. A gust of wind blew down the street, and sparks flew away into the darkness from the torch outside Wylla's hut.

As if the sparks had kindled it, a light shone forth from across the valley. A pinpoint at first, it swelled until it was a harsh blue glow, reaching out to strip the softness of night from the rocky bones of this mountain land.

It came from beyond a high dam of rocks, logs, and rammed earth. The dam blocked the entrance to the gorge across the valley and held within it a deep lake. On one side of the gorge's mouth, the cliffs leaped upward, to form themselves into a jutting crest shaped like a dragon's head.

On the dragon's head, two human figures stood, one tall and one short. The blue wizard-fire glowed on their oiled skins and on the chains that bound them. Bound them for what would soon be climbing up from the lake, to seize them at the Star Brothers' command.

Aybas decided that it was time for him also to be inside his hut. His stomach was not always fit to endure seeing the wizards' pet feed, and the Star Brothers might see this weakness as enmity.

Then, to let Aybas keep the wizards' favor, it would take more gold than his master could afford. With no friends and many foes in this land, it would be time to journey again. Otherwise, *he* might end up on that dragon-headed rock, waiting for the mouth-studded tentacles to claim *his* blood and *his* marrow—

Aybas gagged at the thought and all but spewed. He staggered into his hut and collapsed on his pallet without closing the door. So he heard on the wind the splashing as the Star Brothers' pet heaved itself out of the water, heard the sucking and slobbering as it gripped the rock face and began to climb.

He had stuffed rawhide scraps into his ears before he heard the faint high call of pipes.

The fisherman and his son atop the dragon's head were more fortunate. The pipes came to their ears with a sound clear and exciting, like war trumpets summoning cavalry to the charge.

The fisherman knew that the pipes could not really be making such a sound. Marr the Piper had magic at his command, as much as the Pougoi wizards had.

This did not surprise the fisherman. He had known that he risked much when he and his son went beyond Three Oaks Hill into a land where the man-hunting Pougoi warriors roamed. He had also known that in this land lay pools and streams rich in fat fish; salmon, trout, pike, even fresh-water oysters.

Nothing was ever won without danger in this life. Such was the gods' will. The greater the victory, the greater the danger a man had to face to win it. The fisherman did not mourn his own shortened days. He would have given much to have refused his son's pleas to accompany him.

Now the boy stood in chains beside him, his days about to end before he had seen his fourteenth year. He bore himself like a man in spite of the weight of the chains and the agony of the raw welts across his back. He had been plain-spoken to the wizards, and they did not care for that. Or perhaps they thought to frighten the father by flogging the son.

No matter. That and all other questions would go forever unanswered as soon as what was climbing the cliff reached them.

It was hard to see it clearly. The wizards' magical light had turned the water of the gorge into blue fire, the mist swirling above it into blue smoke. The creature was larger than any riverboat that the fisherman had ever seen. It had tentacles where no creature outside a madman's dream would have them, and neither legs nor eyes.

Its color was that of a fish rotting on a sand spit in the sun; its sounds would have made the fisherman empty his stomach had it not already been empty.

It was then that the magic of the piping joined battle with the spells of the Star Brothers. The chains that bound father and son writhed like snakes. Then they snapped in the middle, leaving lengths dangling from wrists and ankles.

The piping also seemed to give the wizards' creature pause. It halted halfway up the cliff. Its call turned to a rumbling hiss, and its tentacles also writhed.

The fisherman looked about. There was no way down from the rock; a crevice—too wide to jump—sundered it from the hill. The Pougoi warriors had brought the sacrifices to their rock across a bridge of reeds and branches. Now the warriors had drawn the bridge back, and they stood beside the crevice, bows and spears ready.

Down was the only way, and death the only fate, for father and son. The fisherman still called the blessing of his people's gods and the rivers' spirits on Marr the Piper. His spell had given them the choice of a clean death.

"My son, it will be upon us soon. Will you come with me?"

The boy saw his fate in his father's eyes. The father saw knowledge, obedience, and love in his son's.

"Where you lead, I follow."

"I knew your mother and I had made a man."

The fisherman gripped his son's hand and they turned toward the valley. Two short steps, a long third one, and then the final leap out into space.

The fisherman heard the wind in his ears. Its call seemed to him the river spirits welcoming him and his son home. He heard the outcry from the wizards. It seemed that his balking their pet of its prey was not to their liking.

Then the rock of the valley leaped up to smash him from the world, and he heard nothing more.

Aybas heard a great deal during the remaining watches of the night. He did not even try to sleep. Indeed, it seemed likely that the din must be waking babies and distracting lovers in Iranistan! Between the howling of the creature, the gabbling of the Star Brothers, the murmur of the Pougoi, and the uproar of stock from cattle down to cats, the valley echoed until past dawn.

The one sound that Aybas—and, he judged, others as well—were listening for did not come. It seemed that the piper had done his night's work and taken his leave.

This did not surprise Aybas. Marr the Piper had been a legend in the Border Kingdom for a generation, even before Aybas had left his native land. It was only in the last year or so that Marr had seemed ready to contend with the Star Brothers of the Pougoi. There had to be limits to the piper's magic, although Aybas did not imagine that he himself would be the lucky man to reap the reward for discovering them. . . .

As the sun rose, the Pougoi drifted away to their huts and pallets or to their day's labors. The first among the Star Brothers, the man Aybas called

Forkbeard, climbed the street to accost the Aquilonian.

"This is the third time that Marr has befouled our rites," the wizard said.

"The other times must have been before I came among you," Aybas replied.

"You doubt my word?" Forkbeard asked sharply.

"You put words in my mouth," Aybas said, seeking to mix humility with firmness. "I only wish to remind you that I am newly come among the Pougoi. For what happened more than three moons ago. I must trust to you and your brothers."

"Our folk still will not speak to you?"

Aybas shook his head. "About many matters, such as hunting and ale, they are hospitality itself. About your work—" Aybas nodded toward the dam and the gorge "—they are less forthcoming."

Aybas waited, praying that the next question would be, "Do these silent ones seem to have a leader?" Instead, the Star Brother only twisted the brass wires that bound his graying beard into its three plaits.

The man seemed genuinely uneasy in mind and weary in body. Perhaps there was more to Marr the Piper than Aybas thought. Certainly it was not the time to enlist Forkbeard in his quest for Wylla. Aybas prayed that the time would come, before he forgot what to do with a woman when he had one in his bed!

When Forkbeard spoke again, it was not as Aybas had expected. "We must beat the hills and forests about the valley to find the piper or his lair," the Star Brother said.

"That will take many men."

"I see that you have eyes in your head to know the

9

lay of our land. If your master can send more soldiers, archers above all, it will aid us greatly."

Aybas was torn between surprise and fear. Surprise that one of the hill tribes would gladly invite
strangers into their homeland. Fear of what Forkbeard would say or do if Aybas confessed that the
men were not to be had.

His master did not lack fighting men, but for the
work he had in hand, he needed every one of them.
He would have none to spare for chasing magical
pipers up hill and down valley this far into the wilderness.

Forkbeard was frowning when inspiration touched
Aybas. "My master would gladly send every man he
can spare. But what use is even the best warrior
when he does not know your land? I have been
among you for three moons, and your children still
know the land better than I do!"

"There is truth in what you say," Forkbeard con-
ceded. "But our young men who know the land have
other work. If they must leave it . . ." He seemed to
reach a decision. "Can your master send gold, so that
we may fill our needs that way? Then our young men
will be free to hunt the piper."

They would also be free to join with the men of
Aybas's master when his master's plans came to full
bloom. That plain truth might open coffers, if they
were not already empty.

If the coffers were empty, Aybas knew that his time
in the Border Kingdom was drawing to a close. He
had served lords who tried to make fair words and
silken promises serve in place of gold and silver. It
was poor service, and more often than not, it led
unwary folk to unwelcome meetings with the headsman.

If that lay in his future, Aybas would wait among

the Pougoi until whatever his masters sent reached him. Then he would be sure that enough of somebody's gold found its way into his own purse, to buy him a safe passage out of the Border Kingdom.

"My masters will gladly send gold or goods, as you wish," Aybas said. "You have only to say what you need and my message will depart at once."

"No man could do more."

Few would do as much, Aybas knew. The Star Brothers could thank their gods that Count Syzambry had sent them a man who had already closed doors against himself in too many lands!

CHAPTER 1

Dawn touched a pool of clear, cold water at the edge of the trackless dark forests of the Border Kingdom. Dark water turned briefly rose-hued, then sapphire.

A man slipped from the shadows of the forest and crept to the edge of the pool. He moved as silently as a stalking cat, and his wide eyes ceaselessly studied the land about him. Those eyes were of an even colder blue than that of the pool, an odd match with his black hair, at least to those who did not know the look of Cimmeria.

The man's name was Conan. He had willingly used no other name in all his travels. A name was a potent thing in chill, barren Cimmeria, where life and death marched hand in hand. For the son of a blacksmith, closer to the gods than most, a name was best left untouched.

Conan had traveled far from his native village,

learning in many lands the skills of slave, thief, warrior, and captain. Now he was bound southward from his native land after sundry adventures that had left him wishing to taste civilization again. Women, wine, and gold were hard to come by in Cimmeria. Selling his sword in Nemedia might bring him each in abundance.

But to reach Nemedia from Cimmeria, a man who did not wish to cross Brythunia had to brave the mountains and brawling tribes of the Border Kingdom. Conan, a hill man born and never one to shy from a fight, had chosen the straightest route south.

At this dawn, he had been four days within the Border Kingdom. He had seen little to make him wish to tarry, and last night he had witnessed something that made him wish to hasten onward. What could only have been witch-fire had blazed above the hilltops. It had been a long way off, but had it been in distant Khitai, it could not have been far enough for Conan's taste. He loathed sorcery with a passion.

At the edge of the pool Conan knelt to thrust a leather water bottle beneath the surface. It bubbled briefly as it filled. Then he tied it once more to his belt and returned to the forest by a different path than the one by which he had come.

Only when he was safely within the shadowy ranks of the forest giants did he rise to his full height. That was well over six feet, with muscles and sinews to match. A wise man would have given Conan a clear path even had the Cimmerian not carried a well-used broadsword.

His garb was a bearskin, leather breeches and boots, and a jacket of mail as well-used as the sword. A dagger rode on one hip, and a pouch of well-greased cloth held salt, nuts, and the remains of a rabbit he had snared the previous night.

Being no fool, Conan would not gladly walk when he could ride, and he had begun his journey south well-mounted. But he had lost his horse, and nearly his life, in a desperate battle against the monstrous *yakhmar*, the ice worm he had thought a creature of legend.

It had been no legend, as the bones of a girl and his horse proved. Now at least one of the monsters lay dead beneath Snow Devil Glacier, brought down by a gulletful of red-hot coals flung by a muscular Cimmerian arm. Conan was not a man to trouble uncaring gods with pleas for help, but he hoped they had no plans to match him with a *yakhmar* again!

Being otherwise well-accoutred for his journey, Conan had set off for the south on foot. He had sought a chance to trade for a mount in the villages on the northern frontier of the Border Kingdom, but found few openings. None would have given him a mount up to his weight, either.

Chances to earn a mount were fewer still, and as for stealing one, the villagers guarded their horses as if each was worth its weight in silver. Also, the folk were by blood more Cimmerian than not. Conan had little wish to steal from his own people, and no wish at all to do anything that might give him an evil name among them.

The deeper he passed into the Border Kingdom, the less he missed a horse. The entire land seemed to be built at a slant. Thrice he saw a patch of level ground large enough to maneuver his former squadron of Turanian horsemen. The rest of the land seemed to consist of hills either rising to peaks or sloping into valleys, rushing streams with a few quiet pools, and endless forests.

In such a land, a hill man like the Cimmerian could

make better time afoot. Also, in a land not without men but seemingly without law, he was rather harder to see. Twice he had seen the leavings of bandit attacks, once near-skeletons, the other time both living and dead. The living were two men so covered with flyblown wounds that they begged for the mercy of Conan's dagger. He had granted it.

Conan looked up through the treetops at the position of the sun. He had a good half day free for traveling before he needed to think about food. In this forest, those few hours would not take him as far as a man might wish, but the sun would guide his steps southward. The more he saw of the Border Kingdom, the less he wanted to tarry in it.

By mid-morning Conan had learned that the forest he traveled was neither as endless nor as uninhabited as he had thought. Twice he came upon well-worn foot trails, and once he passed a cluster of huts too few to deserve the name of village. A vegetable garden and racks for smoking meat told of how the folk here lived.

Conan's belly was reminding him that his next meal really ought to be more than half of a rabbit. His belly did not command his wits, however, which told him that he would be quickest out of the Border Kingdom if he passed through it like smoke on the wind, leaving no trace of his coming and no one to say that he had ever been there.

This resolution grew firmer about noon, when he left the trees and saw a wooded valley ahead. High on a crag to the left of the valley's mouth stood a ruined castle. At the foot of the same rocky eminence there straggled an abandoned village.

Before the least-ruined hut of the village stood a gallows, the long kind, fit for hanging a half score of men at a time. Three nooses dangled in the breeze now, and only two of these held bodies. Well-ripened ones, too, Conan judged as a shift of the breeze brought a whiff of the corpses.

He wrinkled his nostrils, both at the stench and at the message he read in the dangling bodies. If two bandits were all that the local lord could bring to justice, it was one more proof that law sat lightly on this land. Conan was not one to worship the law when it stood between him and easy wealth, but the Border Kingdom seemed to have neither gold nor law.

It doubtless had archers, though, so Conan took care not to make an easy target of himself as he crossed to the mouth of the valley. The bow was not his weapon of choice, but he had learned its ways well enough in Turan to judge where an archer might lurk.

No arrows or other signs of life came his way before he reached the valley. At the bottom, a stream that almost deserved the name of a river flowed downhill. Beside it was a trail that clearly had borne shod mounts as well as booted feet, and not long ago.

Conan scrambled up the side of the valley as if the trail had been alive with serpents. He would use the trail if the lay of the land forced him to, but otherwise he would leave it to those who wished to make targets of themselves. He had long since learned that he would probably not die in bed from the onset of years. Likewise, he had learned how not to die young from witlings' mistakes.

By mid-afternoon he was well down the valley. He had devoured the rabbit and some wild mushrooms by a small stream. As he washed his hands, he thought he heard a distant bell chiming, but afterward judged it a trick of the wind.

A jagged spur of reddish rock plunged down from the crest across his path. It seemed an impassable barrier, and Conan reluctantly decided that he must at last strike downhill toward the trail.

He had covered perhaps half the distance when he heard the bell sound again. This time it was no trick of the wind. Indeed, it seemed to come from beyond the spur.

A moment later, he heard a bird calling. Or, rather, a man imitating a bird, not so well that Conan's woodswise ears could not discern the fakery. Then an answering bird call came from the trees in front of Conan and not more than a hundred paces away.

Conan's sword leaped into his hand. Then he looked at the thick-grown trees and sheathed it again. For close work here, his dagger would serve better. There would be such work, he was certain, and he'd wager against the bird-callers.

But he'd not put the wager down, though, without asking a few questions first. Dropping to hands and knees, Conan began a slow downhill crawl. He was as he had been by the pool: a stalking cat would have been loud by comparison.

Before he'd covered half of the hundred paces, he heard the bell chiming again. This time he knew the sound for what it really was: a horseshoe striking on rock. Listening intently as the breeze came and went, Conan heard the clinking shoes of several horses. These mounts, too, were beyond the spur of rock, but the volume of their chiming was growing steadily louder.

Had the horses been his, Conan would have muffled their hooves before taking them through this bandit-haunted forest. A grim smile crossed his face briefly. Perhaps some of the steeds would be his after this fight.

The approaching horsemen might well have no better claim to their mounts and goods than did whoever was stalking them. If the Cimmerian chose, he might assist in a change of ownership. He might depart the Kingdom afoot, but with the price of more than one mount in his purse. Then he could begin his career in Nemedia rather less like a beggar and more like a man whom warriors would trust to lead them aright.

Conan was still cat-silent as he crept down the slope to where he had heard the birdcall. No rolling pebble or snapping twig alerted the men he sought. When he found them, he saw that three of them still had their eyes fixed to the front, as though they had no backs that might be vulnerable. The archer among them was looking to the side as he thrust his arrows point-first into the soil.

None of the men looked as if they had bathed or eaten properly for half a year. Their beards and hair would have done to stuff a mattress, and all of their garb together would barely have made one man fit to appear on the streets of a town. Yet their eyes and weapons were bright, and the Cimmerian knew that he faced no easy foes here, if foes they were to be.

The archer—rising from placing his last arrow to unsling his bow—was the first to see Conan. His eyes widened as he saw the Cimmerian loom over him, and he hastened his movement. Unslinging his bow brought it within Conan's reach. A muscle-corded hand, well-furnished with sword calluses, gripped the curved ash. The archer tried to free his weapon. He might as well have tried to loose it from the grip of a troll. His eyes widened more.

"Easy, man," the Cimmerian said. He spoke in a low voice, one clearer than a whisper but carrying no farther. "Who comes?"

18

"A caravan for the king," the archer replied. This drew a glare from one of the others, which faded swiftly as Conan returned it.

"What king?" There were some rulers whom Conan had no wish to turn into enemies. There were also some who had long since put a price on his head.

"The Border king, of course," the archer said as if addressing a witling.

That told Conan little, but perhaps that little was enough. If he would be shaking the dust of the Border Kingdom from his feet within days, did it matter if he took some of its king's goods with him?

"How many are you, and how set?" Conan asked.

The bandits looked at one another. The sound of the approaching horsemen was now an almost continuous ringing, like tiny forges hard at work.

"I'll not be your enemy unless you give me cause," the Cimmerian said. "But I'll be no kind of friend until I know if you're worth befriending."

The bandits looked Conan up and down. One of them shifted position, until a look from both Conan and a comrade nailed his feet to the ground. "Your backs are safe from me as long as mine is safe from you," Conan added.

The sturdiest of the bandits seemed to reach a decision. "Four men on either side of the trail, on this side of the spur," he said. He jerked a thumb toward the spur.

"No more?"

"Half again as many to the other side of the spur. Runs across the valley, it does, with a gap for the trail. The others, they jump out, drive the caravan through the gap. 'Stead o' safety, they find us, blocking the trail."

Then the first bandits would pour through the gap, taking the caravan in the rear. Unable to move, mounted men lost their greatest advantage in fighting those on foot. Conan himself had learned as much in Turanian service, where light-armed foot frequently overmatched mounted nomads if the foot could chose their ground.

"Well and good," Conan said. "Where do you want me?"

The bandit leader jerked a thumb again, this time toward the left. Conan understood. That flank would trap him between the other bandits and the spur. If he had thoughts of treachery or flight, he might not live to act upon them.

Or so the bandits intended. Conan would not quarrel with their folly, or with anything else about them, unless they gave him cause. Before he took his leave of them, though, he might teach them a lesson or two about judging Cimmerians.

The bandits now spread out in a line some forty paces long. The farther end of the line was out of Conan's sight in the underbrush. The bandit leader was just barely in view, and Conan knew it meant that the man probably could not see him. A glance also showed Conan several places where, with a few steps, he could become as invisible as the air. One of the places, he judged, would not only hide him from his new and dubious comrades, but would allow him to see clearly what lay on the trail.

It was no part of Conan's plan to follow the bandits into a fight against impossible odds or against folk he might not wish to have as enemies.

The Cimmerian had just finished settling into place when the bandits beyond the spur launched their attack. Bloodcurdling shrieks rose, echoed by the screams of horses torn by sharp steel or arrowheads. Those men not shrieking hurled war cries at one another, and more than war cries. Conan heard stones cracking hard against shields.

Then he caught a single word in one of the war cries. It was a name, and at the sound of it, Conan's blood leaped in his veins.

"Raihna! Raihna! Rainha!"

CHAPTER 2

Conan had never known the woman by any name save "Raihna," the name a score of leather-lunged men were now shouting as a war cry. But he had known her well as battle comrade, shrewd judge of horseflesh, cheerful bedmate—and companion on an adventure into the Ibars Mountains that had been the stuff of nightmares.

If this was the same Raihna. It was not an uncommon name in Bossonia and several other lands. Conan felt no call to bare steel in defense of a total stranger.

He dropped his bearskin, shifted his sword so that it would not clatter against the rock, and flung himself at the face of the spur. Fingers with an iron grip and booted feet found holds, and the Cimmerian swiftly mounted the height. As he climbed, he drew steadily to the right, to where he could catch a glimpse through the gap.

22

The bandits had once again forgotten that they had backs that might be vulnerable, and this time they also forgot that they had flanks. Conan scrambled up to his intended perch without so much as a glance from below.

It was his Raihna. The woman who sat a scrubby but strong-limbed mare in the middle of the fight wore a helmet that covered a good part of her face. Her breasts now strained a much-repaired hauberk. Conan recognized the wide, gray eyes, the freckles on the uptilted nose, and the long, fine neck.

Then she shouted a string of orders, and certainty became more certain still. The voice had roughened a trifle since they had parted, but dust and winters on the road would leave their traces on a throat of brass.

A man leaped from a tree onto the rump of Raihna's mount. The mare staggered under the assault, but her rider was equal to the situation. Unable to swing her sword for fear of hitting comrades, Raihna drove the pommel into the man's face. His short sword grated on her mail; then its point caught in a broken link and drove through. Conan saw Raihna's lips tighten.

He also saws her hand rise, holding a stout Aquilonian dagger drawn from her boot. The bandit was so busy trying to press home his sword thrust that he never saw the steel that opened his throat. His eyes were wide but unseeing as he toppled off the horse, leaving both Raihna and the mare drenched in another's blood.

Conan sought a foothold with which to begin his descent. He had no bow, nor was he the most accomplished archer. Indeed, it would have taken an archer of miraculous gifts to send an arrow into that tangled fight without hitting friend rather than foe.

23

One bandit exchanging swordcuts with a guard saw Conan. His eyes widened and he shook his head, then opened his mouth to shout. It seemed he could not decide what the Cimmerian might be about. This moment of doubt ended when the guard grappled him and rammed a short sword up between his ribs. The bandit died with his mouth and eyes wide open, his questions about Conan forever unanswered.

As Conan sought his next foothold, an arrow cracked into the rock next to him. He looked down and saw that he could drop the rest of the way in safety. He landed with a force that would have broken the bones of a lesser man, but he rolled and came up into a crouch. He heard shouting from the bandits, with the leader calling the archer the son of more fathers than a dog has fleas and other pleasant names.

Perhaps the archer had not waited for his chief's orders before shooting. If so, the quarrel between the bandits would give Conan his best opportunity to strike.

He would strike, too, for Raihna and her men. Nothing that the Cimmerian believed in, neither honor nor gods nor the simple courtesy due a bedmate, would allow him to do otherwise.

He must also strike swiftly. The bandits on the other side of the gap were doing as they intended, herding Raihna's caravan forward—forward through the gap to what she might be thinking was safety, but to what would instead be more like a killing pen.

The caravan guards would sell their lives dearly when they learned the truth, of course. There would be fewer bandits by the time the survivors of the band laid hands on the caravan. Conan intended that there would be still fewer, and none of them grasping the king's goods.

The quarreling bandits were now making as much of a din as they would in a wineshop in Aghrapur. If the fight beyond the gap had not been making more, they would have given warning of their planned ambush.

As it was, the archer was not too distracted to miss Conan's reappearance. He whirled, nocked an arrow, and shot just as the leader clutched his arm. This sent the arrow flying wildly; Conan's leap behind a tree was hardly needed to save his skin.

It proved useful, though, in surprising the bandits. They stared about them as if the Cimmerian had vanished into the air. They were looking the other way when Conan burst from behind the tree, sword in one hand and bearskin in the other.

The bearskin flew through the air, wrapping itself about the archer's head and shoulders. He fought himself clear of it quickly enough to give him a shot at most men.

The Cimmerian was not most men, as the archer swiftly and direly learned. As he nocked another arrow, Conan's broadsword slashed at his bow. The string parted, splinters of ash flew from the wood, and the archer leaped back, dropping his weapon.

He also leaped back squarely into the path of his leader. For a moment, the two men were as one, and that one incapable of moving against Conan. The leader seemed to believe that no man so large could move fast enough to gain from this situation.

In the next heartbeat, he died of that misjudgment. Conan's sword hissed in a deadly arc, ending with a solid *chunk!* as it clove the man's head. He wore a stained leather cap reinforced with rusty iron bars, but Conan's blade sliced through it as if it were parchment. Indeed, it sank so deep into the leader's skull that for a moment the Cimmerian was not master of his own blade.

With desperate courage, the archer drew his dagger and sought to grapple and stab. He grappled, but the stab ended in futility against the Cimmerian's mail. Then Conan's free hand slammed into the archer's jaw hard enough to snap the man's neck and fling him backward into a tree, thereby cracking his skull as well.

Conan freed his sword, stepped free of the bodies, and faced the next bandit. The man had no weapon fit to face the dark-haired giant he saw before him, and no wish to die before his time. Judging from the crashing in the bushes, his comrade felt likewise.

Much to Conan's pleasure, neither of the surviving bandits thought to shout a warning to their comrades on the far slope. The Cimmerian was free to move against those comrades as he wished.

He knelt and examined the bow. It had suffered more than a trifle when his sword knocked it out of the archer's hands, but the dead man had a spare bowstring wound about his waist. With swift and supple fingers, Conan restrung the bow, then drew one of the arrows from the ground and nocked it.

The weapon would do well enough. It was not the curved horsebow Conan had learned to use in Turan, nor the stout Bossonian longbow. With the horsebow, a man could put five arrows into a man-sized target at two hundred paces from the back of a galloping horse, with the last arrow in flight before the first struck. With the longbow, Bossonian yeomen could drive a shaft as long as a man's arm through Aquilonian mail and a hand's breadth into the man under the mail.

Conan had no need to do either today. All he had to do was to persuade the bandits across the trail that enemies now stood where they had thought friends to be. Their own fear would do the rest, as the Turanian High Captain Khadjar had so often told those he thought worth teaching among the captains of the realm's irregulars.

"He who rules his mind on a battlefield will be the victor in the end," Khadjar once said. "He who lets fear rule it will be either a dishonored fugitive or fare for the vultures."

Wise words from a wise man, now chasing Picts on the Aquilonian border—if no one had sent assassins after him. Perhaps Raihna had heard something?

Perhaps, but she needed to survive this battle to tell it. Conan jerked the string of the bow to his ear, then shot. The arrow darted through a gap in the trees to vanish in the forest across the trail.

It needed two more arrows before anyone over there so much as cried out. Even then, it was a curse on a friend for ill-aimed archery. It was not until the sixth arrow that a scream told Conan of drawn blood.

Two more arrows flew, and he was nocking yet another when the bandits did what he least expected. They attacked.

Not four, but at least twice that many, charged out of the woods. Conan sent the nocked arrow into one man's chest and he fell, writhing. The others came on. It seemed that they had the wits to know how to set their trap anew. Drive off this foe who had sprung from the earth and they would once more command both sides of the trail.

The bandits had more than courage. They had luck, at least at first. Conan had no time to even think of picking his ground before the vanguard of the caravan spilled through the gap.

In a moment, bandits, pack animals, and guards—both mounted and dismounted—were as mingled as a nest of serpents in the Vendhyan jungles. Conan did not dare shoot another arrow. He had worked upon those bandits' minds, but not as he had intended. If this tangle of fighting men and frightened animals lasted for more than moments, it would block the gap as tightly as ever the bandits could wish.

When one road to victory was blocked, the Cimmerian never hesitated to take another. He flung himself downhill, leaping bushes and rocks, darting around trees, both sword and dagger gleaming in his hands. Seeking surprise, he uttered no war cry, but the sound of his passage gave warning nonetheless.

Fortunately, it was warning to friend and foe alike. The bandits on the trail turned to face him. The guards had the wits to see this. When Conan burst onto the trail, the guards already thought him likely to be a friend.

This doubtless saved his life in the next moment. He thrust with his dagger at one opponent, but the man lunged for the Cimmerian's legs. The dagger thrust passed over the man, and Conan's sword was occupied with another opponent. Caught off balance, Conan reeled.

Then a guard vaulted over a pack mule and landed on the back of the bandit gripping the Cimmerian's legs. The guard drew no weapon and needed none. Above the din of the battle, Conan heard the man's spine crack and felt his arms ease their grip.

Conan stepped clear of the dying bandit and held his other opponent at arm's length for a moment with deft swordplay. Then his instincts warned of new danger. He feinted at the first man, whirled, and sliced from a bare, hairy shoulder an arm wielding a tulwar. The man shrieked, tried vainly to stanch the blood, then stopped shrieking as his strength failed him.

By the time Conan could return to his first opponent, the man was dead. He had backed into easy reach of the guard, who had no lack of weapons or dearth of skill to use them. The bandit lay with a gaping neck wound that half severed his head.

By now the outpouring of blood was turning the rocky ground of the path into a ruddy ooze that offered precarious footing. Conan leaped onto a boulder, then down onto drier ground. This not only gave him better footing, it put him closer to the foremost edge of the battle.

A bandit who thought no foe was within reach learned otherwise as he bent to slit the saddlebags of a dying horse. He died before the horse did as Conan gripped a greasy pigtail with one hand and rammed his dagger into the man with the other. The bandit fell on saddlebags already half-open and spilling vials and pots whose seals bore runes Conan did not recognize.

The guard who'd already fought beside Conan came to join him, and now each man had a safe back as he faced the bandits. One of the bandits who had fled emerged from under a tangle of bushes, his courage renewed, or perhaps hoping for easy pickings.

Whether from courage or greed, his return to the battle brought him only swift death. Conan was ready for the bandit's leap into the middle of the fight. A stoutly booted foot shot up like a stone from a siege engine to catch the man in mid-leap. He doubled up with a sound that was half gasp, half scream. As he toppled to the ground, Conan's sword split the back of his skull.

After that the battle swiftly took on the common shape of such affairs: a confused blur of steel flashing and clanging, men shouting and screaming, and bodies writhing or lying still. It began to seem to Conan that he had far more opponents than the bandits could have furnished. He had a moment's chilling thought, that new bandits were indeed rising from the ground, or that those he had slain were coming back to life.

A moment later he realized that the abundance of foes was owing to the bandits trying to flee past him. Raihna, or someone with his wits about him, had blocked the gap and thus the retreat of every foe who had passed through it. The gap was now working against the very men who had thought to use it. Their one remaining thought was to flee, an endeavor that led them past Conan.

This, in turn, led to butcher's work for the Cimmerian. When he finished, he awoke as from a daze to find himself standing in the trail. He was bloody from chin to boots, his weapons hardly less so, and the ground around him a mosaic of blood and bodies.

As the battle rage ebbed, he noticed that the surviving guards were keeping their distance from him. One archer had not slung his bow, although he had not yet nocked an arrow. Another, a dark-faced, bearded man, was making what Conan recognized as a sign against the evil eye, over and over again.

"Raihna!" Conan shouted. The name came out like the croak of a giant frog. The Cimmerian realized then that he must have been fighting like an Aesir berserker. Small wonder that even those he had aided were wary of him!

"Raihna!" This time the name came out as if spoken in a known human tongue. The guards recognized it and stared at him. The bearer of the name also recognized it but did not stare. Under the helmet, her fair, freckled face had its own share of bloody smears. Now her features were drawn together in an intent frown.

Conan laughed. He could almost hear her wondering, "When in my travels did I meet this giant berserker, that he calls my name as if we were old friend?"

"Raihna of Bossonia," Conan said more quietly. "I am Conan the Cimmerian. I swear this, by the gods of my own people and by anything else you want me to swear by."

He knew much about her that would remove all questions of who he was . . . and he doubted that she would much care for having these matters talked of in broad daylight before her men.

Raihna's frown trembled, then vanished. Her full lips trembled also, before curving into a smile. In a single fluid series of movements, she sheathed her sword, slid from her saddle, and crossed the bloody ground to the Cimmerian.

"Conan?" She sounded delighted and wondering at the same time.

"I've no twin brother that I know of, and no sorcerer has ever done much with an image of me. Trust me, Raihna. I am here."

"Oh, Mitra!"

For a moment it seemed to Conan that Raihna would swoon. He raised a hand, ready to save her from this indignity. It would cost her some obedience from her men, that he did not doubt. Without the battle haze in his eyes, he saw them for a stout band who would not readily take orders from a woman. No, better said: would not take orders from *most* women.

But Raihna was not most women. It hardly surprised Conan to see her with her own band of caravan guards in less than two years after she had left Turan as a simple guard in another's band.

What did surprise him was that their paths should cross again here, in this dreary wilderness that called itself the Border Kingdom. Yet that was most probably another tale best saved until later.

Raihna now seemed to have regained command of herself. She reached up and tugged at a stray lock of Conan's black hair.

"Gods, it is no bad thing to see you again. Better still, when you have put me—us—so much in your debt. I swear that I will find some way to—"

"Pay that debt?" Conan said with a grim smile. Again thinking of her authority, he lowered his voice. "Best pay it by rallying your men and moving on." He told of his own battle in the trees in a few words, leaving out altogether his first notions about joining the bandits.

"You have the right of it, Conan. If these wretches have friends, that one you put to flight may send them warning. And we are hardly in a fit state to meet them if they come."

Raihna seemed to grow a hand's breadth in height, and Conan would have sworn that her eyes glowed. When she turned their gaze on her men and snapped out a half-score of commands, they leaped to obey as if a warrior goddess was among them.

Conan resolved to worry less about Raihna's authority among her men and more about his own welcome. He would have her favor, but many in the southern lands did not know Cimmerians. Some of those, like fools everywhere, feared what they did not know.

Seeing that Raihna had matters well in hand,

Conan strode off uphill. He returned with the leader's body and the discarded weapons of the bandits he had slain.

"Best not to leave anything lying about that some witling can pick up," he said of the weapons. Raihna nodded, then looked a silent question about the body.

"He has some rank among these mongrels," Conan said. "There's also a public gallows a bit farther on, at the foot of a hill with a ruined castle atop it. Hang this fellow up and it might send a message to any friends who think of trying us again."

Raihna nodded. "You were always a longheaded man for one of your years."

Conan laughed. "You make me sound like a green lad!"

"No," she said, and both her voice and her eyes held memories that made Conan's blood leap. "No lad."

Then she was the war captain again, calling to her men to contrive a pack animal or a litter for the bandit's body.

Conan stood apart, smiling. The promise had been made and returned. Now they needed only darkness.

CHAPTER 3

A few of Raihna's men wanted to track the fleeing bandits.

"Keep 'em from warnin' their friends, be there any," one man said.

"And loot anything the friends stole from other caravans, I'll be bound?" Raihna smiled as she spoke, but her voice was as hard as the rock where she sat.

"Well—I'll not deny that, Mistress."

"Good. You're truthful, if not wise. We have four dead and six hurt past fighting again today. This forest is no place to be dividing our strength against foes who likely know it well."

The man took the rebuke with a shrug and a smile and set to work mending the harness of a pack mule.

In less time than Conan needed for a meal at a good wineshop, the caravan was on the march again. As they retraced Conan's path from the ruined castle

34

and gallows, the Cimmerian rode in the van. Raihna rode in the center, well out of earshot, which denied Conan the chance for a discreet word with her.

Not that he would have taken it had they been riding side by side. Every eye and every ear would be needed until they left the forest, and every mouth had best remain closed.

Clouds and the passing of the day had brought twilight to the land before they reached the gallows. It was then that Raihna drew rein beside the Cimmerian and studied the ruined village.

"I like not the looks of that place, Conan. Know you anything of it, for good or for ill?"

"You have no one from this realm among your men?"

"Folk of the Border Kingdom who have won free of it seem not overeager to return, I have learned. I had good men of my own, and no wish to burden them with fainthearts."

Conan nodded. One willing man was worth three dragged into an undertaking. Moreover, a native of this land could well have been in league with the bandits.

"Castle or village?" Conan asked.

"The path up to the castle's too steep for the beasts, and I'll not be dividing the men here, either," Raihna said.

"Then it's the village or sleep wet and cold tonight," Conan said, looking at the sky. It had grown yet more sullen in the time they sat their mounts, watching the bandit's body rise to the gallows.

"That would ill serve our wounded," Raihna said. She cupped her hands. "Ho! We camp in the village tonight. Find the softest stones and the driest mud it offers, and see to the animals. Blue Watch takes first guard."

She turned to Conan. "That means me. The sergeant of Blue Watch is among the wounded. But I will not be awake all night."

Conan grinned. "You mean, you'll not be standing guard all night. Whether you sleep or not—"

"You seem sure of your prowess, Cimmerian!"

"Have I no reason?"

Raihna returned Conan's grin. "If you press me for an answer, I would not deny it. But before I see to the men—what brought you from Turan? The service of spylord Mishrak again?"

Conan suggested that Mishrak defiled he-goats and pissed in wells, then laughed. "Not Mishrak, nor anyone in Turan, bade me here. Indeed, the farther the better from Turan for a few years."

He told of his final year in the Turanian service and of how it had ended in flight when a high-ranking officer took offense at the Cimmerian's ways with the man's mistress. He told more briefly of his travels afterward, north to Cimmeria and then south again.

"I doubt not that Mishrak had a finger in one or two of my journeys before I dusted Turanian soil from my boots," Conan said. "But Crom spare me from ever having to serve him again as we once did."

A shadow passed over Raihna's face, and she gripped Conan's hand. Then she smiled again and dismounted. "I must be about my work. You see to our mounts and baggage, and I will join you in good time."

Conan watched Raihna stride toward where her men were tethering the pack animals and unloading them. She was as fair as ever to a man's eye, but it seemed that far more years than before sat upon her shoulders.

No, it was not the years. It was the weight of being

36

a captain, a weight the Cimmerian had come to know rather better than he wished.

If Raihna was southward bound after finishing her work here in this godless wilderness, perhaps he should join her. A captain's burden could be lighter if borne on two sets of shoulders.

Aybas had slept much of the day, for the night before had been as hideous as ever a night of sacrifice could be. It seemed to him that the Pougoi wizards were in fear of something mightier than themselves, or of their sworn foe, or of both. In their fear, they were sending the warriors farther and farther abroad to snatch victims for their beast.

Last night there had been no less than five victims, one a girl-child years from womanhood. Five victims, and no piper playing in the night to give the chained wretches a chance at a clean death. No piper to unsettle the Star Brothers—and Aybas realized more and more that it pleased him to see those bearded bloodsuckers rolling their eyes with fear of the unknown!

The gods only knew that he himself had been doing enough of that since he took the service that had led him here. What kept Aybas at his work now was the knowledge that he might be near to finishing it. He also knew that if he fled without finishing the work, he was unlikely to leave the Border Kingdom alive. He had come too far to leave his bones in the wilderness out of fear or whim.

The knocking on the door of his hut was loud enough to awaken a dead man, so Aybas listened to the voices with his senses alert. He had his sword drawn before he undid the latch to admit a Star Brother. Before he slammed the door behind the man, he saw that the guards standing outside wore long faces.

"What has the piper done now? Frightened your pet into a fit?"

The Star Brother glared and made what Aybas hoped were useless gestures of aversion. Aybas decided to guard his tongue. True, Count Syzambry needed the Pougoi warriors, but he needed the wizards to keep the warriors willing to do his bidding. For that the wizards needed their pet—and their pet needed its horrid food.

"Lowlander, we rejoice in the gold your master sends. But as for you, we can ill-speak you more easily than you might imagine."

Aybas was not sure whether the wizard meant that he would carry tales to the count or cast a spell. The Aquilonian decided not to hazard either.

"Forgive me. I slept ill and have—" not a fever, he would not say that for fear the wizards would try to heal him "—a flux." Yes, a flux. Even here in this wizard-haunted wilderness, they healed fluxes with herbs and wise women's simples, not with spells passed down from places and times far better lost to the memory of man!

"Have you summoned the wise woman?" the wizard asked.

"No, but I will do so at once when you have spoken. The ills of my flesh are of small importance if you bring great news."

The flattery ended the rites of aversion without gaining a smile. The Star Brother inclined his head in what he no doubt thought was a gracious gesture.

"The news is not yet great, but soon will be. The first band is ready and will do its work tonight, at the hunting lodge."

"Is it known if both Princess Chienna and her son are in residence?"

"Of the princess, we can be certain. Of the babe, my Brother seems less sure."

Aybas would have prayed that old King Eloikas's grandson Prince Urras was absent from the lodge where his mother lay. Prayers rising from this land, however, seemed more likely to draw the wrath of the gods than their favor.

So he merely hoped that the babe would be absent and that only his mother princess Chienna would be abducted tonight. That would be enough to either bring the old king to heel and win Chienna's hand for Count Syzambry or to force Eloikas into open warfare against the count. In either case, Aybas would be done with wizards, if not with the Border Kingdom!

But that happy time was yet to come. Now Aybas could not ask even one Star Brother to leave his hut. Indeed, the man seemed to have more news, if one could read as much of his countenance as showed above his beard.

"Has aught gone ill elsewhere?"

"A band of the Free Friends—" the name the bandits of the realm gave themselves "—sought to while away the time by taking a royal caravan. It would have been a shrewd blow had they done the work and lived to guard our folks' path homeward."

"But they did not?"

"All but a handful who fled died. Those who fled spoke of a giant, conjured from stone and set loose among them. Our foes seem to have more spells at their command than we had thought."

"Or more men?" Aybas withheld a sigh. "Look you, Brother. All the gods be witness, you and your comrades know more of magic than I had thought mortal men had it in them to apprehend. But I know rather more of war and battle as they are waged outside these hills. Rather than fear sorcery, fear lest the caravan has taken some of the Friends prisoner and forced them to reveal what they know of our plans. Bid the men who take the princess to retreat by a different route, to hide by day and march by night, to speak to no one, and to delay for nothing save the end of the world!

"That will do as much against our enemies as any spell you can cast or any score of folk you might . . ."— he would not say, "let your pet slaughter"—"take up."

"Will you never be done with insolence, Lowlander?"

It was in Aybas's mind to say that his insolence was a child's compared to that of Count Syzambry. But he held his peace. Let the wizards find out what manner of man they had bound themselves to when the count ruled in this land. It would be a harsh lesson, and by then Aybas would be well-hidden, far from the Border Kingdom.

"Forgive me again if I give offense. It is not my wish to do so. But it is very much my wish that work so well begun should not fail now through simple mischance."

"The message you set forth will be sent, Aybas. Will that content you?"

"Entirely." Aybas knew that he would not have won more had he offered the wizards the treasury of the priests of Set!

The clouds that had loomed overhead through the twilight passed on without dropping more than a cupful of rain. Conan saw lightning and heard the crash of thunder to the west as the storm moved on, but the caravan made a dry camp.

Although Conan had no duties once he had unpacked Raihna's baggage, he took his share of the camp duties nonetheless. It was plain that some among the men had guessed that he and Raihna were once lovers. It was plainer still that all wished to know more about this man to whom they most likely owed their lives.

So Conan drank as much as he wished and could have drunk more than was wise. He brought his sword to the armorer to be examined for nicks. Cimmerian work was not often seen by armorers from the south, and Cimmerian swords wielded with deadly effect by the sons of Cimmerian smiths hardly ever. Conan and the armorer had a pleasant enough chat over the wine.

He helped a groom oil leather saddlebags that showed signs of cracking. He helped two newly hired boys repack vials of herbs and simples hastily scooped up from the ground where they had fallen during the fight. He helped another boy with a potter's deft hands for clay mend a broken jug that held something foul-smelling beyond all belief.

"This will give King Eloikas a great power against his enemies, or so it is said," the potter explained.

"Phaugh!" Conan said, yearning for fresh air or, at least, the closing of the jug. "What will he do? Invite them all to dine and then unstopper this jug at the banquet? Surely enough, the stink will slay them all."

The potter frowned and did not reply. Conan felt a chill of unease deep within. Was King Eloikas dabbling in sorcery? Even if he did so because his enemies had begun it, Conan wanted no part of such duels of magic. If Raihna was going toward the place

41

of such a duel, he was honor-bound to follow her as far as she went. But he would hope that it was not too far, or that if it was, a stoutly wielded sword could win him free again.

In twenty-three years of life, the Cimmerian had learned that sorcerers seldom made a good end. They also made an even worse end for far too many other folk before they came to their own.

"Forget that I asked," Conan said. "I bear King Eloikas no ill will. I will even bear his ill-smelling gifts, if I must."

The potter's frown eased. They chatted briefly, and then Conan moved on to the hut where the wounded lay. There were five of them now, for one had died since reaching the village. As Conan entered, the leech was kneeling beside a man who was clearly taking his last breaths.

Man? Boy, rather; hardly older than Conan had been when he first felt the lash of the slaver's whip. A boy, dying far from home and clearly fearing that he had not done well in his first and only battle.

Conan knelt beside the lad's pallet. "Easy, there. What is your name?"

"Rasmussen, Cap . . . tain."

"Aesir or Vanir?"

"Vanir!" Even dying, the boy had the strength for indignation. Conan smiled.

"Did you . . . did you see me fighting? Did I do well?" Rasmussen gasped. His northern fairness had turned the color of fresh-fallen snow. Only his eyes held color now.

"Twice, when I had time to look about." Conan said. He had not in fact laid eyes on the boy until this evening, but this was one of those lies that any honest man would tell and any god forgive.

"I did well?"

"Rass, your strength—" the leech began.

"I . . . tell me, Captain!"

"You paid your way, Rasmussen," Conan said. "Few can do more in their first fight, and many do not do as much."

"Conan tells the truth," came Raihna's voice from behind Conan. "I made a good bargain when I took you on."

But she was talking to a set face and staring eyes. After a moment, she joined the two men beside the pallet and with her sword-callused thumbs, closed the boy's eyes. Then she swayed, and Conan contrived to keep her from falling without appearing to do so.

Presently Raihna was in command of herself again. No words were needed as they walked back to the hut Conan had chosen for them. Still in silence, they sat across from each other while Conan poured the last wine from a skin into two wooden cups.

"To old comrades," Raihna said. They clicked cups, then drank. When her cup was empty, Raihna wiped her mouth with the back of her hand and regained something of her old manner. Then she shook her head with a rueful grin.

"Conan, I wish I had half your skill in telling lies to soothe the dying."

"What lies?" the Cimmerian growled. "I said the lad had done as well as any man does in his first fight. He did not run, and all of his wounds were in front. That is as well as most men do."

Raihna shook her head again. "Conan, you were born a hundred years old."

Conan threw his head back and his laughter raised echoes in dusty corners. "Tell that to the thieves of Zingara. It was said, when I was learning their craft, that a wise thief would not be caught in the same

43

quarter of the city with Conan the Cimmerian. The great lout would warn his prey, the watch, all soldiers sober or drunk, and even the fleas on the watchdogs!"

"They said that of you?"

"Not to my face, I grant you. But, in their cups, some forgot that I was hearing. I let it pass."

He pulled off his boots. "But telling tales of my past will be dry work with the wine gone. What of you? Caravan guarding seems to have done well for you."

Raihna's men seemed well-seasoned, save for the lads, and they were certainly well-armed. They were also well-furnished with things like purgative herbs and spare boots. Conan had known the lack of such small matters to leave great gaps in the ranks of a company, even if it had no enemy to face.

Raihna wore baggy leather trousers—unable to disguise the long, supple legs within—that hung down over the best sort of Argossean riding boot. The dagger on her belt was of good Aquilonian work, as was the mail now lying in the corner. Her tunic was red Khitan silk, tight enough to set off breasts that seemed as fine as ever.

"I have been one of the lucky ones," she said. Her tale followed swiftly, for it was a short one. Caravan guarding drew many men, but kept few. They fell to bandits, to disease, and hardship, to the temptation to steal from the caravans. If they survived all those, they sometimes fell prey to mere disenchantment at discovering that the distant cities of their dreams had no towers of ivory or women clinking with gold.

"I survived all the perils and thereby learned to keep others alive as well," Raihna concluded. "After that it was a simple matter to win my own band. It was not so simple to win it a reputation."

"Is that why you're here?"

She nodded. "King Eloikas had a fair selection of goods to bring home but only ten of his own men to guard it. His steward would not make a free gift to the bandits. Most guards would not give the steward a civil answer. The Border Kingdom has a reputation as a place of hard rocks and still harder men."

"I've seen nothing to make me doubt that."

"Nor have I. But I grew up poor in Bossonia. A land such as this holds few terrors for me, and where I would go, my men would follow."

"Where are the king's men?"

"They rode on ahead this morning to warn the captain-general of our coming."

"Or so they said," Conan growled under his breath. The unknown captain-general might not be the only one they had warned. And there was the matter of the stuff of sorcery he had seen in some of the bags.

The Cimmerian rose and turned away. Before her men he would uphold Raihna's authority with the last drop of his blood and the last stroke of his sword. Alone with her, he had to ask a few blunt questions, the gods grant without making her fling the wine jug at him—

He turned back to the woman, and thoughts of serious matters fled his mind like rats from a burning barn. Raihna had pulled off her tunic, and above the waist she wore only the dressing over the cut on her ribs.

As Conan watched, she kicked off her boots, then pushed the riding breeches down those long legs. The breeches were a more practical garment than a tavern dancer's silks, but somehow they came off as swiftly.

"You are as fair as ever," Conan said.

Raihna mimed a kick at his manhood. "Shape your

tongue to wiser words, Cimmerian. Few women turn into wrinkled hags in a year. Or spare your words and speak to me without them.''

She held out her arms. The invitation could not be denied, nor did Conan refuse it.

It was long before they slept, and when they did, it was the kind of sleep that is near-kin to death. They did not hear thunder without lightning roll through the hills. Nor did they hear, closer to hand, the soft but insistent call of pipes.

Aybas heard the thunder. He also heard the cry of the Star Brothers' pet. Where he was, a dead man might have heard it. He was standing at the very foot of the dam.

It was a cry unlike any he had ever heard, even from a creature that seemed able to make the sounds of every earthly animal. It was a long, whistling moan, with an ugly bubbling note beneath the whistle and the moan. It was a sound that no human ears should have heard, a sound from another world, where evil reigned crying out to the world of men. Evil for which no human tongue had words, but which Aybas feared he might soon be meeting.

That fear took away much of his pleasure at the news that Princess Chienna and her captors were safely away from their pursuers. He did not know if the babe was also captive, but from the wizards' refusal to speak of it, he judged not. That made the news even better. Or did, until the thunder rolled and the beast cried.

It was some consolation for his own fear that the Star Brothers seemed quite as fearful. Perhaps it was not only Aybas who harbored thoughts of evil reaching out from a world beyond the world, an evil hungry and yearning to feed that hunger, an evil perhaps soon to slip past all restraint.

Aybas spoke more sharply than usual when he addressed the Star Brother who seemed to have the most command of himself. "What is this? Is your pet sick?"

"It is in fear," the other replied. Aybas did not even bother to turn away before making the gestures of aversion. Whatever could put the wizards' pet in fear was something no man in his senses should not also fear.

Thunder rumbled again, and Aybas and the wizards cringed. But the creature beyond the wall made no reply to the thunder. Searching the dark sky, Aybas saw lightning flash beyond a distant peak that bore a rounded bare summit horribly resembling a skull.

It was natural thunder, the gods be praised! Aybas stopped his gestures before the wizards noticed them and took offense. Then he saw that they were too busy jabbering among themselves to notice him even should he begin beating a drum and chanting war songs!

Aybas slipped away and crossed the valley floor toward the village. Halfway across, he saw two figures half-hidden in a stand of spiceberry bush. The next flash of lightning showed him Wylla's coppery hair and long-fingered hands lifted in prayer. Beside her rose the familiar massive bulk of Thyrin, her father.

Prayer, or some woman's rite? The Star Brothers might be interested to know that Wylla could be doing that which they had forbidden. This might be Aybas's long-sought opportunity to win Wylla's gratitude for saving her.

Yet somehow the idea no longer drew Aybas onward as strongly as it had, even though thoughts of Wylla still did. Having unnecessary dealings with the Star Brothers was too great a price to pay for any woman!

With victory so close, it was best to bide his time, then speak to Count Syzambry. The count could deal with the unruly among the Pougoi should any protest at seeing one of their clanswomen sold away from the valley.

Of course, the count might refuse his acquiescence. But even then, Aybas would be dealing with a mortal man—an ambitious man, to be sure, one who would stop at little to rule in this wretched land—but not with a wizard, one who sent messages without a messenger and tamed creatures from beyond the world.

"Mistress Raihna, Mistress Raihna!"

The shouting slowly penetrated Conan's ears. He sat up and willed sleep from his muscles and wits. In two swift strides he was at the hut door.

Behind him he saw tanned limbs flash as Raihna scrambled into her garments. Conan unbarred the door and allowed the man pounding on it to open it a hand's breadth.

"Mistress Raihna! Mistress Raihna!" the man repeated.

"Are we attacked again?" Raihna called.

The man made no answer. Instead his mouth opened slightly as he stared at the Cimmerian looming in the crack. The Cimmerian, in the same hut as Mistress Raihna, and not fully garbed.

Conan heard that thought as if the man had been shouting it. He saw the man bend to peer through a crack between the door's weathered planks. Then the man straightened abruptly as a large hand gripped the collar of his much-mended shirt.

Jerking the man to his feet, Conan opened the door wider but stood to block any view into the hut. "Your captain has asked you a question, my friend," he said with dangerous softness. "Is it your habit to ignore commands from her?"

"Ghhh—" the man replied. Conan realized that his hand on the man's collar was depriving him of speech, and he loosened his grip. The man rubbed his neck, started to glare at the Cimmerian, then seemed to think better of it.

"There's a Count Syzambry outside the village, ah—"

"Conan of Cimmeria, once of the Turanian service," Raihna said. She was only just decently clad as she stepped into the doorway, but she wore sword, dagger, and helmet over scanty garments.

"Ah, Mistress, Captain Conan. Count Syzambry says that the Princess Chienna was abducted last night. He wants to question all of us and search the camp and the baggage."

"I'll see him buried in camel dung first!" Raihna snapped.

"Mistress, he has fifty men with him."

"Has, or says he has?" Conan asked.

The man looked dubious about Conan's authority to ask, then cringed at Raihna's look and shrugged. "No one has seen more than twenty, and they are still outside the village."

"Good. Keep them there until I come," Raihna said.

"Yes, Mistress."

The door slammed behind the man and they heard his feet running off. Conan and Raihna looked at each other.

Even if Count Syzambry had no more than twenty men, that was more than Raihna had. If he had the fifty he claimed to have, he might be a worse menace than the bandits.

Raihna threw her arms around Conan and let him hold her against his massive chest for a moment. Then she kissed him and stepped back.

"Guard my back and your tongue, friend. We haven't brought King Eloikas's goods this far to lose them now to some son of a she-ass calling himself a count!"

CHAPTER 4

Count Syzambry was a small man who sat on a square-built roan stallion as if he had grown in the saddle. He wore a plate back-and-breast, an open-faced helm plumed in scarlet, and a well-used broadsword ready for a left-handed draw.

The helmet hid most of his face but left exposed a bushy dark beard shot with gray, a jutting red nose, and large dark eyes. The count was staring about as if he wished to make folk believe those eyes could see into a man's soul.

Conan, remembering some of the mortal men and other-than-mortal beings he had faced, was not much bothered by the count's playacting.

"Temple pageants are this one's talent, not leading fighting men," the Cimmerian muttered.

Raihna was close enough to squeeze his arm, feel the rock hardness of its muscles, and whisper in his ear. "For your life—and mine, Conan—be silent until I give you leave to speak."

Conan jerked his head in a nod. Speaking out of turn might provoke Count Syzambry to folly. Or it might make a shrewder man wonder if he faced dividing foes, whose quarrels he could turn to his advantage.

Conan now stepped back and studied the count's men without seeming to do so. They were a good twenty and more. None of them was as well-mounted as the count, nor as well-armored. Conan saw much mail among the men and noted a few unfortunates with no more than boiled-leather jacks sewn with iron rings.

Their weapons were better fitted for battle. All had swords, and most of them had either short horse-bows or crossbows. Conan could only guess at their stock of arrows and quarrels. He feared that they had sufficient to win any fight Raihna's men were foolish enough to provoke.

Conan was not the only one to see that. Raihna's men took one look at their visitors, a second at their captain's gestures. Then they seemed to vanish into the air, to put stout walls between themselves and the count's men.

A man darted out from behind Raihna's hut and came close enough for Conan to hear his whisper. "We are gathered in the heart of the village. Shall we start blocking the streets?"

Raihna shook her head. "Put the archers where they can see and shoot in all directions. Don't forget the castle side of the village, either. If His Beardedness has any more men, he may well send some of them over the hill to take us in the rear."

"The gods be with you, Mistress."

"And with all of you, too."

The man vanished. Raihna struck her left arm with her right hand. "I wish we had gone up to the castle. It would be easier to defend."

"We'd still be getting the pack animals up the path . . . if they hadn't fallen off and squashed themselves like grapes," Conan muttered. "Small use to worry about what might have been."

"Another saying of Captain Khadjar?"

"Any man with his wits about him learns that before he's been in five battles, or he's vulture's fodder."

Raihna folded her arms across her breasts. "Count Syzambry. I am Raihna the Bossonian, captain over this caravan and its guards."

"So I have been led to believe. I was also led to believe that you had royal men with you. Where are they?"

Raihna repeated what she had told Conan. Syzambry's laugh was mirthless. Raihna flushed, and it was Conan's turn to grip her arm.

"I am Conan of Cimmeria, once of the hosts of Turan, and under-captain to Mistress Raihna. I ask, what is the jest?"

Syzambry stared at Conan. His laughter this time was forced as the Cimmerian stared back. Ice-blue eyes caught and held dark ones. It was the dark ones that looked away and a gloved hand that twitched as if it sought the hilt of a sword.

"I do not say that you lie," the count said. "But without the royal men watching you, much might have happened against the king's good. Against your good, Mistress Raihna, if you value your reputation as an honest captain."

"Nothing happened," Raihna said. "Certainly nothing that bears on the matter of Princess Chienna's abduction. The first we knew of it was when your man summoned my guard."

"Yes, and if he had let my men into your camp, we would not be standing here glaring at each other like two packs of wolves over a scrawny stag." The count's eyes gave the lie to the soft-seeming words.

"The guard had my orders, and I have orders from King Eloikas. One of them is to let no one question the men or search the baggage unless he bears a royal writ."

Count Syzambry sniffed. "A nobleman such as I bears such a writ by birth. You need have no fear of disobeying the king by obeying me."

"Forgive me, my lord, if I seem doubtful," Raihna said. "We are strangers in this land. We know not its laws or customs, so we cannot judge the truth of what you speak."

Conan saw that she wanted to add, "And we cannot judge whether you are a count or not," but drew back from such an insult.

"I am the judge here," the count said. It was next to a snarl. The fingers writhed again. Conan eyed the distance between himself and the count. The man had made a serious mistake, perhaps without realizing it. He stood between where Conan and Raihna stood and those of his archers who had good shots at the opposing captains.

With only a trifle of luck, Conan could have the little man off his horse and down in the dust before the archers could shoot. If that came to pass, the fight would take a very different path.

The count glanced at Conan again. The Cimmerian tried to look as harmless as a lamb and to stand as motionless as an oak tree. From the rider's change of countenance, Conan thought he had succeeded.

The count opened his mouth to speak. His intended words died unuttered as a pack mule brayed in the village. Shouts echoed the mules, some of them in voices Conan recognized. Others were the voices of strangers shouting "Steel Hand!"

Conan looked to Raihna. She nodded. He whirled toward the village. The count gave a wordless yell, and Conan heard crossbows cocking.

Conan continued to whirl, scooping up a stone as he did. He flung the stone with the force of a sling, driving it into the flank of Count Syzambry's horse. The roan squealed and reared, catching the count unready. He clutched frantically at the saddle, the mane, the reins, anything that would keep him from tumbling to the ground.

Meanwhile, Conan's free arm looped around Raihna's supple waist. Snatching her off the ground, he ran for the cover of the village. Behind him, the count was still struggling to keep his saddle, never mind control his mount.

"If that little jackal in man's shape shields us for a moment longer—" Conan began. The whistle of arrows cut into his words. Arrows and bolts began sprouting from walls and kicking up dust.

Count Syzambry screamed curses. His mount screamed in pain. Conan judged that some ill-aimed shot had struck home in the roan. The archery slackened but did not cease.

Ahead, a vacant hut offered a gaping window. Conan flung Raihna through it like a wharfman flinging a bale aboard ship. Then he followed, landing almost on top of her.

"Ekkkh, Conan!" Raihna gasped. "Watch my fingers if you want my sword in this battle!" Conan stepped back as Raihna sprang nimbly to her feet and drew her blade. Outside, the archery had ended and the count's curses were dying away.

The din from the rear of the village had redoubled. It was still more the hurling of insults and war cries than the clashing of steel. Conan set his shoulder against the sagging door of the hut. Wood and leather gave with a ripping crack, nearly tumbling the Cimmerian onto the ground. Recovering himself, he led Raihna toward the rear of the village.

Conan allowed himself only a glance at the fight there, sufficient to tell friend from foe. The men who had come down the hill numbered at least a dozen; enough to hold Raihna's at bay, not enough to press home an attack.

The attackers also lacked the wits to post flank guards. Conan and Raihna took full advantage of this error. They hurled themselves against the flank of the enemy, wielding the flat of their swords like berserkers. All of Conan's instincts told him to leave foes dying, not merely stunned. But everything he had learned of warcraft since his youth told him that Count Syzambry would stop at nothing to bring him down were he to slaughter the count's men.

Himself and Raihna and Raihna's men. Alone, Conan knew that he could show all the counts of the Border Kingdom a clean pair of heels. He doubted that any Border Kingdom lordling's writ ran far into Nemedia or Aquilonia!

But with duties to Raihna and her men, Conan was not free to wreak bloody havoc among the count's men. He had to use his strength and speed to put them in fear without littering the village streets with their corpses.

This he did with terrifying skill. At least it terrified the count's men, who gave way as quickly as if Conan had actually butchered half of them. He cracked heads, broke sword arms, kicked men in the stomach, and punched them in the back of the neck. Beside him, Raihna did the same with somewhat less strength, but hardly with less speed or effect.

Together they rolled up the enemy's line as quickly as thieves rolling up a stolen tapestry. Those of the count's men who had time to see the fate of their comrades did not wait to meet their own. They turned and fled out of the village and up the hill.

Raihna's archers on the roofs began shooting. Raihna screamed at them to stop. They heard, but they did not obey at once.

"No more blood, you witlings!" Conan roared. "No more blood and we can still win free of this!"

"Tell that to—" someone began.

Conan did not spend time in arguing. He leaped high, clutched the ankles of the nearest archer and brought him down with a crash on the hut's roof. Rotten timbers and thatching gave under the man's weight and he plunged the roof in a cloud of dust. From inside, Conan heard curses that proved the man was shaken rather than hurt.

"Mistress," a man called in a more moderate tone. "Garzo is hurt to death, and two others have shed blood. That says nothing of the pack animals hurt or slain. We owe the bastards for that!"

"We owe King Eloikas the safe·arrival of his goods!" Raihna snapped. "We will fight or not as it will help us honor our bond. You swore to obey me in that. Will you stand foresworn in the face of the enemy and before a man who knows how to use strength and wits?"

This speech drew an eloquent silence. Conan knew that Raihna's power over her men was fraying. He hoped that the last few strands would hold until either Count Syzambry saw reason or the fight began in good earnest.

A whistling warned Conan in time. He flung himself one way, Raihna the other, as arrows from the hill sprinkled the village. More pack animals screamed. A mule cantered down the street, blood gushing from its throat. At the corner, it collapsed. A scrubby but stout-legged pony broke into a gallop, toward the count's men. Arrows jutted from its flanks and rump. As it passed the dying mule, more arrows sprouted from it and it reared, then also collapsed.

"I'd wager they're trying to keep us here if they can't beat us down," Conan told Raihna.

"Keep us here until they can bring up more men?"

"Why not? I'd also wager that if none come before nightfall, we can win clear then. For now, they seem to lack the stomach for a close fight."

"We can hardly win free with the animals to consider."

"There are times—"

"There are times when you are too free in telling me how to do my work, Conan!"

"Truth is truth, whether I speak or stay silent."

Raihna shook her head as if that could make matters otherwise. Then she wiped her eyes with a tattered sleeve. The movement lifted breasts that her garb hardly hid. Bruised, grazed, and dusty as she was, Raihna could have walked into any tavern and danced her way to a purseful of silver.

The archery now slackened from both the hill and the valley side of the village. Conan swung himself onto a roof and lay low enough to be invisible, high enough to see clearly.

The count was waving his arms so wildly that he seemed to have more than two. After a moment Conan realized that Syzambry had the wits to know what he faced here: men who could defend themselves well enough if they had warning of an enemy's plans. Commanding his men by silent hand signals, Syzambry must be hoping for surprise.

That he was planning on attacking at all raised Conan's hopes. Syzambry's men from the hill had lost half of their strength and were past fighting, or they were still fleeing. The count had barely the means with which to attack a foe standing on familiar ground, well-armed and under captains who knew their work.

Conan remained on the roof for some time. The vermin swarming in the thatch left their customary haunts for tastier prey. They drew no response from the Cimmerian, not even a twitch. He had learned the art of silence and stillness while fighting the mountain tribes of the Turanian frontier. Against them, to move was to die.

A whistle, a thump, and the smell of smoke at last made Conan move. Looking to the right, he saw smoke curling up from the thatch of the next hut.

Fire arrows!

Briefly, Conan cursed Count Syzambry's wits and the scantiness of last night's rain. If the ancient thatch of the village had been well-soaked, the count could never have used this trick.

As Conan finished cursing, three arrows plummeted into the thatch of his own hut. All three of them must have struck a dry patch, for flames rose almost at once, then leaped toward the Cimmerian fast enough to singe his hair.

Conan rolled toward the edge of the hut. The thatching sagged under him, and he heard a muted crack of wood. Then a roof beam gave way, and burning thatch, unburned thatch, timbers, and Conan crashed to the floor of the hut.

The Cimmerian leaped to his feet, beating out smoldering patches on his clothes and in his hair. As he finished the work, Raihna appeared. Her light linen trousers now covered less than did most loin-guards, and her shirt consisted of rags that threatened to part company with one another at any moment.

Her garb might be in disarray, but her wits were not. "I have the men gathering the most important goods now. They know what those are." For a moment, her lips trembled. "You were right. We shall appear before King Eloikas as little more than beggers and pray—"

She could not go on. Conan wanted to hold her but doubted that they had the time, or that she would take comfort from it.

"Raihna. We'll need a rear guard to hold the village while the rest of the men go over the hill. That will have to be the way, so that Syzambry's mounted archers can't follow. Give me two or three men, one an archer, and I'll make that rear guard."

"Conan . . . ." She stared at him as if he had started speaking in Khitan, or had turned into a dragon.

"In Crom's name, we haven't the time for arguing!" he almost shouted. "I'm the best man for the work. Give me some good men at my back and flank and I'll do it."

Raihna's hand came up. For a moment, Conan braced himself for a slap. Then her hand came the rest of the way and lightly brushed his cheek.

They were standing there, knowing that time and foes pressed, when deep-toned war trumpets sounded outside. First, one in the far distance, beyond the hill. Then another, answering it from closer by. Finally, two more, which grew louder as they sounded.

By the time the last trumpet blast died, Conan

heard the sound of many horses, swelling rapidly. He pushed Raihna lightly on one bare shoulder.

"Time for you to run and for me to fight. I think the count's friends are coming."

Decius, captain-general of the Hosts of the Border, knew what might come of sounding the trumpets. If Count Syzambry was at the village and had the wits to heed the warning, his men could show Decius's men a clear pair of heels.

The captain-general prayed to every lawful god, however, that Syzambry would be driven to desperation instead of to flight. If the count hurled his men into the village so that Decius could catch them red-handed—

King Eloikas would not much care for a battle if Syzambry escaped. But if the battle put an end to the count and his scheming and treachery, the king would forgive his captain-general much more than that.

Decius leaned forward in his saddle, then drew himself upright. A captain-general could not appear uneasy, not when he led no more than a score of men toward battle against perhaps twice their number. The villager who had warned of Syzambry's march might have miscounted, but Syzambry could indeed have fifty men.

As the trumpets sounded again, Decius nodded to his banner bearer. The banner of the Silver Bear rose and stood out in the wind. Decius nodded to his squire, riding almost boot to boot with him, and the lad handed over his master's shield.

The stout oval of metal-rimmed oak settled on Decius's arm like a familiar friend. He did not draw his sword. It was not yet time to be reduced to guiding his horse with his knees, not over such rough ground.

A final blast on the trumpets echoed from the hillside. The captain-general's men spurred their horses to a trot as they rounded the final bend in the trail.

Before them stood Castle Dembi and the equally ruined village at the foot of its hill. Half of the huts in the village seemed to be aflame. On the hillside sprawled the bodies of men and animals. A column of heavily burdened men on foot was scrambling past the bodies.

Decius reined in before the ruins of the village shrine. The ground about him showed the traces of many shod horses. A cloud of dust on the trail leading into the forest showed where the horsemen had gone.

"Who comes here?" a rough voice shouted from the village.

Decius was not accustomed to being so addressed, not since he had won his spurs at seventeen. But if whoever shouted had just survived a fight against Syzambry's minions, he had good cause for suspicion.

"Servants of King Eloikas," Decius replied. He would not name himself lest it provide Syzambry's rear guard an easy victory.

"Advance and be recognized." The voice was still harsh, but now it sounded like a seasoned captain's.

Decius dismounted, threw his shield in front of himself, drew his sword, and advanced past the shrine. He had taken five steps beyond that when the voice came again.

"Far enough, thank you."

"Easy, Conan," came a second voice, which Decius would have sworn was a woman's. "He bears Decius's Silver Bear, quartered with the arms of the kingdom. I'd wager it's Decius himself."

What sounded like a brief dispute followed, too

low-voiced for Decius to understand. Then two men—no, one was a woman—strode from a hut to face him.

The man overtopped Decius by nearly a head. He wore a sooty shirt and breeches, boots, and a serviceable broadsword. The woman—

"Mistress Raihna! It was you, then?" The villager had also spoken of a caravan sheltering for the night at Dembi village. Catching Count Syzambry looting any caravan could mean the end of the man. Catching him looting the long-awaited royal caravan guarded by Mistress Raihna's company—

"It is," the woman said. "Does that displease you?"

Decius realized that his disgust at driving Syzambry into flight must show on his face. "It does not displease me at all, Mistress Raihna."

He wanted to add, "Nor do you," which would have been the truth, but perhaps one best left to another time. The description of Raihna he had from the steward had said that she was fair to the eye, but not how fair. That was easy to judge now, considering how little she wore.

As Raihna had the reputation of a captain with her wits about her, Decius was certain that this was not her common fighting garb. But there was no denying that in it she both drew and pleased the eye. For a moment, Decius wished the black-haired giant standing at Raihna's shoulder anywhere but here.

"I only wish that Count Syzambry had not fled at our trumpets. I had hoped to drive him into a final, desperate attack. Then—"

"Well, the gods be thanked you didn't," the giant growled. "You'd be laying out our bodies now, as well as our men's."

"Who are you?" Decius asked. Ceremony seemed wasted on this man.

"Forgive me, my lord," Raihna said. "This is Conan the Cimmerian . . . in this band, captain under me."

The last words drew a few bawdy laughs from Decius's men. Neither Conan nor Raihna replied, although Decius saw Raihna's nostrils flare. Her nose, he observed, was as well formed as was the rest of her.

"Well, Captains," Decius said, "I trust that it was Count Syzambry who fled?"

"If he's a small man with large pride whose men shout 'Steel Hand' as a war cry—" Raihna began.

"You have met Syzambry. Tell me more."

The tale went swiftly, and Decius found himself listening carefully to Conan even while he observed Raihna. The Cimmerian seemed to have his wits about him more than most, for all that he could not have seen twenty-five summers. But then, it was battles rather than years that seasoned a captain. Decius knew that well—indeed, better than a reasonable man could wish.

When they finished talking, Decius saw that his men were looking at Conan and Raihna with open admiration. He would have done the same had he not had duties to his king.

"Well, call your hill-climbers back," Decius said. "I think we can be out of here before noon."

"We no longer have all of our mounts or pack animals," Raihna said.

"You just told me that," Decius said, letting impatience creep into his voice. "If some of your men, as well as mine, can walk, we shall be able to carry all the packs."

"And the wounded?" It was the Cimmerian who spoke, in a voice like a grindstone sharpening a war ax.

"They can wait until I reach a castle that has men to spare. There are several on the—"

"No," Conan said, more politely than before. "Raihna, if Decius insists, I will stay behind with the wounded. Otherwise, Syzambry will be sending men back to cut their throats or to torture knowledge from them."

Decius decided that the Cimmerian had passed the test. The man could have proposed that the packs stay behind, perhaps with himself as guard. Or he could have been careless of the wounded.

He had done neither. He had not only his wits about him, but some notions of honor. Raihna had not brought a cuckoo or, still worse, a serpent, into the Border realm. Too many men had come wearing fairer guises than the Cimmerian and left red ruin behind them.

"If most of us walk, your wounded can ride as well," Decius said. "This will mean camping tonight rather than reaching a castle."

"I am sworn to my men and they to me," Raihna said firmly.

"And I am sworn to Captain Raihna," Conan added.

Decius would have given a good sword to know by what oaths the two were sworn to each other. No look had passed between them to hint that they were lovers, but the captain-general would have wagered the same sword that they were. This displeased him, although he could not have said why.

Conan and Raihna walked in the rear of the united bands when they marched out well before noon.

"King Eloikas made no bad choice when he gave Decius his banner," Conan said.

"You think so?" Raihna replied. "When his eyes were on me as they were?"

"A man can be a good captain and also a good judge of women," Conan told her. He did not quite touch her. "Otherwise, where were we last night?" he added softly.

Raihna colored briefly, then laughed. "I stand rebuked. But truthfully, King Eloikas must have made some bad choices—or else had bad luck—to be afflicted with folk like Count Syzambry."

"Had you heard of him before you came north?"

Raihna colored again, and this time her calm did not quickly return. "I—we were eager to start. Eager to make our name. We were told that . . . that the Border Kingdom had powerful robber lords. But we did not think . . . we did not think that they were more than what is commonly found in wild lands."

Conan saw pain and shame on Raihna's face. She would not make that error again. Besides, he wanted no more rebukes for telling her how to do her work.

"If I make no mistake, Syzambry is one who fears neither god nor man nor King Eloikas," Conan said. "That sort is less common, and always worse."

Raihna's face twisted briefly into a mask that might have frightened children into fits. Or the mask of a child who *had* been that frightened—by what, Conan did not care to ask.

He knew that Raihna had left Bossonia in haste for reasons of which she did not care to speak. He had met her when she served as bodyguard to the sorceress Illyana on their quest for the Jewels of Kurag. What she had done between leaving Bossonia and taking service with Illyana was a mystery that she chose to leave dark.

So be it. Raihna was bedmate, battle comrade, and captain fit to follow. That was enough to tell Conan that whatever happened to her had not turned her wits. More than that he would not ask of man, woman, or god.

But he would ask a few questions of King Eloikas, or of someone close enough to him to know the answers. As long as he was sworn to Raihna, Conan cold not return to the road south. He was bound to the Border Kingdom, and if need be, to the fight against Count Syzambry.

Such a fight was always chancy, more so than a pitched battle by daylight against an open foe. Out of such a fight, though, a shrewd man might snatch something worth having.

Conan knew that he could rise again in the south if he entered the southern realms as a beggar. He would rise faster if he entered with a clinking purse.

CHAPTER 5

The coming of Princess Chienna to the Pougoi village did not awaken Aybas. He had been unable to sleep since he had seen the Star Brothers preparing for a sacrifice to their beast.

He lacked the courage to ask if they intended to sacrifice the princess herself. He told himself that even if he possessed the courage, it would make no difference in the end. He had made clear Count Syzambry's wishes many times over. If the Star Brothers ignored both him and the count, there was nothing to do but bear word to the count.

Bear word to the count, and then swiftly take himself out of Syzambry's reach. The little lord would not thank the bearer of bad news any more than would most ambitious men.

Gongs, drums, and that hideous wooden trumpet signaled the coming of the warriors. The common battle trumpet of the Border Kingdom was an offense to the ears. What the warriors of the Pougoi used was beyond Aybas's powers to describe.

Would he ever hear an Argossean flute-girl or a Nemedian lyre-maid again? Would he even hear the wailing pipes and thudding drums beating for the march of the Aquilonian foot on a bright autumn day? He doubted it.

He also doubted that he would accomplish much by feeling sorry for himself, save to fuddle his wits at a time when he needed them clear. Taking a deep breath, Aybas pulled his cloak about him and stepped into the village street.

Heads were thrusting out of doors all the way down to the valley. A few folk even stood in their doorways, staring into the darkness. Aybas saw some of these make gestures of aversion as he passed. He wondered if the gestures were against him, against the Star Brothers, or simply against whatever ill luck might come to the Pougoi through meddling in the affairs of kings and counts.

Aybas had long since realized that these hill folk were more longheaded than Count Syzambry realized. No amount of gold could silence their tongues or blind their eyes. If the count gained what he sought, he would have a reckoning with the Pougoi as well as with the other hill tribes they had preyed on for a generation to feed their wizards' pet.

A stand of spiceberry hid Aybas, as it had hidden Wylla and her father two nights before. From within it, he stared out across the rocky fields of barley as distant fireflies grew into crimson-hued torches. The pungent reek of the herbs the Pougoi used in steeping their reed torches made Aybas sneeze.

This drew no attention. The warriors of the Pougoi marched up to the wizards, and the leader raised his spear crosswise in both hands.

"Hail, Brothers of the Stars. We bring what we have sought. Bless us now."

It did not sound like a suppliant coming before a priest. It sounded more like a captain commanding something he would take if it were not given freely.

Aybas would not pray that the Star Brothers take offense and quarrel with the warriors. Such a brawl would end Count Syzambry's hopes by ending the life of the princess, if indeed it was she within the covered litter. Aybas's reward would die with her, and so might he.

The fall of the Star Brothers might also unleash the beast. The creature might rampage through the hills, devouring all in its path, with neither men nor magic able to bind or slay it.

One by one, the Star Brothers nodded. As the last bearded head bobbed on the last thin neck, the principal Brother raised his hands. A globe of fire, vermilion flecked with gold, sprang into being between them. It turned wizards and warriors alike into figures of blood and shadow.

The Brother with the globe raised his hands higher. The other Brothers began a chant that Aybas had never heard, and he liked it even less than the rest of the wizards' music.

The globe leaped into the air and rose higher than the top of the dam, higher than the uppermost pinnacle on the tower of the greatest temple in Aquilonia. It screamed as it soared, a scream that seemed to come from a living throat, a scream that the beast echoed.

Then the globe was no more, and fire was raining down on the warriors. Gold and vermilion mingled in the fire, and the warriors raised their faces and weapons to it.

The fire descended upon the warriors. It turned

their eyes and mouths to pools of fire. To Aybas, it seemed that the Pougoi warriors were now some man-shaped breed with cat or dragon blood, or both.

Their weapons did not turn to fire. They rose from their wielders' hands, as gently as soap bubbles, glowing softly. Aybas watched, breathless, as they ascended, rising almost as high as the globe of fire had done.

When the weapons finished rising, they bobbed about for a moment like twigs in a swift-rushing stream. Some of the spears turned end over end. Some of the swords danced as if sorcerous hands wielded them.

One sword clashed in midair with a battle-ax. The sparks they struck from each other poured down upon the torches. As if the sparks had been water and not fire, the torches died.

Crouching like an animal on all fours, Aybas briefly shut his eyes. He did not see the glow die from the weapons and all of them plunge out of the sky and into their masters' hands.

He did hear the *crunch*, like a rotten melon bursting, as the battle-ax clove the skull of its owner. He also heard the scream as another warrior's spear plunged through his outstretched hands and drove into his belly.

Every mortal ear in the valley must have heard that scream, and likewise the beast's reply. Aybas would have sworn that the sounds of slobbering and sucking could not roll like thunder if he did not hear them do just that. A moment later he realized that he was also hearing witch-thunder, which had come without lightning several times before and considerably frightened the wizards.

Both wizards and warriors seemed stricken mute and motionless by the uproar. One warrior finally

71

broke into movement, bending over his screaming comrade and silencing him by cutting his throat. As silence returned, another warrior opened the curtain of the litter.

The woman who stepped forth moved with the grace of a queen, for all that she was barefoot and wore only a soiled nightshift. Her dark hair would have flowed down upon her shoulders under other circumstances. Now it made a bramble-bush tangle. Bloody streaks on neck and ears told where jewelry had been savagely wrenched off.

On one slim arm rode a swaddled bundle. Aybas uttered a short prayer that the bundle was only clothing that Chienna had been allowed to bring away. Then the bundle wailed and the princess changed her grip that she might soothe her baby.

Aybas felt strangely calm. Prince Urras's crying was the first wholly natural, wholly human sound that he had heard in this valley in many days.

Then the drums and that hideous raw-throated trumpet raised their din again. Aybas realized that it was time that he make himself seen, even at the side of the Star Brothers. It would not do to let the wizards wonder if Count Syzambry truly valued the princess. Death would come to her very swiftly if they began to doubt that.

Aybas rose, brushed dirt and the dust of spice-berry flowers from his clothes, and strode toward the Star Brothers with his hand on the hilt of his sword.

Princess Chienna took no comfort from seeing a man in civilized garb approaching her. She had two causes for this.

One lay in heeding Decius's wisdom, likewise that of her father and of her late husband, Count Elkorun. All three had said that false hope in a desperate situation brings deeper despair. Since despair would slay her child as well as herself, she would fight it as long and as fiercely as possible.

The other reason for denying herself hope came from no one's counsel. It came from knowing that a man such as she saw before her could only be serving her enemies. Count Syzambry, most likely, or another lordling in the tumbledown alliance the count had raised against her father.

Their alliance would fall, the princess was sure. She was not sure that she would see its fall with living eyes, but she swore now to all the gods that she would see it from beyond death if she had to.

As his mother's rage touched him, Prince Urras forgot that he had been soothed into silence and began squalling again. With a fierce will, Chienna calmed herself and began rocking the baby in her arms.

He went on squalling. She decided that he was probably hungry.

"Is there a wet-nurse among you?" she asked. She wanted to say, "in this accursed pesthole of a village."

"I will inquire, Your Highness," the man said.

Chienna hid surprise. By the Great Mother's Girdle, the man knew the forms of courtesy!

"Do you that," Chienna said graciously. She bounced the baby up and down. "He hungers, and I am sure it is no part of your plan to encompass his death."

"None of mine," the man said. He was clad in a mixture of new hill-folk shirt and cloak and the ruins of civilized breeches and boots. His sword seemed a new one that had seen much hard service in little time.

And was there a slight emphasis on the word "mine"? Chienna dared a look at the ... the Star Brothers, they called themselves. The hill wizards, the villains of tales that had been old when her nurse was a babe.

Yes. They seemed to be displeased with the man, as if he had spoken out of turn.

A dispute between them? Not likely that it was open enough to give her any advantage, but it might be made worse. Not at once; all those who had taught her war craft had counseled against attacking before knowing the battlefield or the foe.

Afterward, though. ... She remembered Decius saying, "Nothing is worse than sitting and letting the foe do as he pleases. Even if you can strike only the smallest of blows against his weakest part, strike it!"

The captain-general would in time know that he had taught her well, although it was unlikely that she would tell him herself.

The man raised his voice. "Ho, summon a wet-nurse for the babe! At once!"

The princess noted that the wizards again looked displeased. But their displeasure did not stop the man, nor several warriors. The warriors ran off toward one side of the valley as if the ground was spewing flames at their heels.

The man stepped forward. Closer at hand, he showed a pinched, pale face above a scraggly brown beard shot with gray. Yet there were good bones in the face and in the hand he raised in greeting. A nobleman who had come by long and sorry roads to this wretched place, she would wager.

"I am Aybas, formerly of Aquilonia." The accent was not only Aquilonian, but courtly. "The warriors

74

will see to it that your babe suffers for nothing. Can I do aught for your comfort?"

Short of releasing her, or at least taking the hobbles from her ankles, she could think of nothing. Chienna shook her head.

"Then I might suggest, Your Highness, that you sit on the softest rock you can find." He smiled faintly before his face and voice alike turned hard. "The Star Brothers wish to show you the powers they command to punish those who disobey them or make themselves enemies."

Aybas pointed upward, toward the dam of rock and earth that blocked the mouth of the gorge to the left. As he did, something rose above the top of the wall. Something that writhed like a snake but was longer than any snake Chienna had ever seen.

A second writhing thing joined it, then a third, then too many too quickly to count. A body not meant to be described in human tongues followed, climbing the vertical cliff above the wall. Water poured from it as it rose, and it made sounds even less fit to describe.

Prince Urras sensed his mother's fear by her quickened heartbeat and wailed louder yet. The princess sat down, forswearing dignity for the sake of her babe. She rocked and dandled and bounced him, but nothing soothed the infant.

Yet all was not lost. She did not dare to close her eyes to shut out the scene on the rocky crag that was shaped like a dragon's head. She knew that to do so would mean punishment, and punishment so soon would take strength she might need later.

She was not forced to hear the cries of the sacrifices, however. Her babe's wailing drowned them out.

* * *

Wylla heard the end of the sacrifice from her perch on a branch high above the valley. Once again she thanked the gods that she had told no one of this dead tree and the view it gave her. She could see much, without ever being seen.

One day a strong wind would bring the tree down, and then she would need to seek another vantage point for spying on the wizards. Until that day, she would use this perch, with the knowledge of no one else in the village, not even her father.

She waited until the last trace of the beast vanished in the mist gathering over the gorge. That mist always seemed to come after the beast fed. Was it part of the Brothers' star-spawned magic?

She did not know. She could not even be sure that the woman and babe she had seen were Princess Chienna and her son. She only knew that she had to bear the news of what she had seen swiftly out of the valley, to where Marr the Piper waited.

She would not have to go far. The pipes had not sounded tonight, but the thunder and the havoc wrought on the weapons told of Marr's near presence.

Wylla wore a warrior's cloak, the shapeless dress of the Pougoi women, and hard-soled leather shoes beaded with colored stones from mountain streams. She cast aside the cloak, then drew the dress over her head.

Under the dress she wore only a birdskin belt, with a dagger of finely shaved mammoth ivory thrust into it. The starlight played delicately over her body as she stood for a moment naked in the night.

Then she bound her cloak about her loins, knelt, and took several deep breaths. As Marr had taught her to expect, the life force flowed into her, making her blood tingle.

When it seemed that her limbs would take fire in the next moment, she leaped up and began to run.

From far ahead in the darkness, the pipes called softly.

CHAPTER 6

Close to the time that Wylla met Marr the Piper, Conan met King Eloikas's Palace Guard.

The caravan and Decius's men had camped for the night about double bowshot beyond a small village in the lee of a thickly forested ridge. The village was inhabited, but it was hardly less ruined than the Dembi village where they had fought two days before.

The villagers' surly looks would have told Conan of years of hard living had their rough huts and scanty garb not done so. A few chickens and some half-ground barley were the best that Decius's coins could pry loose from them.

If this was the common run of folk in the Border realm, Conan decided, he was not going to profit much from it. King Eloikas's gratitude would feed no horses and burnish no armor. That needed gold, something that the Border Kingdom seemed unlikely to offer.

So be it. Honor bound him to Raihna's side as long as she needed him. He could contrive some other way of filling his purse or take his luck in Nemedia with an empty one. He had wrested gold out of poorer lands after entering them with no more than his sword and the clothes upon his back.

Conan was inspecting the sentries when the Palace Guard appeared. Decius trusted the caravan men to share the watch with his men, but not Conan to keep a watch by himself. The Cimmerian had judged it best to hold his peace on the matter.

Decius's men were clearly masters of their craft. Conan was advising one of Raihna's archers to hide himself better when the wind had borne to the Cimmerian's ears the clatter of hooves and the thud of boots. He had waved both pairs of sentries into hiding, seen both obey, and strode up the path toward the sound.

A hiding place in the roots of a great gnarled oak offered itself. Conan crouched there, cupped his hands, and hailed the newcomers.

"Halt! Who is there?"

"The Palace Guard, Captain Oyzhik commanding."

"Advance and be recognized."

Conan heard one of Decius's men scuttling off to summon his chief. He also heard the hooves and boots fade raggedly into silence.

The Cimmerian's keen night sight pierced the darkness. He recognized the royal banner, a sadly tattered one drooping from a crooked lance. He also recognized a company that numbered a handful of veterans and a great many new recruits. He had seen enough of both in Turan to be able to tell the one from the other, even in the darkness.

The man who had replied, naming himself Captain Oyzhik, was also a type that Conan recognized. Too

Roland Green

bald and too fat for his years, he wore fine armor and sat a horse worth as much as three of Decius's. But the armor was undented and the sword slung across his back showed gilding and jewels that could not have survived a single real battle.

"Captain Oyzhik," Conan shouted. "Captain-General Decius has been summoned. I ask you to hold where you are until he comes."

"My men have traveled fast and far on urgent orders from the King's majesty," Oyzhik replied. His voice was as round as the rest of him. "They must have their shelter at once."

Conan doubted that such a mob of old men and boys could have traveled fast or far had a god commanded it. Oyzhik no doubt wanted to get his plump arse out of the saddle and into something more comfortable.

The Cimmerian laughed softly. Oyzhik had a surprise coming if he thought the caravan's camp offered what could be called "comfort" in any tongue Conan knew.

The sound of a firm stride coming up the trail warned Conan that Decius was at hand. The Cimmerian rose to greet the captain-general, then fell behind him as Decius went to meet the Palace Guard.

"What brings you here, Oyzhik?" Decius asked.

"Tales came of Count Syzambry's friends and allies gathering men. We did not know what strength the caravan might have. So King Eloikas decreed that the palace would bar its gates and send forth the Guard to be your shield at the end of your journey."

Conan hoped that King Eloikas had been speaking for the ears of the doubtful rather than out of any real belief that this Guard could defend an apple orchard from a band of small boys. Serving a master

80

who had neither silver nor wisdom in war could end in filling a rocky grave in this godless land.

"We thank you, Oyzhik," Decius said. "Captain Conan, return to the camp and wake Raihna and my second. We break camp and march at once."

"At . . . night?" Oyzhik's question came out more squeak than words, as high-pitched as if he had been gelded.

"We are now in good strength, Oyzhik," Decius said. "The trail is clear, or you would not be with us. And our foes will not be expecting us to march by night, so it is the wisest thing we could do."

To Conan, struggling to choke back laughter, a night march seemed to have another virtue. It might cause the plump Guard captain to fall down in a fit, or at least to faint from weariness.

The Cimmerian held his peace, though, until Decius dismissed him. Then he hastened down the trail toward the camp. When he finally saw the campfires glowing ahead, he let out such a roar of laughter that half the men jerked awake at once.

Raihna thrust her head out of the tent they shared. "Share the jest, Conan, if it is so fine."

Conan merely shook his head and laughed harder. It would not do to insult the Palace Guard before the captain-general's men.

"An old tale, Raihna. But the new one tonight is that Count Syzambry's friends may be waiting for us. The Palace Guard has come out, and Decius wants us on the march before he can take a deep breath!"

Raihna's head bobbed and vanished, and all around him Conan saw and heard men garbing and arming themselves.

* * *

Conan's first sight of the palace of King Eloikas made him wonder if it was worth guarding.

He had seen mere noblemen keep larger hunting lodges, and not only in wealthy lands such as Turan. He had known of Vendhyans who would not have housed their tiger-hunters in something so wretched.

The gates hung ajar. The outer wall crumbled so that in some places an agile man might have walked over it upright. Holes gaped in every roof that Conan could see, and he did not doubt that under each hole was a puddle of muddy water from every rain in the last ten years.

A beaten-down patch of earth set about with thorn hedges might have been a drill ground. A collection of huts that a swineherd would have disdained might have been a barracks. Otherwise, Conan had no idea of where the Palace Guard lived, or of where Raihna's men might find quarters.

Since Decius's men joined them, he had heard muttered tales of "the secret hoard" of the Border kings. Some folk, it appeared, believed that the palace was so wretched because Eloikas was saving his gold for a time of need.

Conan would believe in that hoard, as he would believe in the will of the gods, when he saw it with his own eyes. For now, he suspected that the cache was so secret that even King Eloikas had forgotten where to lay hands on it.

Oyzhik hurried into the palace to report their arrival to the king. Conan and Raihna busied themselves with their men and beasts. They were careful to avoid the boggy fields and wretched hovels stretching downhill from the palace. They were likewise careful to keep the caravan beyond bowshot of the brooding forest uphill. The forest held trees Conan had never seen before, in shapes he did not wish to see again, and no birds sang within it.

Conan let Raihna stand close to him, but he laid no hand on her. Both were aware of Decius's eyes upon them, more especially upon Raihna.

"This land pleases me less with each new turn of the trail," Raihna said. "Will you come with me and my men if we choose to leave at once?"

"Best wait for your pay if you want—forgive me, that's telling you your work again."

It was also not noticing her unease, bordering on fear. Gratitude for that shone in her smile. "Unless that means waiting so long that it will buy nothing but a burial shroud, and a poor one at that!" she said.

Then, "Conan," Raihna went on, raising her hands as if to grip his shoulders, "if we leave, would you come with us as far as the nearest civilized land? I think you have hopes to win something in this land—"

"An empty belly and an untimely grave? That's what this land seems to promise. Raihna, I said in plain words that I would be at your side wherever you went. Does a shield jump off of a man's arm because it thinks he's overmatched?"

Raihna might have embraced him in spite of Decius's presence, but at that moment a palace servant appeared in the gateway, Oyzhik behind him.

"Captain-General Decius, Captain Raihna, Conan of Cimmeria. You are summoned to audience with His Sacred Majesty, Eloikas, King of the Border, Fifth of That Name."

The outer parts of the palace were much as Conan had expected: courtyards where weeds sprouted as high as a man's waist and trees overtopped what was left of the walls; chambers all but open to the sky, with stagnant marshes where once gentlefolk might have taken their pleasure on silk-swathed couches, drinking perfumed wine from gilded cups. One chamber still had much of its fine tile floor intact, and Conan had to call his men away from gaping at it as though it were a rare and wondrous treasure from a distant land.

How much of this they passed, Conan did not know then or afterward. He knew that he was beginning to feel an itch between his shoulders that no scratching would soothe. With every step he was farther from even the modest protection that Raihna's men might offer him and deeper into a place where foes, human and magical, might wait.

Some of them at least, he vowed, would live only as long as he needed to teach them not to lay traps for a Cimmerian. Or a Bossonian swordswoman, he added, taking in how Raihna's face also grew more somber with each step.

A final step took them around a corner, and both Conan and Raihna stopped as if they faced a pit of fire. Beyond them lay a courtyard clean of dust and weeds alike. Opening off of it were chambers that seemed at least fit to belong to a decent merchant's home.

Every door of these chambers was guarded, and the guards were also unlike what Conan had seen so far in Eloikas's palace. Most of them were past youth, but not past bearing good armor and stout swords or bows, with an occasional halberd to season the mix. Conan judged them with a soldier's eye. He would wager that most of them were of a type he had met before, those who might have lost swiftness but had gained experience and would not be opponents to take lightly.

The guard with the most ornate halberd brought it up in salute.

"Hail, Decius. His Majesty awaits."

The captain-general nodded and fell back. Guards took their place around Conan and Raihna, so close that the two could not have drawn a weapon freely had they wished to. Thus hemmed in, they entered the throne room of King Eloikas.

The throne room was about the size of the dining room in a good inn, and so clean that one might have eaten off the floor. One could see that here, at least, silver was spent to keep the dust away, the tapestries mended, the paint of the murals fresh, and the gilding of the bronze throne unscarred.

One could also see, as Conan did at once, a strong resemblance between the man who sat on the throne and the captain-general who knelt before it. Conan and Raihna followed Decius's example, but the Cimmerian did not take his eyes off their two hosts.

If they were not father and bastard son, Conan swore, he would drink nothing but water for a year. Both were of medium height but of soldierly bearing. The king was somewhat scanter of hair, and that more gray than black, but the chisel-shaped nose, high cheekbones, and wide gray eyes were common to both.

Conan was so intent on discovering further resemblances between Eloikas and Decius that the command to rise caught him unaware. Raihna had to dig at his ribs with her elbow to bring him to his feet, a gesture that drew a royal laugh.

It seemed the laugh of a man who had found little to laugh about for far too long but who had not altogether lost the habit. In spite of his suspicions, Conan found himself warming to Eloikas.

Decius presented Conan and Raihna in a few sol-

dierly words. They knelt again. Eloikas greeted them
in still fewer words, then bid them rise.

"Mistress Raihna, you have Our gratitude, and you
will have your promised fee and more. You have not
only brought Us what We put in your charge, which
will strengthen Our blows against those who have
taken Our daughter and heir . . . but you have struck
shrewd blows yourselves against Our common foes.
It is Our wish, Mistress Raihna, that you and your
men remain within Our realm to aid us in striking
further blows. We expect to be able to reward such
service most generously."

Eloikas then folded his hands across a belly re-
markably flat for a man of his years and clad in a
robe of Brythunian style much patched and dyed
over many years. His gaze passed over Conan's head
and seemed to fix itself on some detail of the mural
on the wall behind the Cimmerian.

Conan could tell that Raihna would have given half
of her pay to be alone with him, able to speak freely.
She also seemed to be gazing at something far away,
then drew heself up.

"Your Majesty, I am honored by your confidence.
But I beg you to answer two questions."

Captain Oyzhik hissed like an outraged goose, but
Decius waved him to silence. The captain-general did
not, however, take his eyes off the king. Nor did he
fail to make certain subtle gestures to the guards.
The guards held their places, but their hands crept
closer to their weapons.

Eloikas nodded, and Conan saw Raihna quiver like
a released bowstring. "Our gratitude to you extends
to answering many questions. But let Us hear your
first two."

Raihna wasted no words. She wanted to know if
her caravan fee would be paid at once so that she

could divide it among her men. Some had not been paid since long before they joined her company, save in clothing with which to make themselves decent and weapons with which to make themselves fit for battle.

"I would judge also that some may not wish to remain in Our service and that you wish them to travel safely," Eloikas said.

This time Raihna's reply was as swift as a runner's start. "I cannot swear to that, Your Majesty. But if there are such men, would you ask me to hold them in your realm against their will?"

"We would not. We suspect that if We did, We would hear plain words on the matter from Lord Decius."

The only word for Eloikas's look at his captain-general was "fatherly."

"Your Majesty is gracious," Raihna said. "I would also beg that you consider taking my under-captain, Conan of Cimmeria, into your service."

This time Eloikas's look was that of a king asking advice of a trusted counselor. The captain-general shrugged.

"Conan might have my voice in less troubled times. As matters stand, when a stranger might have more than one allegiance—"

Now it was Conan's elbow that prodded Raihna's ribs. Her outraged look did not turn into outrageous words.

"Your Majesty, if I may speak for myself . . . ?" Conan said.

Oyzhik hissed again. "Who asked you—?" he began.

"Peace, Oyzhik," Eloikhas said. "Even a condemned man may ask one final favor of the judge."

"Your Majesty, before you condemn me to leaving

Mistress Raihna's service, to which I am sworn until she sets me free, please hear from my own lips what I did."

"You may speak."

Conan obeyed. His account of his deeds since entering the Border Kingdom was as plain as a halberd head. No gilding that he could give it would make it more convincing. He could hope for no more or no less than persuading the king that he was not in Count Syzambry's service and never would be.

When Conan finished, the king nodded. "You speak very freely before a king."

"Your Majesty, I've faced men, and more than men, far more to be feared than just a king."

"And learned flattery from them?"

"Call it what you will, Your Majesty. I call it the truth."

Eloikas laughed softly, but it seemed that his eyes were not altogether dry. The silence lasted some good while until the king spoke again.

"We think that this Cimmerian can be trusted sufficiently to be offered a post in Our service. Oyzhik, you have spoken often of needing more seasoned soldiers in the Guard to instruct the recruits."

Oyzhik was silent. He looked ready to deny that he had ever said any such thing until he saw Decius's eye upon him. The captain-general might have been shouting, "Lie at your peril!"

"It is true that I can instruct the recruits only by plucking the ranks of the veterans," Oyzhik said sullenly.

"Then We think the favor of the gods is evident in sending Conan the Cimmerian to Our realm. Conan, if it pleases Mistress Raihna, would you become Sergeant of the Second Company of Our Guard?"

Conan looked a question at Raihna. She nodded.

Conan knelt again. "I accept with pleasure, Your Majesty. By all the lawful gods of this and other lands, I swear that you'll not regret this decision."

"Then rise, Sergeant Conan."

The gods might keep King Eloikas from regretting his decision. One look told Conan, however, that the same could hardly be said of Captain Oyzhik. Had he been able to conjure the roof down on his king and his new sergeant alike, he might well have done so.

As Conan expected, his quarters and those of the Guard lay outside the palace, while Raihna's men would seek a dry room within it, if such existed. It was hard upon sunset before they had a chance to speak without fear of eavesdroppers by dint of taking a light supper out onto the drill ground and eating it while sitting on a blanket.

"I wish we could serve together," Raihna said.

"Missing a bedmate already?" Conan jested. "Cast one of your languishing looks at Decius and you'll not—*ufff*!"

He broke off as she punched him urgently in the ribs. "I am not blind to his desire for me. I am also not blind to his kinship with Eloikas."

"I wonder. Could Decius have something to do with Princess Chienna's abduction? Bastards have won thrones before this when there were no legitimate heirs."

"My gratitude to you overflows, Conan. You know perfectly how to give me a sound sleep at night."

"Yes, and I'll have no chance to use it tonight, or for many nights to come. If Decius is no enemy, best we not make him one."

"I fear Oyzhik more."

"An open enemy's easier to watch than one biding his time. Turan taught me that, if nothing else. Moreover, I'd wager all the wine in this realm that Eloikas or Decius have men among the Guards to watch Oyzhik. Unless his chiefs want me dead, Oyzhik might find a few obstacles in his path."

"Wager more than this wine," Raihna said. She spat into the dust and rinsed her mouth from the water bottle. "In some lands, this would not pass even as vinegar."

"I've heard a score of tales of the Border Kingdom," Conan said, "but none of them ever claimed that it was a great land for fine living."

He did not add what most of the tales did say: that the Border Kingdom reeked of ancient and unwholesome sorcery. Or sorcery even more unwholesome than that commonly found, at least since the fall of the nighted realm of Acheron.

Was this the secret truth about the Border Kingdom? That when the tide of the dark hosts of Acheron drew back from civilized lands, some of its leavings remained here among the sharp-peaked mountains and the forests as dark as a death-spell?

It was, as such things went, a warm night for the Border Kingdom. But the Cimmerian felt more than an itch between his shoulder blades at the thought of Acheron yet living here. He felt a chill, as from the breath of the wind off of a Hyperborean glacier.

CHAPTER 7

Conan began his new undertaking as Sergeant of the Second Company of the Palace Guard the next day.

Indeed, he began it before the roses of sunrise touched the eastern sky and the fanged peaks jutting against it. This was not much to the liking of some of the recruits, who had been accustomed to rising when whim or wine allowed.

"From this day forth, you've no whims unless I order you to have them," Conan roared at the staggering, bleary-eyed men. "I'll not give that order."

He spat on the ground in disgust. "Or at least I won't give it until you sons of flea-ridden wolves are closer to being soldiers than you are now. From the looks of you, I'll have a long gray beard before that happens!"

He put his hands on his hips and raked the line with his eyes. No one laughed, no one flinched, and several men looked him in the eye as if daring him to put them to the test.

Good. They might lack training but perhaps not spirit. Seen by the dawn's light, indeed, they looked a trifle closer to being soldiers than they had when he first met them.

"Very well. Now, let me see your weapons."

Conan remained silent until it became clear that fewer than half of the men had brought their weapons. That, and the condition of many of those that were displayed, drew another sulphurous blast from the Cimmerian. He eloquently described the ancestry of soldiers who went about without their weapons. He added predictions of the fate awaiting them, barring the favor of gods sometimes charitable to fools.

When Conan told the unarmed to run back to their quarters and bring their weapons, most of them actually ran.

The first day was a tale of errors and omissions, intermingled with minor catastrophes and follies. By the second day, the Second Company had mustered its wits and concluded that its new sergeant was serious.

By the third day, it dawned upon them that neither Captain Oyzhik nor the captain of the Second Company was going to lift a finger to save them from the Cimmerian. The choice was either mutiny or obedience. Somewhat to Conan's relief, those who favored obedience outnumbered those who favored mutiny. He suspected that a reluctance to face Decius's seasoned veterans had something to do with the matter.

After the third day, Conan's work with the Second Company marched forward swiftly and, for the most part, steadily. It was work he knew well, having learned it from a master, High Captain Khadjar in Turan. It was work that needed doing if the Second Company was to be worth even its scanty rations.

Most of all, it was work that Conan enjoyed and that the men of the company came to enjoy also. They were not so lost to pride that being a company of soldiers instead of a rabble did not put heart into them. By the fifth day, Conan had appointed four under-sergeants from their ranks. Three of them were men who had on the first day brought clean weapons to muster; the fourth was the one who had first returned from quarters with his.

By now, Conan had concluded that nothing could be expected for good or ill from either Oyzhik or the company's captain. The latter spent most of his time in his quarters and most of that time either drunk or sleeping. It passed belief that anyone could stomach enough of the Border wine to fuddle his wits, but it seemed that the man was made of stout stuff.

As for Oyzhik, it was said that he was being kept busy strengthening the palace's defenses against an attack by Count Syzambry. This left the captain-general's men free to take the field against the count and on the trail of the lost princess.

Conan might have believed those tales except that Decius seemed to be present at the palace almost every day. He seldom missed spending at least a moment with Raihna, either—or so the Bossonian told Conan.

"I no longer wonder why you suspect Decius," Raihna added. "I sleep no sounder because of it, but that is hardly your fault."

Conan grinned, and as they were alone, slapped her smartly on the rump. Raihna was no woman for sleeping alone unless she had to. But with so many doubtfully friendly eyes around and about, a cold and narrow bed was also the safest.

Some of the village girls had eyed the Cimmerian's massive frame with open approval. But Conan had soon thereafter seen soldiers of both the Guards and Decius's troops eyeing him in a rather less-than-friendly fashion. Clearly, bedding one of the girls would be poaching. Conan could live with a cold bed if it meant a safe back.

He also kept a watchful eye and a keen ear for any opportunity to win enough gold to free Raihna's company from any need to remain in this land. Once the need for gold no longer bound her men to Eloi-kas's service, they would hardly let another sun set before they marched south.

It was the eighth day of Conan's service in the Border Kingdom. The sun was well up, and he was watching over an archery match. Not all of the Guards had bows, and not all of those who had bows had any skill with them.

Conan, however, had gone to Turan barely knowing the point of an arrow from the fletching. Little more than two years later, he was an archer fit for the battlefield. He vowed that every man of his company could achieve at least that much mastery of the bow. Then the company could hurl forty arrows at a single command, two hundred paces in any direction.

That would be no small gift to King Eloikas, Conan judged. Archers would be useful in every kind of fighting the king faced, beginning with the defense of the palace against Count Syzambry.

The contest was not yet half done when Kalk, the senior sergeant, approached Conan. "Sergeant

Conan, I have sighted men skulking up toward the ridge. I am sure they are none of ours."

Conan turned his eyes toward the hillside, which sloped up toward a knife-edged ridge. The slope was covered with small trees or large bushes. Call them what one would, they were abundant enough to hide a company.

"We need not raise the alarm yet," Conan said. "Pick five men and tell the rest to continue the contest. Then meet me here, and we'll go teach these uninvited guests better manners."

Kalk nodded, then remembered to raise his hand in acknowledgment and respect. He also seemed to be smiling as he turned away.

Kalk was like many of the recruits of the Guard, fit to learn the arts of the soldier if someone was ready to teach him. Oyzhik never had been, and Conan wondered how many Guards had died through Oyzhik's sloth. Their kin would owe Oyzhik a blood-debt, that he knew.

Conan led the six men toward the hill as the sun finished burning off the mist. When they struck the steepest part of the slope, he allowed Kalk to take the lead. Careful not to be noticed, he dropped back to the rear. From there he could study the ground both uphill and down. He also had no man at his back.

The recruits set a good pace in mounting the slope. The Border Kingdom was home to all. As children, they had climbed its hills, and as men, they could teach even a long-limbed Cimmerian something about moving on rough terrain.

Beyond the line of the ridge, the ground plunged away into a cliff. Only a bird, or perhaps an ape, could descend the drop. The cliff was so high that the stream below was a silver thread winding through gray rocks dwarfed to pebbles and dark green trees that might have been flowers in a garden.

The slope behind Conan lay silent in the sun. If the skulkers were not Kalk's fancy, they had either departed or lain quiet as the Guards passed them.

Conan frowned at Kalk. The sergeant spread his hands. "It was not the sun," he said mildly.

"I didn't say it was," Conan replied. "We'll spread out as we go down. Grow eyes in the backs of your heads and ears in your arses and we may find something."

Six men was a jest for a real search of the slope. Sixty would not have been too few, and three times that many might not have been wasted.

The men had finished spreading out along the ridge line when Kalk shouted.

"Sergeant Conan! I was not deceived. Come and look just below the top of the cliff!"

Conan thought of drawing his sword but realized that he would need both hands for a secure grip. He stepped cautiously toward Kalk, but no caution could have saved his ankle from the snare Kalk had set the night before.

What caution could not prevent, strength and speed did. As he felt the leather thongs coil serpentlike around his ankle, Conan flung himself backward, away from the cliff. With his sword still at his waist, he had both hands free to break his fall.

The Cimmerian landed, rolled, then lashed out with his feet. The savage lunge of powerful legs snapped the thongs like twine before Kalk could draw his steel. The sergeant's blade was still coming clear when Conan's feet lashed out again.

This time one boot drove against Kalk's knee. He screamed at the pain of his ruined kneecap, then toppled sideways over the cliff. Kalk went on screaming all the way down, until the scream ended in a distant sound, like a ripe melon flung down on a stone floor.

Conan did not wait to listen to the would-be assassin's fate. Kalk had friends, and the Cimmerian had other matters at hand.

He dealt with two of the friends in a flurry of steel striking sparks from steel, then slicing flesh. Both men were down and bleeding when a shout made Conan turn.

One of the Guards was grappling with an archer who had an arrow nocked to his bow. Conan hurled himself at the men as his ally drew a dagger and stabbed the archer in the thigh. The man screamed but lashed out with his bow. The other man fell backward, to land on the very edge of the cliff.

Then he was over the edge as the stone under him crumbled. Conan was barely in time to grab the hand that was the only part of the man visible. The man's bloody fingers made Conan's grip uncertain, and he shifted to using both hands. Thus he pulled the man up until he could firmly grip a wrist. Then the sound of boots in dry grass drew Conan's attention to his rear.

The archer had retrieved his bow and arrow and lurched to a sitting position. Well beyond the reach of Conan's sword, he was trying to draw and shoot. If he succeeded, the arrow could hardly miss a vital spot.

Conan knew that his death might be no more than a few-score heartbeats away. But he did not have it in him to send the man who had saved him plunging after Sergeant Kalk. That might not save him either.

What saved Conan was a man who burst from undergrowth the Cimmerian would have sworn could not hide a squirrel. The man jumped on the archer, lashing out with hands and feet. The archer seemed to leap upright, then to topple. When he came down, he landed squarely on Conan's rib cage. The Cimmerian's breath came short, and for a moment he had to fight for his grip. Then he saw, with staring eyes and doubting mind, who had come to save him.

The man wore sun-bleached leather leggings and a sweat-stained linen jerkin. He looked twenty years younger than usual, but he was nevertheless Captain-General Decius.

"If dangling your friends over the edge of a cliff is sport to you, Conan, no wonder you walk alone."

Decius knelt and caught the loyal Guard's free arm. The double pull had him safe in another moment, whereupon he fainted.

Conan rose cautiously and retrieved his sword. "So this is where you've been in days past, when you were not flattering Raihna?"

"Here and there and other places like it," Decius said. "My men are out and about, however. I mean no insult, Conan, but I can trust my sergeants more than yours."

Conan remembered his glimpse of Kalk's body, bent backward over a blood-spattered stone. "By Erlik's brass tool, I should hope so!"

While they spoke, Decius tore strips from the archer's shirt and bound his bloody thigh. Now he wiped his hands on the remnant of the shirt and stood.

"He will do long enough for questioning. I doubt that we will learn many of Oyzhik's secrets from him, but Kalk is silent forever."

"I didn't send him—" Conan began, then realized that Decius was smiling. The smile broadened, and Conan knew that his own face must have said more than he wished.

"I have shared your doubts about Oyzhik, Conan,

if you were wondering. As for your doubts about me—'' Decius shrugged.

"I'm done with those," Conan growled. He thrust his sword back into its scabbard with a thump. "What of your doubts about me?"

"I have none," Decius said. "Not anymore. But . . . I do have a favor to ask of you."

The words came out strangely, and Decius's look was stranger still. He was sweating even more than the sun could explain and seemed unsure of what to do with his hands.

Conan knew a moment's unease at not knowing what the favor might be. Then he decided that the gods forbid he should be ungrateful to the man who had saved him from joining Sergeant Kalk on the rocks below.

"You can ask, although I don't promise to grant," the Cimmerian replied.

"What lies between you and Raihna?" The words came out in a rush as if Decius feared his voice would betray him otherwise.

Conan wanted to laugh. Decius was not much younger than the Cimmerian's father would have been were he alive. He was also a widower who had buried three sons as well as his wife. Yet the captain-general was asking as if he were a love-stricken youth.

He would also be as easily hurt as any such youth, and he would not forget such an injury. That thought made it easier for Conan to find words.

"By all the lawful gods of this realm and my homeland, I swear that Raihna and I are not bonded, hand-fasted, betrothed, dedicated, wed, married . . . have I left anything out?"

Decius smiled uncertainly. "Not to my knowledge. But . . . you are bedmates?"

Conan swallowed a peevish reply to the question. Decius had not only saved him from Kalk's fate, he had done so at the risk of meeting it himself. Decius might not have come to the hill alone, but he had surely hidden himself far beyond help by any companions. That courage called for at least a civil reply to the man's uncivil question.

"We have been, and may be again. It was the choice of both of us."

"Well, then," Decius said. Relief seemed to leave him speechless and unsteady on his feet for a moment. "Then—it is much to ask you, Conan—but will you press my suit with Mistress Raihna?"

Conan silently invoked the names of a number of gods of love and desire. All of them seemed to have led Decius's wits astray. He hoped they would shortly lead them home again. Meanwhile, he could at least answer this question from sure and certain knowledge.

"I will not, and for two good reasons. One is that the lady would not think the better of you for lacking the . . . for not speaking for yourself. The second is that I doubt you saved my head today so that Raihna could break it tonight!"

"I suppose that is the best I can hope for," Decius said. He cupped his hands and gave a war cry that had either no words or none that Conan understood.

Three heads popped up from the scrub and three hands rose beside them. Conan judged distances and saw that Decius had not in fact put himself beyond help. His men had stayed hidden while their captain-general inquired if Raihna was a free woman!

So Decius was not altogether foolhardy. Conan still muttered another prayer that the love gods would undo their work on Decius's wits. The Cimmerian had never heard of good coming of mixing love and war, least of all for captains with other men's lives in their hands!

"So Oyzhik has fled," Raihna said grimly. "Do we have much to fear from those he may have left behind?"

"Oyzhik was a fool and likely to choose other fools to do his work. We have more to fear if Count Syzambry chose them," Conan said. He drained half his cup of wine at a gulp, as if this could wash the words from his mouth.

At least it was wine good enough for a man's tongue and belly instead of for scrubbing the jakes! The wine was one of the fruits of Conan's work the day before, along with the furs on Raihna's bed and the embroidered Khitan-silk chamber robe she wore.

"We'll learn more in the next day or two," Conan added. "My company.has the work of studying all those traps Oyzhik promised to set. We know that he planned to either make them harmless to Syzambry's men or to turn them against us. Beyond that, we've yet to learn."

Conan poured more wine into Raihna's offered cup. "Decius simply wanted to ruin all the traps. He said they were no honorable way of fighting. I told him that Syzambry had already pissed into the wind what honor he had. Didn't we owe the king and the princess at least the knowledge that we gave the son of a hundred fathers a decent fight?"

"Decius seems to know what—"

"In Turan, Decius would be called a child! Pitied or ignored until he offended someone who'd squash him like a cockroach!"

"Conan, I think the wine speaks now, not your heart. I was going to say that Decius seems to know what will let him sleep of nights. So do you. Or was it another Cimmerian named Conan whom Decius snatched from death today?"

Conan confessed his guilt and begged for mercy. Raihna laughed. "I will grant it if you pour yourself more wine and join me in a toast." He obeyed and she raised her cup.

"To Captain Conan and the Second Company of the Palace Guard of the Border Kingdom! May they both continue to rise!"

Conan drank, but not without some doubts. Giving him the Second Company was just and wise, if the men would obey him. Making the company's old captain chief over the Guard in Oyzhik's place was not so wise, unless one believed that the honor would sober the man.

Decius would surely end having to be captain over the Guard as well as his own men. As good a captain as he was, he still lacked the art of being in three places at once, or of doing without sleep, food, and visits to the jakes! The best captain could not defy nature without someone paying a price, most commonly in blood.

It was also somewhat in Conan's mind that Decius was following in an ancient tradition. If you wished to court a woman, and had it in your power, you advanced, honored, or enriched her kin.

Well, Decius would learn that he could not follow that path very far before he ran afoul of worse dangers than any of Oyzhik's traps. Raihna's tongue would be the first, but hardly the last.

Raihna had stood beside Conan while they drank. Now she rested one hand on his right arm and leaned gently against him. Not much to Conan's surprise, it seemed that she wore nothing beneath the chamber robe. He slipped a hand under the garment and found that he'd judged rightly. The hand wandered up across a firm flank, then climbed a supple back.

Raihna turned, opened the robe, and slipped out of it. It made a blue and gold pool as she climbed onto Conan's lap. Then she let out a yelp of mock fear as the Cimmerians' massive arms caught her up and flung her across the room onto the bed.

"I think it's lying down that was on your mind, woman!" Conan said. Raihna laughed, and she was still laughing when her arms and lips welcomed him to her bed.

CHAPTER 8

Good wine and long loving meant late sleep for both Conan and Raihna. It was as well that the summons to an audience with King Eloikas came well into the morning and that the audience itself was not before noon. The Cimmerian and the Bossonian alike were able to break their fast and garb themselves in their best without haste.

King Eloikas greeted them with something very like a smile. Decius, standing beside the throne, had his face set in a blank mask, but Conan judged that he was not displeased either. The captain-general's eyes followed Raihna, however, from the moment she entered to the moment that Eloikas bid her step back while Conan knelt before the throne.

Decius handed the king a linen bag. Swift movements told of strength in the royal hands as they opened the bag and drew forth an elaborate necklace. It was made of links of heavy gold, with a medallion in the center in the form of a comet. The head of the comet was a great polished blue stone, set about with fresh-water pearls.

"This is the ceremonial necklace of a captain in Our Guards," Eloikas said. "Oyzhik fled with his, and I would not shame you by giving it to you even had he left it behind."

For a moment Conan would have sworn that the king's eyes glistened. "This was the necklace of my son, Prince Gulain, when he had a company of the Guards. It was not buried with him, because the gods sent me a vision that it might be needed for a worthy man."

The royal eyes were definitely moist now, and Conan noted that Eloikas had dropped the royal "we." The Cimmerian had heard more than a few tales of the valor and wisdom of Prince Gulain, Chienna's brother, who had met his death in a riding accident. So Conan replied with an easy mind and a clear voice.

"Your Majesty, I pray that I may be worthy of this honor. I know that I walk in the footsteps of a better man. But I think I can give your enemies some sleepless nights and busy days, with the help of some other good men—and women." He nodded at Decius and Raihna.

This speech went over well, although Raihna had to stifle giggles when they were alone. "Anyone would think you had been raised at some court and were a royal page in your childhood," she said at last.

Conan snorted like a mired ox. "Say rather that I know what will help keep daggers out of my back. The fewer tongues that wag about my new rank, the fewer daggers behind me. We'll have all we can handle with the ones in front!"

It would not do to tell Raihna some of his other thoughts. Such a necklace told its own tale. The hoard of the Border kings might not be altogether wine-flown babbling. Good service might bring more of that hoard into the Cimmerian's hands.

Nor might that be the only gold to be won in these mountains. Conan would not steal a rusty horseshoe nail from Elpikas or anyone sworn to him, but Count Syzambry and his friends were another matter. Their coffers were fair game and might repay a visit, if the chance came.

What might happen if the little count had all that the sorcerous allies' rumor gave him was another matter, of course. But Conan would think of that when he had to. Sorcerers appeared more often in tales than in truth, and quick wits and a well-wielded sword lost little power even when a sorcerer did appear.

Aybas did not bow before Princess Chienna. That was against the custom of the Star Brothers for their prisoners. In vain Aybas had railed at them, pointing out that the princess was more Count Syzambry's prisoner than theirs.

Worse than in vain, Aybas realized. He had made the wizards yet more suspicious of him. They would be less charitable toward him now in other matters—such as that of Wylla.

If Aybas wanted the wench, he would have to hunt her down himself. The Star Brothers would now most likely send her straight to the beast and be done with her. If he offended them further, Aybas would be lucky not to follow her!

Meanwhile, Aybas's not bowing clearly offended the princess. "I hear Aquilonia in your voice, Aybas," she said. "I was taught that Aquilonia was a land of civilized manners. Before a princess, a common man, or even a noble, showed more courtesy than seems to be in you."

Drawn up to her full height, she was as tall as he and hardly less broad across the shoulders. That she was fair to look at did not make Aybas less reluctant to step too close to her. Her ankles were still hobbled, but he did not care to test the strength of those arms, for all that scant rations had thinned them and dirt caked their skin.

"Your Highness," Aybas said. The title at least had not been forbidden, or if it had been, then for once he would say curse the Star Brothers! "I fear that those who rule here in the Vale of the Pougoi recognize no rank save their own."

"Not even that of Count Syzambry?"

"Why do you name the count, Your Highness?"

"Because I am not such a fool as to think that you and the wizards contrived to bring me here without his help. You both serve him. The wizards because they think he will enrich the Pougoi, you . . . the gods only know your reasons."

That was too close to the truth for Aybas to keep his countenance. The princess pressed her advantage. "I think you can trust neither the Pougoi wizards nor the count to keep any promises they have made to you. My father and I, however, are more honorable. What—"

"Enough!" Aybas's hand came up as if it had a will of its own. Had the princess spoken another word, he might have actually struck her.

"There will be no punishment for this rebellion," Aybas said, praying that this was a promise he could keep. "But I will not come here alone again." That was a promise he would have to keep, or he would be closer to the chains on the rock and the sucking mouths of the beast's tentacles than he cared to think about.

The princess tossed her head like a fly-beset horse and looked meaningfully at the door. Aybas was through it and bolting it behind in between two heartbeats.

Outside, he found himself sweating, even in the chill of the mountain evening. At least he would have proved his loyalty to any unseen eyes or ears. Beyond that, no good would come of making an enemy of Princess Chienna.

"But what other path is there for me, oh gods?"

Neither the skies, the wind, nor the rocks beneath, answered Aybas's cry.

Conan had hopes of taking the Second Company out into the field to put a final polish on its new skills. Decius had other plans.

"If Syzambry has half the men we think he does," the captain-general said, "we have no hope against him in the open. The more we guard the palace, the less harm he can do."

"The more we guard the palace, the more we leave the count a free hand everywhere else," Conan replied. "I'm a stranger here. I don't know how many friends Eloikas has outside the palace—"

"That's King Eloikas to you, Cimmerian," Decius snapped. "And you say truly, you are a stranger here."

"A stranger who's seen his share of battles and intrigues," Conan reminded the older man. "Such a share that His Majesty made me captain over a company of his own Palace Guard. Did you argue against that, or are you regretting it now?"

That was pushing a man of higher rank rather hard, but not harder than necessary, or so it seemed to Conan. If Decius was letting a boy's passion for Raihna addle the man's and the captain's wits—

Decius shook his head. "I spoke for you then, and I will speak for you now whatever you say to me. Just think before you speak, if you have it in you to do so."

Conan gave Decius a tiger's grin. "Well enough, my lord. I think that His Majesty must have some friends in this realm. Otherwise, Syzambry would have plumped his arse down on the throne years ago."

"Not unlikely."

"Cursed near certain, I'd say. Now, what will these friends say if they see us hiding in the palace like a mole in its burrow? I know the king's no coward. You know the king's no coward. What about our friends? Even if they think that the king's worth helping, what will they do if Syzambry's men are free to roam the land? If any of our friends so much as give the count a sour look, they'll be dead, or running for their lives. Running to us for help, when we've enough to do for ourselves."

Decius looked the Cimmerian over with great care, as if the younger man had just grown bright-blue scales or a long, spiked tail. Then he shook his head again.

"Conan," he said, "if you ever 'plump your arse' down upon a throne, I would not like to be the man called on to move you from it."

Conan shrugged. "I've seen a few men win thrones or lose them. I'd be a fool not to learn from that. One thing I've learned is that a throne makes a man a big target, and a sitting one. The day my arse and a throne do make friends, you can call me a fool!"

"Small chance that either of us will ever have the chance," Decius said. "But it is more than likely that

Count Syzambry will be visiting us soon. Your company's work for now is to make sure that our hospitality is worthy of him. We will speak later of taking the field again."

"Later," it seemed, might be in the next age of the world for all Conan heard of the matter in the next few days. He had little time to concern himself with it, however, for the work given to the Second Company kept captain and men alike as busy as galley slaves.

Oyzhik's traps were many, but for the most part they were poorly made, and too often poorly concealed. Conan wondered if Oyzhik had planned this to be sure that his master's men would not spring the traps even if he could not wreck them on the night of the attack.

Be that as it may, one cunning and well-concealed trap was worth a dozen that any child could avoid. Conan made sure that no child would find any of the ones he set. Some were Oyzhik's deadfalls—pits, hidden crossbows and the like—done over with greater skill and bloody intent.

Others were altogether new. Conan had to be cautious there. The palace was vast, built in days when the Border Kingdom bore another name and its main defense lay with armies that marched where other realms now held sway. It was also ancient, and it had been several generations since the Border kings had had the gold to pay masons to repair sagging arches and cracking walls.

There were parts of the palace unvisited by any living man. Conan judged that the count would seek entry by these long-unused paths, and he gave most of his attention to them. Care was needed to avoid leaving suspicious traces. Still more care was needed to avoid bringing entire corridors or chambers down on the heads of the workers instead of on the count's men.

Raihna visited Conan one day during the noon meal. She found him stripped to a loinguard, sword, and a liberal coating of dust and plaster, sitting with a company of Guards similarly clad. The fruits of their morning's labor yawned before her, a pit with a spiked log in the bottom.

"When we've closed the pit, we'll lay on another surprise," Conan said, pointing toward a side hall. "An old catapult cord with a trip release and a barrel of tar. We'll have a lighted candle in a clay pot set into the barrel. When the barrel breaks and spills the tar, the candle falls into the tar and the whole chamber's ankle-deep in flames."

Several of the Guards cheered at the picture. Others called greetings to Raihna, inviting her to join them at their work—

"—'specially if you get into our workin' garb," one added.

Raihna clapped her hand to her sword hilt and stepped back, nostrils flaring in mock fury. She set a boot heel into a pile of rubble, and dust flew up like smoke from a fire. She took in a good breathful, coughed, then began sneezing.

Near the ceiling, a crack appeared in the wall to the left. It ran as swiftly as a hare fleeing a fox, down the wall to the floor. Then a slab of wall gave a mighty groan and topped outward, crumbling as it fell. Part of the ceiling followed, but only after Conan and Raihna and the workers were safely clear of the fall.

As the dust settled, Conan looked at the pile of rubble, then spat to clear his throat. "Well, men," he said, "I've been warning you that a sneeze could bring this ruin down on our heads. Now you see that I was speaking the gods' own truth."

Some of the men still made gestures of aversion, but most of them laughed. Since none of them were under the rubble, they could turn it to a joke.

The men salvaged such of their food as wasn't buried or too dusty to eat and resumed their meal. Conan led Raihna aside into an empty chamber with a stone bench built into one crumbling wall. The bench creaked as they sat down on it but did not tumble them to the floor.

"I'd best see Decius about going on with this work," the Cimmerian said. "We've already laid traps in every part of the palace that's not this ruined or worse. If we go on into the old warrens, we'll have the place down on our heads before Syzambry comes to take them!"

"Let me speak to Decius first and see how the land lies," Raihna said. "He has heard enough about your notions of going into the field against our enemies. He will not be gracious if he thinks you are putting the matter forward again."

Conan cursed—softly, out of fear of provoking another collapse. When he spoke, it was also softly, but more out of fear of listening ears.

"Mitra bury Decius in mule dung!" he said. "There's as much sense in striking first as ever there was. And as little sense in waiting like rats in burrows for the ferrets to come down and snatch us!"

Raihna put a hand on Conan's arm. "I think you do him an injustice, Conan."

The Cimmerian shot Raihna a sharp look but said nothing. With another woman, he would have reasoned that Decius had begun to turn her head. With Raihna, he knew that he would hear what she believed to be sense, even if he did not agree with it.

"How?"

"The Palace Guards are not fit for the field. He would be taking his own men and them only on any such raid. That would make the Guards stronger."

Conan nodded slowly. He had seen enough intrigues in Turan to know that Decius was not starting at his own shadow. But—

"Does he fear the captains, me among them, or the men, or what?"

"The men Oyzhik may have left behind and whom you might not discover in time. He trusts your sword and your honor, Conan, but he also knows that you are a stranger here."

"Yes, and men who might have been loyal before they saw a stranger made captain can turn to treason overnight." Conan wished greatly for some wine to wash both dust and the taste of plots from his mouth. He had to content himself with spitting again.

Then he rose. "Perhaps Decius has the right of it. But I still won't put my company at hazard from this tumbledown palace. Loyal men or not, they don't deserve to be squashed like grapes in a winepress!"

Raihna squeezed his hand. "I'll say as much, and you'll lose nothing with Decius by his hearing it. That I can swear."

She strode off, as graceful as ever, leaving Conan to ponder briefly how she could be so sure of Decius's goodwill. Of course, women had their ways—

And if he gave way to jealousy over that, he'd deserve to have the next piece of ceiling drop on his head, for all the use he was making of it! Raihna would go where she pleased, and he could no more chain her than he could command the mysterious thunder that had now begun to roll through the hills at least once a night.

That thunder was worth a thought or two, for it reeked of sorcery. What Raihna might do to soothe Decius had naught to do with such matters.

Conan walked back to his men. They were already at work again, although slowly and casting doubtful looks at the walls and ceiling.

"Good news, men. We're done for the day. Decius is thinking about putting the rest of the traps where they'll take Syzambry's men, not us!"

"I'd work here a moon and more if it'd build a trap for the count himself!" one man shouted. Others nodded.

"You may get that chance, but tomorrow," Conan said. He set the example by starting to bundle up pry bars and hammers.

As the tools clinked into the baskets, it came to the Cimmerian that Decius might have another reason for not taking the field. Eloikas's handful of good men might chase the count's retainers all over the hills for many days without ever coming up against the count himself.

If the little man with the great ambitions escaped, he could find another army. If he died, his cause was finished. And what better way to kill him than to let him come to the palace, as he must if he wished the final victory?

Perhaps there was nothing wrong with either the captain-general's wits or his loyalty. It did not make Conan any happier to think about being immured in this crumbling palace against all of his instincts for taking the fight to the foe.

Outside the chief's hut, thunder rolled. Aybas, peering through the chinks between the logs, saw no lightning, so he knew it was the witch-thunder again.

Had he doubted, the sounding of horns and drums from the village would have ended his doubting.

Count Syzambry let the thunder—and the din of the Pougoi trying to fight it—die away before speaking. He did not take his eyes off of Aybas and Oyzhik, sitting together on the straw at his feet.

If Aybas had not long since given over flinching at the witch-thunder, he would have nerved himself to sit still under the count's scrutiny. Oyzhik was clearly as uneasy as a man on hot bricks, and the chill of the mountain night did not keep the sweat from his brow. Rather than seem less brave than Oyzhik, Aybas would have climbed the dam and cast himself into the slime-dripping grip of the beast.

"The Pougoi can be trusted?" Oyzhik asked for the third time.

Something that had no name flickered across Syzambry's face. In the dimness, Aybas could not read the little count's countenance, nor did he really wish to try.

"They can be trusted for all that I have asked them to do," Syzambry replied.

Aybas had the sense not to ask Syzambry what the Pougoi were expected to do to help lift the count onto the throne. In any case, there would not have been time for an answer even had Syzambry wished to give one.

Heavy footsteps thudded on the beaten earth outside, and the door opened with squeals and groans. Half a score of Pougoi warriors marched in, with one of the Star Brothers bringing up the rear. The warriors carried spears and stone-headed axes, the wizard a leather sack.

"Him," Syzambry said. The warriors surrounded the seated men. The count motioned Aybas to rise and step forward. Aybas commanded his legs to uphold him and his knees not to rattle together, and obeyed.

Oyzhik's mouth opened, but before he could cry out, four warriors were upon him. A leather gag stifled his cries, while leather thongs bound his wrists and hobbled his ankles. Then the warriors gripped the thongs and Oyzhik's travel-stained clothing and dragged him out of the hut.

Aybas remained motionless until the heavy tread of the warriors faded into the night. Stepping back and looking nowhere and everywhere, he said quietly: "Decius would have given much to see that."

"Pah!" Count Syzambry moved nothing except his mouth. Then he crossed his thin legs in their dyed riding leathers and shrugged. "If our lord captain-general had blood instead of milk in his veins, he would long since have taken his rights. Had he done so, I would have served him gladly."

Aybas thought that Count Syzambry would gladly serve another man the day vultures gave over their lives to fasting and prayer.

"Is Oyzhik to go to the beast?" Aybas asked.

"You presume to question my judgment?" Syzambry purred.

"I question nothing," Aybas said, "least of all your judgment. Were it not sound, we would hardly be so close to your victory. I merely remind you that too many among the Pougoi are uneasy about the sacrifices to the beast."

"They are cowards," Syzambry snapped.

It could be said that with enough cowards, the best army might become a rabble. It could also be said that any man who had watched the princess's coming to the valley could be excused for wishing himself elsewhere.

Neither could be said to the count's face by one

who wished to see another sunrise. So the Aquilonian merely shrugged.

"They will not release Oyzhik, that I can promise you," he said. "His kin played no small part in driving the Pougoi from their ancestral lands and into this valley. These folk have a long memory."

"But the lowlanders have a short one," Syzambry said. He seemed to be almost grinning. "When they see Oyzhik go to the beast for his treasons, they will forget how I gained the throne. They will think there may be some truth in what I say, that I stormed the palace to save it from Decius and Oyzhik, that the king died and the princess needed consoling. These are matters of ill fortune, of the gods' doing and not mine."

Aybas thought of men he had seen and heard in his long journey from his father's estate to this wretched valley. Compared to some of them, Count Syzambry's intrigues were those of a child cheating at a game of toss-pebble. Yet this child had the power of life or death over Aybas, and would toss him away like a pebble if he ever guessed the Aquilonian's thoughts. Aybas feigned good cheer when he next spoke.

"May it be so, my lord. Now, how may I next serve you?"

"I shall depart to join my men at cock crow. Is it prudent to find me a woman?"

"None you would think pleasing, I fear," Aybas replied, praying that the gods had not granted Syzambry a glimpse of Wylla.

"I supposed as much," the count said. "Very well. Then guard this bag with your life until I come for it. Farewell, and my thanks for good service."

Syzambry spoke as if "my" should in truth have been the royal "Our." Aybas bowed and remained bowing until the door slammed, then knelt to study the bag.

It was of plain leather, bound shut with an iron band. The runes on the band were such that Aybas did not care to look at them too closely. Even in the dim light of the single oil lamp, he could see that they were kin to the runes on the face of the dam. He could also feel that the bag held something heavy, as stone, but he would not even think of opening it.

Count Syzambry was now quite without restraint in using the Pougoi wizards' magic to lift him to the throne. The Aquilonian was also sure that the count was quite without real knowledge of what he was using—or of what its real masters might ask of him as their price.

CHAPTER 9

Conan awoke in darkness, at first not sure why he had awakened. It might be only the bed, which was stoutly built but overly generous in size. It might have been comfortable for the Cimmerian when he first left his native land. For him now, it was a minor torture, and only his ability to sleep anywhere allowed him to endure it.

Before retiring tonight, he had sworn a solemn vow to see the palace carpenter about a new bed. He was even prepared to endure the man's witless jests about who Conan might be planning to share the bed with.

Conan set feet to the cracked tile of the floor, drew on breeches, belted on his sword, and listened. Nothing uncommon reached his ears. A slop-pot gurgled, then banged against stone; someone cried out in a nightmare or in passion; mice or rats scurried in a corner.

The knowledge that he had awakened for some good reason remained with Conan. All of the instincts that had kept him alive now called warnings. They would tell him no more, so it was best to seek out true knowledge of the danger.

He drew on his shirt and thrust both daggers into their sheaths. He thought of taking his bow, but in the end, he left it with the bearskin and riding cloak piled at the foot of the bed.

Conan knew that danger stalked the palace. Others did not. Seeing him roaming about full-armed would only raise questions he could not answer. Ignorance and fear together were the sparks to ignite a panic, which could leave the palace defenseless.

Conan's grim thoughts went no further. Horns and drums sounded in the distance and were echoed closer at hand from within the palace. Also from within the palace, shouted messages and war cries reverberated. Conan heard too many screams as the weaker among the palace folk let fear master them.

The Cimmerian had no need to wake the portion of his company lying in the next chamber. The first sergeant was already cursing, kicking, and as needs be, dragging the men off their pallets and into their war harness.

The sergeant raised a hand as Conan appeared. "I have sent a messenger to the barracks. The men there are to rally on the palace," he said.

"Good. But send a second man in case the first meets with ill luck. I am going to Decius. Our rallying point is the Chamber of the Red Fish."

"So be it, Captain Conan."

Conan thought of giving a second rallying place, outside the palace. But that would be admitting doubts about the outcome of the battle before it had even begun, an admission that stuck in his throat.

In silence the Cimmerian stalked toward the Chamber of the Red Fish. Taking its name from the mosaic in what had once been an ornamental pool, the chamber could be defended by a handful against a stout band. It also had a staircase, battered by the years but still fit to let a nimble man climb to the roof and look about him.

Conan reached the chamber to find that half of Raihna's men were already there. Leaving them to build barricades of stone and ancient furniture, Conan scrambled up the stairs.

The horns and drums in the distance were silent now. Darkness hid whatever they had been rallying, be it men or monsters. Conan looked at the sky, where lowering clouds veiled the moon more often than not. He half-expected to hear the witch-thunder.

Instead, he saw a pinpoint of ruby-tinted light spring to life in the darkness downhill from the palace. The pinpoint grew into a ball of fire, and its color changed from that of rubies to that of old wine.

By that light Conan saw what seemed a mighty host drawn up before the palace. A second look showed him that it was not mighty, and indeed barely a host.

Count Syzambry was well to the fore, mounted on his roan stallion and surrounded by some two-score riders. Many more men stood behind the horsemen, most of them archers, bearing scanty armor and few weapons save their bows. A final band of perhaps three-score had surrounded the huts and the remainder of the Palace Guard there. From the way they kept their distance from the huts, it seemed that the Guards were neither asleep nor yielding.

That was enough for Conan. Syzambry might command sorcery, but all it had done so far was to reveal how few men he had. They were no band of

121

beardless boys, but neither were they the predestined victors of tonight's battle.

Now, if only the Guards in the barracks could strike into Syzambry's rear at the moment his men went forward—

The globe of light had turned the hue of old blood. It spread so far that Conan could barely make out the count. Then the little man flung his hands wide apart and something fell smoking from the globe of light.

A vagrant breeze brought the Cimmerian the smell of heated metal and burned grass. An angry hiss rose, along with clouds of smoke and steam, as what had fallen struck a puddle.

Then the globe of light shrank back to barely more than a pinpoint. The smoke curled up to form a stalk swaying in the breeze, the light bobbing at the end of it like a flower.

The earth quivered. Smoke and blood-hued light began to move toward the palace as if drawn inexorably forward by something just out of human sight.

Not quite out of sight, either, as Conan saw in the next moment. What drew the fire-flower after it was also making a furrow in the earth, an arm's length wide. Smoke poured out of it, stones and earth flew to either side, and the quivering of the earth doubled and redoubled.

Conan abandoned thoughts of rallying the Guards to surround Syzambry's men. The first task for all of the king's captains now had to be keeping their men clear of this sorcerous monstrosity rumbling toward the palace. If that meant leaving the palace so that it would not topple on their heads and bury them in the ruins—

One of the barracks huts did collapse, the sound lost in the rumble of the ravaged earth. Dust and smoke swirled up, and Guards poured out like ants from a kicked hill. They came with their weapons in hand, though, and dragging or carrying wounded comrades.

Conan forced himself down the stairs. For better or worse, the Guards caught in the barracks would have to make their own way tonight. His battle would be here, so far as a man could fight sorcery.

The Cimmerian was three steps from the floor when the earth heaved fiercely. The steps cracked. So did a section of wall and several sections of roof. Conan leaped as the stairs sagged under him, leaped again to avoid falling stones, went down, caught himself on his hands, and ended kneeling at Raihna's feet.

She had a grin for him, but he could see that she was trying to hearten herself as well as her men. He returned the grin and sprang to his feet.

Most of the men who'd been in the chamber when Conan climbed up were there when he came down. Few had fled, and Raihna had brought the rest of her band with her. But there was more than one man who had remained because falling stone pinned him to the floor.

Conan gripped the nearest such stone, wrapped his massive arms around it, and heaved it clear. In the last moment of silence before the fallen men began screaming, Conan heard his own breath coming hard.

He also heard, so faint that it might have been a trick of the night wind, the distant trill of pipes.

The pipes were indeed distant and faint. But to Count Syzambry, they might have been shrilling in his ear.

He knew what they meant. He also knew what the

Pougoi wizards had said, so many times that he had become weary of hearing even the truth.

"Let fear break your will, and your will drags down our power with it. Wield what we have given you without fear, and it will do what must be done. We cannot keep our promises to a man who lets fear rule him."

That was as close as any man had come to calling Syzambry a coward since he had been old enough to know that he could have blood for such an insult. He let it pass, for he did not doubt that the wizards spoke the truth and that all of his schemes would fail if his courage faltered.

So the count willed himself to shut the piping out of his mind even if he could not close his ears to the distant, silvery voice. He would not let it surround him, enwrap him like swaddling clothes on a baby, echo within his skull until all awareness of anything but the pipes fled—

Between one moment and the next, Count Syzambry knew that he had won the first victory. The pipes now seemed a long, wailing lamentation for the dead and the dying, for the doomed who knew not their fate. They did not master the count's thoughts.

Instead, the power flowing from the pipes turned against the Pougoi magic unleashed against the palace. The furrow had almost reached the outer wall of the palace when the earth itself heaved up into another wall. Stones poured down from the new wall and into the furrow.

The furrow vomited smoke, so thick that it seemed almost solid. The stones flew out as fast as they fell in, and so violently that some of them nearly struck Syzambry's men. Horses reared, their panicky squeals lost in the din of the tormented earth, and even men began to turn pale faces toward one another.

Syzambry once more found himself battling fear that threatened to eat not merely his magic, but his very wits from within.

Furrow and earthen wall now seemed to fling themselves at each other like maddened monsters. Stones flew high over the ranks of Syzambry's men, dropping among the Guards' huts.

One smashed a hut to rubble, and the count thought he heard the cries of men trapped within. He would have prayed that the stones bury the rest of the Palace Guard, except that praying to god, or even to demon, seemed unwise in the presence of the star-magic.

Syzambry forced himself to look beyond the duel of magic, trying to pierce the palace's veil of dust. In places, the night breeze had torn the veil, and there the count saw what made his heart leap.

The palace was crumbling before his eyes. It could hardly have been crumbling faster had it borne the full weight of the sky-magic. Walls sagged, roofs gaped, whole chambers opened themselves to the sky in the moment before they crumbled into rubble. More dust streamed up, renewing the veil until the count's eyes could no longer penetrate it.

They had no need. There must be defenders ready within the palace. But those defenders would have to fear peril not merely at their flanks and rear, but from the sky above and the earth below. They would be in no condition to make a determined fight.

The wizards had said that the count's will was all that mattered, not where he stood. What better way to steel his will and that of his men than to lead the way into the palace?

Count Syzambry flung the reins of his mount to

the horse-holder and scrambled from the saddle. The earth rocked under his feet like the deck of a boat in a flood-swollen river, but he would not let himself fall.

Instead, he drew his sword with both hands, tossed it, caught it by the blade, then raised the point toward the palace.

"The gods themselves cast down Eloikas and all his men! Follow me!"

For a heart-stopping moment, Syzambry heard nothing save the roar of the embattled earth. Then, behind him, blades rasped from their scabbards and the war cries rose.

"Steel Hand! Steel Hand! Forward, the Steel Hand!"

In the palace of King Eloikas, chaos reigned. Chaos past description of belief, even for seasoned warriors such as Conan and Raihna.

Not that either of them gave a thought to describing what was happening about them. Their thoughts were wholly aimed at keeping their men from being caught under the falling rubble.

Then they heard the war cries, louder even than the rumble and crash of stone and the roar of the tormented earth. Out of the thundering darkness, out of the blood-tinted clouds of dust, Count Syzambry's men swarmed to the attack.

If they had begun in any sort of order, they had little or none by the time they came within sword's length of Conan. Their order had not survived scrambling over the upheaved ridge of earth. From the screams heard even over the war cries, it seemed that some of the men would not survive either.

Conan wished that the palace's unknown ally were not using sorcery nearly as dreadful as Count Syzambry's. Defending a place by casting it down upon its defenders was to Conan neither honorable nor wise.

At least the sight could leave the men under Conan and Raihna no doubt that any chance of safety, let alone victory, lay to the fore. To the rear lay only a palace sinking into ruins even as they watched. To the fore lay a human foe, and above that foe, the open sky.

"Eloikas!" Conan roared, his voice rising over the battle din. He hurled himself forward. As a lodestone draws iron, so the Cimmerian drew after him the men who saw him. Raihna was not far behind Conan, and she did as well with those who saw her.

Count Syzambry's men were scattered, unsure of their footing, and, in places, actually outnumbered. They had better armor and weapons, and more skill, but at first these were not enough.

Nothing save massed archery or overwhelming numbers would have been enough against the Cimmerian. His broadsword hummed through the air, clanged against armor and other blades, and tore flesh and bone with slaughterhouse sounds. When the fighting grew too tangled or opponents too close for proper sword work, it was the turn of his dagger or massive fist.

Together, the Cimmerian's weapons stretched half a dozen foes helpless on the ground before any of the men following him reached an enemy. When they did, it was with hearts raised by the sight of Conan's work, against foes equally cast down.

The count's men were actually withdrawing when their lord scrambled over the ridge and saw what seemed to be rout and ruin. He heard war cries giving way to shouts of warning, even to stark terror.

He saw the Cimmerian storming forward like an elemental force of nature.

He shouted an order, and the top of the ridge sprouted his archers. They cocked or drew, and arrows and bolts sleeted down into the ranks of the palace's defenders. Now the warnings and screams were not only from the count's men. Beneath his dust-caked beard, he smiled.

Conan had hoped that in the dust and confusion, the count's archers would be holding back for fear of hitting comrades. They were doing this, to be sure, but they were also bringing down too many of the Guards. The Guards would be spent and broken before "friendly" archery wasted the count's ranks.

The Cimmerian judged as best he could the distance to the count. If a man could just cross the broken ground and scale the slope to bring the count down—

Arrows thudded into the earth and *tinged* off chunks of rubble by way of a warning. The archers had picked the Cimmerian out of the ranks of his men. If he tried to grapple the count, he would be an arrow-sprouting corpse long before he covered half the distance.

Conan withdrew, more slowly than he had advanced in spite of the arrow hail. It was against his nature to retreat at all, ten times over to start a panic among his men.

The Guards' archers went to work as their comrades retreated. Caught standing in the open, with only luck and armor between themselves and steel-tipped shafts, many of the count's archers quickly lay sprawled on their high ground. The rest hastily sought the protection of the reverse slope, and not all of the count's curses and entreaties could bring them back.

Thus Conan and Raihna, and more than half of their men, returned to such safety as the palace still provided. In the swirling din of the fight, Conan had not noticed that the duel of earth-magic seemed to have ended. But as he helped Raihna bandage an arrow gash in one of her arms, he realized that the earth was both still and silent. Also, the palace was no longer raining stones and tiles!

"What now?" Raihna asked, gritting her teeth as Conan tightened the bandage to hold the lips of the wound together. "We've barely won a skirmish, let alone a battle."

"I'll wager that's more than Syzambry expected," the Cimmerian grunted. He would have given half the hoard of the Border realm, if he'd possessed it, for some wine to rinse dust and grit from his mouth.

"If the lads in the barracks have held their ground, they're in the count's rear," Conan went on. "Curse it! I'd deal with a sorcerer myself, if he could just take a message to—"

Raihna put a hand on the Cimmerian's arm and pointed. One of Decius's under-captains was picking his way cautiously through the rubble. He kept looking up to see what was about to tumble on him, and each time he looked up, he stumbled on something that had already tumbled down.

At last Raihna took pity on him, scurried down the hall, and led him the rest of the way. Behind what had once been the wall of a sculpture gallery, the three leaders took counsel.

"Decius wishes you to bring your men back to join his so that we may retreat as one—" the messenger began. He said no more before a Cimmerian roar interrupted him.

"Has Decius turned—lost his wits, or sent a coward as his messenger?" Conan thundered the question loud enough to raise echoes and bring down loose pebbles from half-ruined walls.

Raihna gripped his arm again, and this time she put her other hand over his mouth. "Conan, for the love of the gods! You want to tell Decius, not the count!"

The messenger had turned pale at the Cimmerian's look, and he still had a corpse's hue as he continued.

"Captain Conan, the lord captain-general did not ask. He commanded."

"I don't care if Mitra and Erlik together are commanding it," Conan snarled. "We've a good part of the Guard out there, and the gods only know how they're faring. If they could break out into Syzambry's rear—"

"King Eloikas cannot move as fast as one might wish," the under-captain said doggedly. "He must leave the palace now, to escape the men Count Syzambry is bringing against our rear."

Perhaps it was just his blood being roused, or the fact of the sorcery so close at hand. Conan still thought that the man knew something he was not saying about Eloikas's reasons for this hasty departure.

"I wasn't asking the king to lead our charge himself," Conan said. "Only to remember men sworn to him, and to make one last try for victory. We can still bring down the count. If we can't do that, we can hurt his men and slow their pursuit."

"Perhaps—" The messenger seemed torn between fear of Decius and the king and fear of Conan. Or was it knowledge that the Cimmerian's counsel held wisdom?

"Raihna," Conan said. "Gather a half score of archers and hold them ready. I'm going to climb as high as I can to see how the men in the barracks fare. If they've fallen or fled, we'll do as Decius wishes."

The messenger opened his mouth to argue, then saw Raihna's hand rest lightly on her sword hilt. His mouth shut again, with an audible click.

Conan saw on Raihna's face a wish that he send someone else. He also saw the knowledge that nothing she said would lead anywhere, save perhaps to a quarrel in their last moments of life. Conan would not readily ask a man under him to go where he would not, still less when the man was barely fledged as a soldier.

Conan dropped his bearskin and slung on a quiver and bow. He kicked off his boots, to bring toes as well as fingers to his climb. Then, as the archers gathered, he picked his stretch of wall.

As Raihna raised her hand, he stepped to the base of the structure. The hand came down, arrows hissed into the night, and Conan began to climb.

CHAPTER 10

Count Syzambry was no man to admit failure, let alone defeat. He could alter his plans if they went too plainly awry.

The way in through the front of the palace would need more men than he had in hand. He must not only beat down the king's men, including that black-haired giant who seemed to be worth half a company by himself. He must also face losing men to falling walls, traps, ambushes, and the gods only knew what else as he made his way through the palace.

If he held the defenders he faced, the men he had to the rear of the palace would close the trap. Even holding where he was promised stout fighting, but not beyond what he could ask of his men.

Syzambry's decision had come swiftly. His orders were swifter still.

"Bring half the men from the Guards barracks into line. Move the rest so they stand between our rear and the Guards. Then every man prepare to advance.''

Some thought him mad, or at least foolhardy. He could see it in their eyes. But they remained silent, so he need not fear losing any fighting man by summary execution for disobeying orders.

Weakening the watch on the Guards' barracks might let their survivors escape. Every servant of the king who lived through this night would be one more to hunt down later. The Pougoi warriors had refused to march with him against the palace, but they would not scruple at hunting down royal soldiers. If they did, the Star Brothers would remain them of the need to feed the beast.

Conan was perched as securely as the wall allowed before Raihna's archers had time to shoot three times. As the third flight of arrows whistled toward the enemy, he saw that Syzambry's archers were not shooting back.

Indeed, it seemed that the count's men had abandoned the fight, though not the field. Conan strained even his excellent night sight, trying to make out what might be happening beyond that magic-spawned earthen bank.

The dust was still settling, but the magical light was altogether gone and the moonlight turned fitful and dim. Conan would not have light at the price of another duel of sorcery, but he misliked planning his battle like a blind man groping in a rat-infested cellar.

The Cimmerian realized that what his eyes could not provide, his ears might. Cautiously he stood upright, unslung the bow, and nocked an arrow. Drawing back to the ear, he sent the shaft whistling toward the Guards' barracks.

Five arrows drew enough noise to tell Conan that the count still had men watching the barracks. The Guards must yet be there, or perhaps had left so cunningly that the count's men had not heard them.

The count was also moving men toward Conan's right. Had fresh men joined him, or was he drawing men from before the barracks, or both? In either case, the count's men would not likely be thinking of attacking, but of keeping up with their comrades.

Now would be a good time to surprise them, and surprise could be half of victory.

Conan waved Raihna and the under-captain who'd brought Decius's message over to where they could hear the faintest of whispers. They listened to him in silence, although doubt showed on the man's face even in the darkness.

"What of Syzambry coming behind us, between us and Decius?" he asked when Conan was done.

Conan decided that he had thought worse of the man than he deserved. "You should return to Decius and warn—"

The under-captain shook his head. "One of your men can take the message as well. I will not run from this fight. Also, I know where we are to meet Decius and the royal party, if we both win free of the palace."

Conan was certain now that he had doubted the man's courage without cause. "Very well, then. But if you want to test your steel against the count's, then tell me and Raihna of the meeting place. Then you can go to the gods leaving everything behind you fine and tidy!"

The under-captain grinned as Conan tossed down his bow and quiver, then followed them in a panther-like leap.

* * *

134

Count Syzambry cursed the unknown archer, but did so silently. More silently than his men had endured the arrows plunging among them, at any rate. Two men had died screaming, and the unhurt were more than a trifle shaken.

Useless to tell them that the dead were unlucky, victims of a man who could no more see his hand in front of his face than they could. Too much sorcery wielded by friend and foe alike had unsettled his men. Nothing but a hard, close fight with honest steel against opponents of flesh and blood would bring them back to their manhood—

A whisper crept along the ranks of the count's men, to reach the count where he crouched behind the crest of the earthen bank.

"The king's men are moving. They know we are coming. They are setting a trap. If we advance, it will be to our death."

Count Syzambry replied with a whispered threat of horrible punishment for cowards.

Silence fell on his ranks. The count turned his eyes to the front. The palace lay before him, a maze of shadows that might conceal anything and certainly hid a determined foe. His men would need torches to shed light as they fought their way into the palace.

The maze of shadows seemed to be even more tangled now. Indeed, some of the shadows were—moving?

"Steel Hand! Cry!" The count kept his voice from screeching like a woman's. But he had to take a deep breath before he could shout again. "Up! Up and on guard! They're coming out!"

The enemy's giving the alarm did not slow Conan. Nor did recognizing Count Syzambry's voice. The

Cimmerian had time for a brief thought that the count must be almost within reach if his words came so clear.

Then chaos erupted again.

Half of Conan's men were not as battle-seasoned as the Cimmerian. Some stood gaping, others cried out, a few began to run. Altogether, they brought the advance to a noisy halt.

At the same time, fire arrows began to plummet onto the Guards' huts. The uppermost layers of the thatch were as dry as tinder and took fire as readily as straw. In moments, flames were creeping across the roofs of half the huts that had survived the shaking of the earth.

Somewhere among the count's men was a captain who wanted light at all costs. He was gaining it, but the cost included revealing his own men to Conan and the archers at his command.

These archers needed no orders to begin shooting at the men who menaced their comrades. They shot, in fact, with such zeal and so little aim that they were as great a menace to friend as to foe.

Conan left to Raihna the task of bringing the archers to order. He sought to form his men into a solid band that could strike a shrewd blow. The light from the burning huts had shown him what he hardly dared believe: the count at the near end of the earthen bank, with barely a handful of men about him.

"Haroooo!"

It was the under-captain shouting as he plunged forward up the bank. He continued his wordless cries until he was almost within sword's reach of Count Syzambry. Then his steel blazed in the fire-light.

"I am Mikus, son of Kiyom, and I am death to

traitors and rebels against King Eloikas Fifth of—
aarrgghh!''

The count had stood as death closed with him. Not
so one of his guards with a short lance slung across
his back. Its blade sparkled in the firelight, vanished
int Mikus's belly, then burst forth bloody from his
back.

Ere the sword fell from Mikus's limp fingers,
Conan was charging up the slope. Before he reached
the top, the count vanished, and in his place stood a
dozen of his men. They made a wall of steel, armor
and blades alike, between Conan and Syzambry.

Still, Conan hacked three of them out of the fight,
two dying on the ground and the third withdrawing
with a useless arm and dragging leg. But the others
were hemming him in, and arrows began to fly as
the count's archers found a target.

The archers did not cease shooting as Conan
plunged downhill. Indeed, they did not cease shooting after Conan reached safety and the count's men
came downhill in pursuit of the Cimmerian. The
archers made better practice against their friends
than against their foe, or perhaps the nine men made
a larger target than a single Cimmerian.

Regardless, it seemed for a while that the next battle would be between the count's archers and the
count's men-at-arms. While the count's captains
sought order, Conan was doing the same among his
own men. Only then could he study his intended battlefield.

The huts were now well ablaze, and the count's
men who had watched them were now falling back
on their comrades. From the far end of the huts, figures darted off into the darkness, the last of the
Guards taking to their heels.

Conan cursed, not much caring who or what heard

him. If the Guards had not been fleeing, they could have given him the strength for an attack. As it was, by the time the Guards rallied and returned to the attack, Syzambry's men would be in the palace.

The Cimmerian cursed again, this time softly. He was cursing himself more than anything else. Decius might well have had the right of it, and Mikus had shown both sense and courage. Compared to them, Captain Conan of the Second Company had not made such a great name tonight!

Little to be done about it, either. If only the united strength of King Eloikas could face Syzambry, then best unite that strength as quickly as possible. The palace could always be retaken once Syzambry's host was gone. If the king lost his fighting men, however, he lost everything.

"Where now, Conan?" It was Raihna, and for a moment the Cimmerian's tongue could not shape itself to the only sensible words.

"To the meeting place with Decius. He may not thank us for this night's work, but we'll be there for him to say so!"

"As the gods will. Who takes the lead?"

"I'll take the rear. My night sight's the keenest and we'll need it against pursuers."

Raihna loped off toward the front of the line. Conan waited until the last man was past the midpoint of the huts before he rose from his hiding place to join the retreat.

As he did so, he heard the rumble and crash of falling masonry from well within the palace. A moment later he heard shouts and screams.

He did not know if the commotion was due to one of the traps or merely to a careless warrior leaning against a weakened wall. It did not matter. Every one of Syzambry's men who found a grave inside the palace would be one less to fight the next time battle was joined.

The scream from within the palace echoed in Syzambry's mind. He wanted to echo it.

He bit his lip, and the scream died unborn. The swordcut he had suffered from that young fool Mikus's blade was not the first battle wound he had taken. It would not be the last, even though victory was dawning before him. No usurped throne was ever held without fighting.

But gods, the pain! No wound had ever hurt so much. The count would have prayed that no wound would ever hurt so much again, but he doubted that his prayers would be answered. He could not even shape his lips to the proper names of the lawful gods.

Chills gripped his heart and belly, almost making him forget the pain. Had magic entered into him so much that he was unclean in the sight of the gods? Had he done what was forbidden and now was cursed with this dreadful pain from a simple swordcut, and might he be cursed with worse—?

Count Syzambry still did not scream, but he groaned.

From what seemed a vast distance away, a voice that might have been a ghost's uttered sounds without words. Count Syzambry thought he heard what might have been "sleeping draught," and even "Pougoi magic."

Pougoi magic. Yes. That was it. The magic of the tribe's wizards was making him hurt so much. The same magic would take away the pain.

It would take away the pain or he would not be the friend the Pougoi expected. It had been his intention to arm the Pougoi and use them to uphold his throne. He would still do that if their wizards would heal him. If they did not, he would say nothing.

But he would heal himself, or seek the aid of the leeches and surgeons. The healing would take longer that way, but vengeance lost no sweetness with the passing of time.

Yes, the time would pass, his wound would be gone, and he would use the power of the throne to arm all the enemies of the Pougoi. Then those enemies would fall upon them and cast them down, even their beast.

It would not do, after all, to leave the beast alive and a prey to someone who might think he was meant to rule in the Border Kingdom.

A voice spoke again, with nothing remotely like sensible words. A rim of cold metal pressed against the count's battered lips. He smelled herbs and strong wine, then tasted them as the cup was tilted to trickle the potion into his mouth.

For a moment he thought he would choke. He did not, and the cup was empty almost before he became used to the harsh taste. He was already sliding down into sleep as the cup left him, although even after he slept, it was a while before the pain no longer troubled his dreams.

The last sounds from the battle of the palace were long since left behind. Nothing but the sounds of the night disturbed the march of Conan's band of survivors. The night breeze whispered across the bare hillsides, and in the forests below, the night birds called to one another.

Once a wolf howled, long and harsh. The reply came not from another wolf but from something that seemed as vast as a mountain and growled like the heaving earth during the battle. Conan saw the fear-stricken looks on his men's faces and growled curses under his breath.

As they skirted a field of straggling grain, Raihna dropped back to walk beside the Cimmerian.

"The gods seem far away tonight," she said. Her face was such a mask that it seemed the movement of her lips would crack it.

Conan lifted a hand to wipe blood-caked dust from her cheek. "They're never as close as the priests seem to think. We're alive without their help, so I'm wagering on our—"

"Hsstt!"

Raihna did not grip Conan's arm this time. There was no need for it. Both had seen alike: a line of shadowy figures straggling out of the forest. The faintest of moonlight was enough to reveal swords and spears, as well as ragged clothes, scanty armor, and no banner or device that Conan recognized.

Raihna ran like a doe up to the head of the line, waving the men to a halt as she went. They halted, not without a clattering of weapons and thumping of boots that would have alerted trained men below.

The men below, Conan judged, were even less battleworthy than the recruits of the Second Company had been. He saw them staggering with weariness, sometimes falling out of line to drink from leather jacks. He saw them alternately gathered into ragged clumps like bunches of grapes or strung out like a serpent. He saw all of this as he walked along the line of his band, warning the men to be silent, but ready.

"I'm going down when they're all in sight," he told Raihna at last. "When you see me draw my sword or hear me shout Count Syzambry's war cry, come at a run!"

"Count Syzambry's—?" Raihna began, but she was

141

talking to the Cimmerian's broad back as he strode downhill.

Conan was not so foolhardy as to walk up to the newcomers without marking each rock and stump that might hide him as he went. There were enough of those, so that with the favor of the gods—

"How goes the fight at the palace?" someone called, sounding as if he had already emptied more than one leather jack of something stronger than water.

Conan was silent for another moment as he studied the hundred-odd men before him. Most of them were the rabble they had seemed, but here and there, he noted, was a man who carried himself like a seasoned free lance.

King Eloikas had hired no free lances. Count Syzambry, however—

Conan's sword rasped free and leaped high, opening the throat of the nearest free lance. At the same time, he roared, "Steel Hand! Steel Hand! Steel Hand!"

From uphill, Raihna replied, her voice as shrill as any she-demon hovering over a battlefield to snatch the spirits of the dead and dying. After a moment other voices took up the cry, and with their enemy's war cry on their lips, Conan's men thundered downhill to join him.

They arrived just as the foe realized that they were in a battle, even if they were a good way from the palace and the attackers had feigned friendship! Whoever was in command began shouting orders, and some of his men seemed to obey him.

The real peril to Conan was the free lances. They were rallying around the body of his first victim, half a dozen or more. Conan had a busy time of it, working hard with both sword and dagger to keep the free lances from creeping around his flank.

Then Conan's men struck the ranks of their foes, which in a moment ceased to deserve the name. Eloikas's men had speed, the slope, and an ordered line on their side. They also had a king slain, or driven into the wilderness, to avenge, and their own reputation to restore.

Syzambry's rabble vanished like a dancer's silken veil flung into a blacksmith's forge. Flight did not save a good many of them. A score or more died in the first shock, and as many more died with wounds in their backs. The Guards' blood was up, and they were a pack that no hunter could easily call off from their prey.

Conan did not try to. He held the free lances in play until Raihna joined him, turning their flank as they had sought to turn Conan's. Two men died with Raihna's steel in their back before the rest knew of the fresh danger. Then the four survivors divided, two against each opponent.

Two skilled free lances was no light matter even for the Cimmerian. When one of them was almost as big as he, it was a serious affair. Conan had the edge in speed, though, and he used it to hold both men at a distance while he sought an opening.

It came when the larger free lance crowded his comrade away from Conan, jealous of the right to deal the Cimmerian what he thought would be the final stroke. This left a gap between the two men. Conan hurled himself into it, feinting with his dagger to draw the smaller man still farther out of position.

The feint succeeded. Facing only one dangerous opponent now, Conan beat down the larger man's guard, hammered his sword from his hand, then

143

chopped the hand nearly from the wrist. The man reeled back, gaping at his spouting arm and dangling hand. He was still gaping as Conan slashed him across the face, and he fell back screaming and spitting blood and teeth.

Conan whirled, certain that the smaller men would have returned to the fight. Instead, he saw a tangle of arms and legs as four of his Guards swarmed over the free lance.

"Don't—" the Cimmerian began.

"Conan!" It was Raihna, putting into his name the cry for help she was too proud to utter.

Conan wasted no time in joining Raihna and her opponents. Nor did he waste the opportunity one foe's back gave him. He leaped, jerked the man's head back, and heaved him off his feet. The man went down with a thud and a clatter of armor, and Conan finished the hapless fellow's fighting by hammering his head on the ground.

By the time Conan knew that they had a prisoner, Raihna had opened a safe distance from her surviving foe. The man had a longer blade than she, though, and seemed to have no purpose left in life but to sink it into Raihna's flesh.

He signally failed in that purpose. At the sound of Conan's footsteps, he left an opening for Raihna. Her sword opened his neck, and his head wobbled as strength left him. Then he toppled, and Raihna's dagger ended his last writhings.

The mask was gone from Raihna's face as she rose to face the Cimmerian, her expression like a she-wolf that had just brought down the finest stag in the forest. Rents in her clothing showed more blood-smeared skin than before, and her breasts rose and fell with her panting.

She stepped forward and for a moment stood in

the circle of Conan's arms, sword still in hand. Then she threw her head back and brushed sweat-matted hair out of her eyes.

"Time enough when we make camp, my friend. Now tell me, why did you shout Syzambry's war cry?"

"If they were his men, as I thought, they'd lose time guessing who we were. I reckoned that the men could put that time to use."

"You reckoned right. But what if they'd been friends?"

"Then they'd have offered proof and joined with us. Either that or run off, and if they ran, at least they'd be clear of the palace. There's nothing there for any man loyal to King Eloikas save a hard death."

Conan felt Raihna shiver as the truth of his words struck home. Then she kissed him, stepped free, and cupped her hands.

"Ho, the Second Guards! Rally to Captain Conan! We've not done with this night's work!"

They had not, Conan knew, and the end might yet be death for all. But Count Syzambry had lost a hundred men, dead or taken or driven into flight. They were a rabble, but even a rabble could be a loss a usurper might not bear easily.

CHAPTER 11

At most times, Conan would not have asked of his Guards an all-night march after two battles. Moreover, some of the Guards bore wounds that would have commonly put them in bed. Others were borne on crude litters by comrades who would not abandon them to wolves, bandits, or the scanty mercy of any men Count Syzambry might have still roaming the palace precincts.

So the march continued until dawn, although it ended with some of the men stumbling along more asleep than awake; a hand on the shoulder of the man ahead was enough guidance. And by the gods' mercy, they were out of the worst hills.

In an empty village on the edge of a wilderness of virgin forest looming higher than temple towers, they met the Guards who had fled the burning huts. They were some seventy strong—most of them armed and only few wounded—under the command of the veterans.

The sergeant of the First Company raised a hand as Conan strode up. "Hail, Captain Conan. I await your orders. You are the only captain of Guards here."

Conan wanted to order the sergeant to put his men on guard so as to let the Second Company sleep, captain and all. He judged it more prudent to listen to the man's report.

It was simple. Once away from the palace, the sergeant had looked about for a captain to rally the men. Not finding one, he had taken the command himself. The men had formed up and marched in fairly good order until about the hour of false dawn, when they came upon the village.

"It was already deserted, so we saw no harm in settling down."

"It was?" Conan had little stomach for a quarrel with a man who might be valuable help in days to come. He also had little stomach for serving with a man who had robbed his own countryfolk.

"By the Red Rock, I swear it."

The ancient throne of the Border Kingdom was something that few men would invoke to uphold a lie. It seemed best to leave the matter.

"Truly, Captain Conan, they had gone with just what they could carry on their backs, and not much of that," the sergeant added. "We saw some men with spears who might have been the rear guard, but they weren't after staying to answer questions. I would not send the men running about the forest after them, either."

"Wise of you."

Returning favor for favor, Conan told the story of the Second Company's adventures. "I'd wager that the village folk ran when the rabble we fought came by. We'll have some more of the truth out of the prisoners, with luck."

The sergeant led Conan to a hut that had a straw-stuffed mattress in one corner. "Fear it's rat-ridden, too, but—"

Conan lifted the sergeant's jaw with one hand to cut off the flow of apologies. "Sergeant, if the rats aren't bigger than I am, I can face them."

The Cimmerian remained on his feet until the two companies of Guards had divided sentry duty. Then he kicked off his boots and crawled under the molting sheepskins on the bed.

His sleep was sound, though not unbroken. He awoke to find that he was sharing the bed with Raihna. She had taken off rather more than her boots, and as if that message might be too subtle, she then embraced him and drew him hard against her.

Both slept even more soundly afterward, but when the pipes sounded again, the notes were so faint and distant that even the sentries doubted that they heard anything. The sergeant heard nothing at all, and he misliked waking weary captains at the best of times. Conan and Raihna were allowed to sleep until the sun was far toward the west.

Aybas wished that last night's dream would depart from his memory. Even more, he wished that he had never had it in the first place.

Both wishes, he knew, were futile. His wish to be of service to Princess Chienna was not so futile, if he did not let the dream unman him.

It still would not leave him. Random fragments of it would return unbidden, no matter what he was doing. Now he was standing at the princess's door, and he was reliving the moment of the dream when he leaped from the cliff after her falling baby.

He remembered the wind bearing him up, but also blowing him away from the babe. He reached out his arms to grip one tiny foot, but the tentacles of more beasts than all the wizards of the world could keep were also reaching out, clambering from livid swamp and flames the colors of burning rubies and solid rock blacker than a starless night—

"The Princess Chienna bids you enter."

The voice and accent were a hill woman's, but the words were those of a royal maid of honor. Aybas had fought fear. Now he fought laughter. The princess exacted proper service and obedience so firmly that the idea of refusing never came to anyone's mind.

Anyone's, that is, except the Star Brothers—and Aybas was here tonight in the hope that he could make even the wizards' whims miscarry.

The door swung open on its leather hinges. Rush tapers cast a fitful light but showed the princess seated on her usual stool. She wore Pougoi dress now, even to the leggings and the bird-bone combs thrust into her long black hair. But she sat as if in her father's hall, receiving a guest of state while clad in silk and cloth of gold.

"I would bid you welcome, Lord Aybas, if I thought anyone coming in the service of your master deserved such a greeting."

"Your Highness, I—" Aybas looked at the serving woman, who made no move to leave.

"I would have her tell you her own story if we had time," the princess said, "but, in brief, she is kin to a warrior who died on the night of my arrival. Who died of the miscarrying of the wizards' magic. You may speak freely."

149

This command rendered Aybas briefly mute. If it had reached the princess that he was no great friend to the wizards, had it reached other ears as well?

If one could be hanged for stealing a cup of wine, why not steal the whole barrel? Aybas nodded.

"I understand that your son has been wet-nursed by women of this tribe. Now, by the customs of the lowland, that makes him nurse-brother to the Pougoi. By the customs of the Pougoi, a nurse-brother is next only to a blood-brother in kinship."

"So I have heard," the princess said. Aybas was sure that she was hiding ignorance, since few of the lowlanders thought it worth learning much about the mountain tribes. The Border Kingdom might be more peaceful if it was otherwise, Aybas thought.

But ignorant or not, the princess was playing her part well. Aybas judged it time for the next scene of the pageant.

"A nurse-brother of the Pougoi is under Pougoi laws in many ways. Among these laws is one that even the wizards have obeyed since the first days of their star-magic. Man, woman, or child, one of the Pougoi may not be sacrificed unless he gives consent or has committed a great offense."

"A babe at the breast can consent to nothing!" the princess snapped. Then she smiled. "Except perhaps to go to sleep before driving his nurses and mother distracted with his crying."

Aybas held his peace until he was sure that no more would follow. The princess was silent, but he saw her face grow taut as she struggled to hide her fear for her babe.

Then the struggle to hide fear turned into a struggle of another kind. Aybas could read her thoughts, almost as if they had been carved out of the air in runes of glowing fire: *If I admit that Prince Urras is bound by any laws of the Pougoi, this may cause some to doubt his right to the throne. There are already many who fear the reign of a babe. There will be more if they think he must do the bidding of a louse-ridden, rock-scrabbling mountain tribe. Yet if I call my son one of the Pougoi, the wizards cannot sacrifice him without defying their own laws. Their own folk will draw back from them. And if my son cannot be sacrificed, then the wizards' greatest strength against me is a broken reed!*

"Indeed," Aybas whispered in agreement to the princess's unspoken wisdom. She herself was safe as long as the count intended to wed her. Her son, heir to the realm, had always been in a different and worse circumstance.

Without words, Aybas prayed that she would see the way to what must be done.

"The customs of the Pougoi have always been held in honor by me and my kin," the princess said as if speaking to the whole court. "Therefore it is only fit and proper that my son be proclaimed a nurse-brother of the Pougoi. He shall have the rights of any Pougoi male child of his age, and he shall assume his lawful duties when he is of age."

The servant appeared to be ready to fall down in a fit, and for a moment Aybas grew fearful. Then he realized that she was only trying to hold in wild laughter. The idea of a royal princess claiming to honor the hill tribes was too much for her.

"Mistress—ah?"

"Myssa," the woman said as she realized that Aybas was addressing her. "I bear witness to this oath. I will stand, speak, and shed blood to uphold it."

Aybas wondered whose blood she was swearing to shed but decided that his ignorance was best not revealed. He had not inquired too closely into the customs of the Pougoi after he had learned of the one that might save Prince Urras.

"Very well," Aybas said. "I swear to lay this matter before the lawful men of the tribe, for hearing this oath according to custom. I also swear to regard Prince Urras as a nurse-brother of the Pougoi from this moment forth."

That could prove an unfortunate promise should a direct command concerning the prince come from Count Syzambry. Aybas, however, had little fear of such a command being issued at any time soon. He had overheard enough about the count's wound to doubt that the man would be ordering more than an empty chamberpot for some while. The man might even die.

Then it would be well for Aybas if he had Chienna's goodwill. Count Syzambry would have merely cast the realm into chaos rather than usurping its throne, and an exile who wished to survive that chaos could not have too many powerful friends.

With some of his most courtly phrases, Aybas bowed himself out. It was full dark now, and he stumbled twice before his night sight returned.

The dream did not return, however. This was a blessing Aybas had not expected. Perhaps he had found favor in the gods' sight?

Perhaps. But the Star Brothers were closer than the gods, and they would need much more persuasion than Chienna. As he ascended the village street toward his hut, Aybas began to rehearse in his mind a speech to the wizards.

He was so caught up in it that he stumbled twice again. He also passed Wylla as if she were invisible, and he did not hear a single peal of the witch-thunder that rolled across the sky as he reached his hut.

* * *

Conan marched his men and Raihna's hard for the next two days. He turned a blind eye to the Guards who slipped off during each night, and sometimes by day, when forest or rough ground hid them swiftly.

Raihna fretted both at the deserters and at Conan's apparent complaisance. "If this continues, we will have none but a handful of veterans in ten days."

"We will still have your men."

"Of course." But she was near to biting her lips as she said it. Conan would not press her, since the truth would be out sooner rather than later if their roaming the hills continued.

"We've no place to go until we know if the king and Decius won free of the palace," Conan said. "The men understand that. They also know that if Syzambry wins, anyone still mustered as a Guard will have a short life and a long death. A man who has drifted homeward to get in a crop and be a peaceful farmer—he may save his kin, if not himself."

The Cimmerian did not add that Raihna should have known this herself. The daughter of a Bossonian yeoman (at best) must have lived all her girlhood knowing that an extra pair of hands at the harvesting could mean life or death for a family through the winter.

After a moment, Raihna knew what Conan had not told her. She blinked, then rested a hand on his shoulder.

"Forgive me, Conan. I fear that I am too ashamed of how I have misled my men to have all my wits."

"Well, chase them down and bring them back," he said, slapping her on the rump. "You muster a pretty fair strength of them when they're all present."

Conan did not look the other way when some of the Guards talked openly of looting villages and farms.

153

"There'll be none of that, for three reasons. One is that we want the villagers' friendship. Or at least we don't want them running to Syzambry with tales of our whereabouts. The second is that we can scrape by with game, fish, and berries for a while longer."

"Long enough to find the king?" someone asked, from safely back in the ranks.

"The king or his grave," Conan said. "As long as King Eloikas lives, our oath as Guards binds us to his service. If he's dead, our oath binds us to rescue his heir and put him on the throne."

The silence that last vow produced was so complete that a snapping twig sounded like a falling tree. Conan rested a sooty hand on the hilt of his broadsword.

"The third reason for leaving the villagers in peace is that anyone who doesn't answers to me, and to my friend here." The sword leaped from its scabbard, flashed in the sunlight, and returned to rest in a single fluid motion.

The band resumed its march in a more sober mood. Even Raihna seemed to have been affected by the Cimmerian's words when she dropped back to walk with him in the rear guard.

"Will you really—?" she began.

"Hsst!" He put a finger to her lips, and they slowed their pace until the last of the rear guard was beyond hearing.

"Why not, by Crom? If Eloikas is dead, the babe is king of the Border Kingdom. He deserves a better court than the Pougoi. If Eloikas isn't dead, Syzambry still has a hold over him as long as the princess and babe are in the hands of the wizards."

Conan did not add that he would have risked his life to snatch a scullery maid or a spitboy from the hands of the Pougoi wizards. Being in their toils seemed something an honest man shouldn't wish on his worst enemy.

"And if Syzambry's dead?"

Conan jerked his head, dismissing that rumor.

"But if he is alive, wouldn't his men be scouring the countryside for us?"

"We don't know how many men he has left," Conan said. "Besides, I hate to speak well of that misbegotten son of a Kushite camel thief, but he'll be a hard man to kill."

Raihna grimaced. "You're full of cheery counsel this—"

The reproof died on her lips. Faint and far, but beyond mistaking, they heard it.

The pipes.

Conan's hand went to his sword again. He did not draw. He took a deep breath instead, then let it out with the curses in his mind unuttered. But they echoed within his skull as loudly as they could ever have echoed from the hills.

"Show yourself, you whistling jester. Show yourself, you goat's-kin. Show yourself, and show your true colors if you bear any!"

The Star Brother Forkbeard stared at Aybas. The wizard's face held every emotion that Aybas had ever seen on a human countenance . . . save one: it showed no surprise.

Aybas did not pray. Prayers to lawful gods seemed themselves unlawful in this damp grotto, with the smell of the beast hanging heavy in the air. He only commanded his stomach firmly not to disgrace him.

If Aybas had doubted before that the wizards ate flesh from their star-beast, he doubted it no longer. What he had seen in the shadowy corners of the grotto and what he smelled with every breath he took could not be explained in any other way.

Aybas's throat contracted and his stomach twitched. The gods showed some mercy, even if unasked. Forkbeard was looking down at the rough-hewn oak table before him and saw nothing of Aybas's struggle for self-command.

When the wizard looked again at the Aquilonian, he looked with a face twisted by fury and frustration. His hands slapped the table, making a bronze bowl topple over and roll until it clanged on the floor. It rolled again until it reached Aybas's foot. The Aquilonian forced himself not to flinch when the bowl touched his skin.

"Aybas," the wizard said. No "lord," and the name itself sounded like a curse.

"I am here, Star Brother, and at your command."

"At . . . at . . . my—?" Forkbeard's fury altogether took possession of his tongue, and he sputtered into silence. Aybas thought of asking forgiveness for unintended offenses, but he also lapsed into silence. He much doubted that he could utter such words and still command his face.

With neither man able to break it, the silence drew on. It began to seem to Aybas that the rocks overhead would crumble with the passage of the years and allow the lake and the beast to come roaring into the grotto.

"Aybas," Forkbeard snapped then. "Did you speak to anyone of this notion that Prince Urras is nursebrother to the Pougoi?"

"Other than to the princess and her servant, I spoke no word to any living creature, or even to the air. I do not know what the women may have said, where, or to whom. But my tongue has been guarded, and I will swear it by whatever you hold most sacred."

"That would not be lawful, since you are not a Star Brother." The wizard seemed to be speaking merely to avoid looking witless. Then he sat down abruptly and twisted his beard with the fingers of both hands.

"Perhaps you are blameless. But your ... the scheme ... this truth ... it has escaped to the warriors of the Pougoi. They think it the truth. They think well of a future king of the Border being nursebrother to the Pougoi."

Forkbeard did not add, "They think ill of sacrificing him to the star-beast." He did not need to. The very air shouted it in Aybas's ears. He was hard put not to grin in triumph.

To give his mouth some occupation, Aybas inclined his head and spoke. "I rejoice that there is peace between the Star Brothers and the warriors of the Pougoi. Great will be the Pougoi when their strong right hand and their strong left hand wield the same weapon."

Forkbeard shot Aybas a look that made the Aquilonian wonder if he was suspected of jesting. Then the wizard rose.

"You speak the truth. The warriors are our right hand, and the left and the right hands cannot quarrel without leaving the Pougoi helpless in the face of their enemies."

Those might just be the words flung together to sound well, but Aybas thought he heard more in them. Certainly he had not had any messages from Count Syzambry since the night the palace fell and the king fled. Indeed, he had not even heard of any messages.

Had Syzambry perhaps not survived the moment

of his victory? Or was it merely that some aspect of the piper's magic kept messages from passing between the count and the Star Brothers? How much magic did that cursed Marr have at his command?

"Prince Urras is nurse-brother to the Pougoi," Forkbeard said. "This shall be proclaimed so that all may know it. Go in peace, Aybas, but guard your step and your tongue. You are no nurse-brother to anyone, save perhaps a flea-ridden bitch weaned on . . ."

The wizard went on at some length in describing all the various unlikely and unclean animals that were near-kin to Aybas. Aybas submitted to the insults with dignity and did not laugh aloud until he was far across the valley toward his hut.

Then he laughed until he had to lurch to a stump and collapse upon it until his breath returned. As it did, so did a clear mind.

Who had spread word of his stratagem among the warriors of the Pougoi? He knew none whom he could trust with the matter, and he doubted that the princess did either. She was a shrewd woman, notwithstanding that she was young enough to be Aybas's daughter. But shrewd enough to understand the ways of the Pougoi after only a few days' captivity among them? Aybas doubted that miracle.

Then the name burst into his mind like a thunderclap.

Wylla!

She had heard, perhaps by magic, perhaps by being in the right place with a ready ear. Her father was not least among the Pougoi warriors, in spite of his advanced years. He would surely listen to her, would know warriors whom he could trust with anything, and would speak to them. With law and custom giving them a weapon against the Star Brothers, the warriors could be counted on to finish the work that Wylla had begun.

Aybas knelt and rested one hand on the stump, placed the other over his heart. For the first time since he left Aquilonia, he swore an oath by the gods of his childhood, in the manner he had been taught as a boy.

He would speak no word and do no deed to harm Wylla, and he would guard her from the words and deeds of others as best he could. He would not touch her without her consent, nor allow others to do so.

If he was forsworn in this, might he end his life here in this valley, without name or honor or any fit prayers and sacrifices.

It was the fourth day after the fall of the palace and the flight of the king.

Rumors flew now like geese bound south in the autumn. It was said that Syzambry was ensorceled, dying, dead, sick abed, or all of these at once. Conan wondered aloud how much truth there might be behind all these words, thinking to keep his men from hoping for too much.

To Raihna, he spoke his mind more freely. "Something has gone awry with Syzambry or his plans or both. I'd wager my manhood on that. But what it might be, and what good we can take from it—" He threw his hands into the air.

Raihna slipped down off the boulder where she had been perched whetting her dagger. "I'll pray you do not lose the wager, if that is the stakes."

"What, no thoughts of Decius?"

"A woman can think of a score of well-looking men, Conan. But she can only bed one who is present."

Conan put an arm across Raihna's shoulders, but

she slipped from under it and darted down the path. "There's a pool down there where the stream makes a bend. Race you to a bath."

Raihna had a head start, but Conan's long legs quickly made up the distance. They finished the race running side by side, with Conan's arm around Raihna's waist.

They were splashing in the pool when Conan thought he heard a footfall. He took his eyes from Raihna's sun-dappled shoulders and freckled breasts and studied the trees around them.

The mountain wind gave a stately motion to the branches high aloft. Conan did not think he'd heard the sound of either wind or forest. A deer, perhaps, since he and his companion were farther from the main camp than usual, and upwind of it as well.

Nevertheless, Conan reached down to be sure that the well-greased dagger on his ankle was still there and drawing freely. As he did, Raihna popped up directly before him and threw her arms around his neck. She not only pulled his head down between her breasts, she pulled him off balance. He tumbled forward, and they both went down to the bottom of the pool in a warm tangle.

When they rose, Conan could see in Raihna's eyes the thought that they were now clean enough. He drew her against him, then looked beyond her for a soft patch of ground. He found it, but he also found something that drove all thoughts of bed sport out of his mind.

A man was standing on the patch of needles. He was not a man easy to describe, save that he was shorter than Conan and slighter of build. But then, so were most men.

His garb was more uncommon. He wore a loose tunic and looser trousers, homespun and dyed in motley green and brown. A leather sack swung from one shoulder, and he held a long staff of well-seasoned wood in his left hand.

He seemed to be unarmed, but wore on his belt what drew and held the Cimmerian's eyes: a set of pipes, seven of them, the shortest no longer than Conan's thumb, the longest nearly half the length of his forearm. Pipes carved with vast care and cunning from some dark wood, then given silver mouthpieces and silver bands. Bands of silver spun as fine as thread and then braided and knotted—

"I crave pardon if I surprised you," the man said. "I am Marr the Piper."

"Tell me something my own eyes can't," Conan growled. He was edging toward the bank of the pool, moving slowly, refraining from any sudden gesture that might surprise or alarm this visitor. He wished that Raihna had not kept him from drawing the dagger from his ankle.

He could not wish more of Raihna. She was standing waist-deep in the pool, making no effort to cover herself as she wrung water out of her hair. She bore no weapon, but a woman like her was well-armed enough without steel as long as she was also without clothing. A man's body might be safe from her, but his mind—

Conan reached the bank. With a single lunge he was out of the water and gripping his sword. Marr looked his way.

"That will not be needed."

"Needed, or useful?"

"Why do you think it might not be useful?"

"If you aren't a sorcerer or near-kin to one—"

"Whatever else I may be, I am no enemy to you or your friends."

Conan did not lower the sword, but when he spoke,

his voice was less harsh. "That will take some explaining."

"If we have the time—"

"We'll take the time, my friend. Either that or you'll take your leave."

The piper looked from Conan to Raihna, found no more mercy in her face than in the Cimmerian's, then nodded. "Very well. You have been witness to much of my work. Then I heard you, Conan, summoning me to show my colors—"

"What!" The word shot like an arrow from both Conan and Raihna's lips. It raised echoes from the rocks. Marr shook his head.

"If you break in on my speech at every other word, we shall be here too long. Far too long, when I can lead you to Decius and the king."

This time neither Conan nor Raihna said a word. They merely stared at each other, then at Marr. When it seemed to Conan that both he and Raihna were seeing and hearing the same thing, he nodded to her. She climbed out of the water, silver drops beaded on her skin from forehead to toes. Conan cast her sword down to her and bent to don his clothes while she stood guard, then returned the favor.

When they were both garbed, they turned to find the piper sitting as if he had been turned to wood. Only the play of a thin smile on his face told them that he lived.

Conan sheathed his sword and glared at Marr. "As you can see, we'll not tarry here. You say Decius and the king are safe?"

"Alive, I said. I did not say safe. I do not know what dangers might beset them, either."

"Be that honest with one more question and we can strike a bargain, sorcerer or no."

"What kind of bargain?"

"Answer the question first," Conan growled. He liked men who talked in riddles about as much as he liked sorcerers.

"Ask, and I shall answer." The piper's voice itself had a musical quality to it that made it unlike any human voice that Conan had ever heard—man's, woman's, or child's.

"Can you read a man's thoughts?"

"When he wishes me to read them, as you did when you asked me to show myself, I can read them at some distance."

"But not when he wants to keep them to himself?"

"No."

Something in the man's tone hinted that it was a matter of "would not" rather than "could not." Yet— curse it, trust had to begin somewhere! The closer and the sooner the better, if indeed this woodland wizard could pipe them along a path to Decius and Eloikas!

Conan ran fingers through his mane of black hair, wringing out the last water. "If you told the truth, here's my bargain. You guide us to the king and De- cius. Guide us as if you were a common hunter or charcoal burner who knew the land. Not a breath, not a blink, about magic, and that means keeping those pipes out of sight!"

"You bargain hard, Cimmerian."

"I've more than a hundred good men that I don't want scared into flying for their lives. Them I know. You could be much or little. Even if you're much, we haven't forgotten the chaos you sowed at the pal- ace."

"I will prove that I am much before we find Decius and Eloikas. What will you do when I have led you to them?"

"Speak for you to them, and leave the rest to them."

It was clear that the answer did not altogether content Marr. Conan wondered if Decius and Eloi-kas knew something about the man that he did not. Most likely they did. But they could not tell him what it was unless he put himself in the piper's hands long enough to find them.

After a moment, the piper nodded. He swung his pack down from his shoulder, drew out a dagger, some bread, and a linen bag with runes embroidered on it in blue thread. He thrust the pipe into the bag and the whole affair into the sack, then cut the bread with the dagger and handed each of the others a piece.

"If this is to be binding—" Raihna began.

"Of course. Salt." The piper held out both hands, palm upward. In an eyeblink, his palms turned white with salt. He shook it on the pieces of bread, then motioned the others to eat.

Conan ate, but the bread kept wanting to stick in his gullet. If the man could conjure salt out of the air, did it matter if his pipes were hidden?

CHAPTER 12

Count Syzambry awoke to pain that was hardly greater than what he had endured several times before. He still lacked the strength to do more than mutter answers to the surgeon's questions. He contrived not to cry out, or even to groan, when rough hands heaved him about like a sack of barley as they changed his bedclothes and dressings.

Cleaned and somewhat restored by a cup of broth and a draught of poppy syrup, the count lay as if senseless. He feared there was no other way of bringing those about him to talk freely. The surgeons and guards had ignored a direct order to do so.

What he heard was less than soothing. It seemed that nearly five days had passed while he lay unwitting. His wound was grave, and it was not healing entirely as the common run of such wounds did.

No one said the word "magic." Syzambry hoped

that this came from having found no traces of it rather than from fear of the word. If he needed to seek the aid of the Pougoi wizards, he did not want the fears of his men standing between him and the cure he needed to reach for the Border throne.

Even when he was healed, the battle would be longer than he had expected. King Eloikas, Captain-General Decius, and a good company of fighting men had fled the palace in two bands. The earth-magic had bought them that much time.

To be sure, the two bands together were only a few hundred men. But they had already cut to pieces one company of free lances that Syzambry had expected to be ready to hand for harrying the countryside. Now his men were hard-pressed to hold the ruins of the palace and the land about it.

Beyond where the count's writ ran, the country-side was not rallying to Eloikas. It was not rallying to the count, either.

He could not strengthen his hand, to be sure. He could strip not only his own lands, but the lands of every man who had sworn or promised or even hinted allegiance. Strip them of even the boys and the graybeards, strip them of even rotten bows and rusty swords that might avail against bandits.

Strip them, indeed, so that they would be naked to any blow that Eloikas or Decius might chose to strike.

Another source of strength lay in free lances. Word could go out that there were rich pickings in the Border Kingdom for those who would come to follow Count Syzambry's road to the throne. The free lances would come.

They would also come expecting ready gold, and unless he found Eloikas's hoard, Syzambry would have no such thing.

The groan that he had been holding back finally escaped Syzambry's lips. It was not the pain of his wound, but fury at what that wound might do to his ambitions. It would keep him chained to a bed or, at most, a litter, when swift movement alone would save him. How else to save his cause with his loyal handful but to lead them swiftly against his foes, sword in hand?

He groaned again, but more softly, even to his own ears. Perhaps the sleeping draught was taking hold, easing the poisonous thoughts from his mind. . . .

He fell asleep wishing that it could leech the poisons from his body as easily.

Captain-General Decius awoke in his tent to hear the sentries bawling like branded calves. His first thought was that Syzambry had found the royal camp and was hurling his men at it in a final desperate effort.

Decius rolled out of his blankets, jerked on breeches over his loinguard, and left the rest of his harness save for helmet and sword. He plunged out of the tent, nearly sprawled on his face as a toe caught a rope, but saved his skin if not his dignity.

He thereafter walked a trifle more cautiously, though not less swiftly. His men and the handful of Guards and armed servants were turning out as if half of them had not spent the night on sentry duty. His place was at their fore.

Decius reached the head of the path immediately behind the first half-dozen men. He waited long enough to be aware of the chill dawn breeze on his bare chest, then ordered one of the sentries to take a message to the king.

"Tell him that a strong band of strangers is close

at hand. Scouts will go out to learn more. All of the men are on duty and ready for battle."

He did not add that he would lead the scouts himself. Eloikas would most likely forbid it. That would waste the time needed to choose another man, when they might have no time at all to spare.

"That all, lord?" the messenger asked.

"Isn't that—?" Decius snarled, then caught himself. "Tell the king that the moment we know more, he shall know it—"

Decius broke off because his jaw had sunk onto his chest. Nor was his the only jaw agape.

Captain Conan of the Second Company was striding up the path, looking weather-worn and leaner than before, but alive and ready for battle. Behind him, shapes in the dawn and clatters and clangs farther down the path told Decius that Conan had a following.

Decius mustered his wits. "Well, Captain Conan. You—" He decided that "you finally stopped running" would be a mortal insult, and possibly a false accusation as well. "You have come, I hope, to give some explanation of your conduct?"

"That, and more," Conan said. He seemed as impervious to Decius's scorn as a castle keep to a child's arrows. "My conduct includes chopping a band of Syzambry's free lances to rags, as well as some other matters best not talked of before everybody. When you've heard them, I think you'll say I've explained enough."

Decius began to believe that the Cimmerian spoke the truth, and not only because of his assured tone. The royal party had heard rumors of the shattered free lances, as they had heard tales of Syzambry's having been wounded almost to death.

A figure behind Conan removed a helmet and shook

the tangles out of fair hair. Decius's heart leaped within his breast, and he could no longer command his face.

"Welcome, Mistress Raihna."

Her smile made the captain-general's heart leap again. Then a man clad in green and brown, with a sack over one shoulder and a staff in hand, stepped through the ranks of Conan's men. From the manner in which they gave way for him, Decius judged him to be one who had served them well.

"This man is a woodcutter who guided us to your camp," Raihna said.

"He knew where we were?" one of the sentries growled. His hand was not far from his bow.

"Peace," Conan said. "The woodcutter's a loyal man. Hot pincers and the rack together wouldn't give his knowledge to Syzambry."

Decius was willing to take that on faith. What he doubted was that this man was a woodcutter, or anything else that it was wise to speak of before others. Conan and the "woodcutter" were indeed going before the king, although they might not care for what came of it.

Decius called the eager sentry over. "Go to His Majesty. Tell him that Captain Conan has returned with survivors of the Second Company and knowledge he wishes to lay before the king."

As the man scurried off, Decius resumed his contemplation of the "woodcutter." This was not as pleasant as the contemplation of Raihna would have been, but duty before pleasure. The woodcutter stood as if it was nothing new for him to be inspected like a pack mule or a bale of cloth.

He continued to stand under Decius's scrutiny until the messenger returned with the summons of the king. By then, Decius had decided that the man

169

would reveal nothing he did not choose to . . . which meant that it would be well to deal generously with Captain Conan, unless he had done something altogether disgraceful. Generous dealing might open *his* mouth, at least!

The tent of King Eloikas had three walls and a roof, made of stout cloth dyed with herbs until it shared the color of the forest floor. The rear of the tent was the solid rock of the base of a cliff. In that rock was a narrow cleft: the king's path to safety in the last extremity should the camp be falling to his enemies.

To Conan, the rock cleft seemed more like a path to a quicker and more merciful death for Eloikas. The Cimmerian doubted that the king could survive a long scramble through the bowels of the hill.

Eloikas had looked a hale sixty when Conan had last seen him. Now he looked a feeble and sickly seventy, and his hands were so thin they seemed almost transparent. His lips held a bluish tinge, and his breath came with a painful effort.

He still commanded, for which Conan was grateful. The Cimmerian told the tale of his journey from the palace briefly, so as not to tire the king. Whatever Conan had done, or what might be done to him, he suspected that what Marr the Piper had to say would prove of importance.

Decius, he suspected, was not of the same mind. The Cimmerian no longer doubted the captain-general's loyalty. He had, by all accounts, fought too hard and endured too much in Eloikas's cause to be any kind of traitor.

But a man smitten by Raihna and seeking a chance to disgrace a rival—the captain-general might still be so described. Men could make as great mischief out of jealousy as out of treason, as Conan knew all too well. Were matters otherwise, he might still be a captain in the Turanian service instead of climbing the hills of the Border Kingdom.

The captain-general heard Conan out in silence, then waited while the king asked a few shrewd questions. Eloikas's body might be failing him, but his wits were not.

"It seems to Us that you have done good service, and that your skill and loyalty are not in doubt," Eloikas said at last. "Lord Decius, do you have aught to add to what We have said to this worthy Cimmerian?"

In his mind, the worthy Cimmerian performed rites of aversion to keep Decius's mouth shut. The rites, the tone of the king's voice, or perhaps merely Decius's good sense, did the work.

"No, Your Majesty. Few men could have done as well as Captain Conan. Fewer still could have done better."

"Thank you, my lord," Conan said with elaborate politeness. "The woodcutter who guided us here is without, along with Mistress Raihna. May I have the king's leave to bring them within? I believe that the king himself should hear the woodcutter's tale."

That tale was shorter than Conan had feared it might be, for Marr entered the tent with his pipes on his belt. Conan heard Decius suck in his breath, and the king's eyes widened.

"I had thought I was unknown," the piper said calmly, sitting down without asking leave. "It seems that my knowledge was not complete."

"Your pipes have been a legend in the land since before my daughter was born," Eloikas said. He was trying to seem at ease, but Conan noticed that he said "my" instead of the royal "Our."

"You yourself are not much less of one," Decius added. "What brings you here, piper? Consider that your magic shook down the palace and slew a good number of the king's men, and give a civil answer!"

"He will give no answer at all unless you are silent," Raihna said. Her eyes locked with the captain-general's, and it was not the woman who looked away.

Marr sighed. It was the most human sound Conan had heard from him yet. "I have walked a long road to come to a place I had hoped never to see. I beg you not to make the road longer."

He touched his pipes. "May I play a trifle? I think I know a tune or two that will make matters easier among us."

"A spell-weaving tune?" Decius muttered. But Eloikas looked at the Cimmerian and Raihna rather than at his captain-general. The two outlanders shook their heads. Eloikas nodded, and Marr began to play.

Afterward Conan remembered few of the sensations that flowed through him like an underground stream as the piper played. One was surprise that the music sounded so much like common piping that any shepherd lad might have played to soothe himself when twilight drew near and the wolves approached.

Another was an amazing sense of being at peace with himself and every other creature in the world. He would not have embraced Count Syzambry as a brother, but the count would have been safe from the Cimmerian's steel while the music played.

Much beyond that, Conan could not have found words to name what he felt. He only remembered clearly that when the music ended, all of the people in the tent looked as if they had just waked from a healing sleep.

Marr wrapped his pipes and returned them to their bag. "I have done as much as I can for now," he said. "I would rather hear Captain Conan speak. I am sure that on the road here he has devised a plan to rescue Princess Chienna and Prince Urras."

Conan muttered something best not said aloud in the presence of either kings or sorcerers. Trust a sorcerer to call for a miracle and then lay the burden of its performance on a common man's shoulders, with royal wrath awaiting failure!

Yet it seemed to Conan that he had more thoughts on the matter than he had suspected. It also seemed that they came to his lips more swiftly than usual. Had Marr put them there? Or had the piper merely made it easier for Conan to say what was already in his mind?

The smells of woodsmoke, heating stew, and pine needles reached Decius's nostrils as he strode through the camp. As he approached the Cimmerian's tent, the aroma of leather and oil joined the others.

"Captain Conan," Decius said. "Are you alone?"

"Yes."

"Then I wish—may I enter?" Decius chose prudence over rank and turned an order into a question.

The tone of the Cimmerian's reply told him that he had chosen wisely. "You may."

Conan was sitting cross-legged on the floor, wearing only a loinguard. He was rubbing oil into the various leather items of his harness. His sword, already sharpened and oiled, lay on a linen cloth beside his sleeping pallet.

"Greetings, my lord Decius," Conan said. "I fear

that my hospitality is poor. But what I have is yours."

Decius took that as an invitation to sit. "Captain Conan, I will be brief. What I would most like from you is for either you or Raihna to remain behind. Both of you going into the jaws of the Pougoi—I like it not."

"Does it matter which of us remains?" Conan asked. His tone made Decius wary; then understanding dawned. The captain-general laughed.

"I wasn't planning on courting you, Cimmerian!" Decius said. "Nor will I be courting Mistress Raihna until I can be sure I have something to share with her besides an unknown grave in the hills."

"Decius, I don't envy anyone the work of burying you," Conan said. "Your corpse might bite the grave digger."

"I thank you," Decius said. "Now, a little plain speaking. Both you and Raihna are seasoned captains. We have few. To put each of you in danger imperils the king's very cause."

"We've the best chance of winning through and bringing out the princess and the babe," Conan said with a shrug. "If it can be done at all, we're the best to do it. If it can't be done, does it matter how many captains the king has?"

Decius sighed. "No. The doctors say that he will be lucky to see the first snow at best. If he loses hope of seeing his daughter again . . ." Silence said the rest.

"I'd not complain about taking one of your veterans and leaving Raihna behind," Conan said. "But Marr says that it must be she and I, and no others."

Decius frowned. "Does this mean that either of you . . . has . . . is . . . ?"

"I'm no more a sorcerer than I'm a tavern dancer,

and Raihna likewise," Conan said. "What the piper sees in us . . . it's one of the things he doesn't speak of. What it would take to make him speak, I don't know, and I'm not going to spend time in searching for it."

Decius wanted to curse the gods, the Pougoi, their wizards, Count Syzambry, and everything else that had brought matters to this pass. He had the sense of throwing a better man than himself into a pit of venemous serpents, with scant hope of seeing the man climb out again.

"Eh?" the Cimmerian said.

"I was thinking that there ought to be a farewell for the three of you. Wine, meat, music, anything else you desired."

"Don't tempt the gods," Conan said. He stood up and stretched. His head nearly touched the roof of the tent, and his outflung hands did touch either side. "Save the feasting for when we're safe in the palace again. But if there's any wine in the camp—?"

Decius remembered a jar of the best Nemedian vintage that he had saved for the departure of men on desperate ventures. It was buried, and probably shattered by now, beneath the ruins of the palace, along with so much of the past.

CHAPTER 13

Among them, Conan, Raihna, and Marr had faced every peril that a land such as the Border Kingdom could offer. Had they provided themselves against every one of them, they would have needed a pack train for their baggage.

"We'll see about a riding mule for the princess when we come out," Conan said. "Best we go in traveling light and fast. Syzambry may still die, but he may also heal. By his own strength, perhaps, or with the help of the Star Brothers."

"The Pougoi wizards have no healing magic," the piper said. "Their star-magic is—"

"Who asked you?" Decius said. He was sitting by the tent entrance as the three travelers packed. Conan judged that this was to avoid the king, and also perhaps in hope of Raihna's defying Marr and remaining behind.

He was hoping that pigs would fly, Conan knew.

Nothing save a threat to her guards would force Raihna to turn back. Decius was too honorable to use that trick.

"No one asked me," Marr said. "But then, does a wise man wait to be asked when there is truth to be spoken?"

It was in Conan's mind that a man who wanted his teeth in his mouth and his bones unbroken might know that truth was not always welcome. He remained silent and studied the stitching of his sword scabbard. It would not last beyond this journey, but it would do for that.

In time, all the work was done, some of it twice over. Conan stepped outside to permit Decius and Raihna to say what they wished. He bid Marr to follow him.

It was nearing twilight, for the three would-be saviors of the princess and her son intended a night departure. If any unwanted eyes or ears were close at hand, the night and Marr's pipes should make them blind and deaf.

"Who are you, Cimmerian?" the man asked. In the fading light, his face might have been that of a youth or an ancient. Only the eyes denied the youth. They were wide and dark, and clearly had seen much commonly hidden from men.

"My true name is the same as I am called," Conan said. "If sorcerers have tried to use this against me, nothing has yet succeeded. Are you hoping to better them?"

"That was not my question," Marr said. "Who are you, to be here now, embarking on this venture laden with risk?"

Conan shrugged. "I suppose no more than a man who won't run from a fight when his friends are already in it."

"On the rock of such strength, mountains have broken and kingdoms fallen. Am I one of those friends?"

"You will be if you stop talking in riddles and stop asking questions you don't need answered."

"Who are you to judge which questions need no answers?"

"Crom! I'll certainly be no friend if you talk like a sorcerer or a priest, full of mystical wind that blows you where no one can follow. At least no one with his wits about him. Now, for the last time—what do you need to know for this journey?"

"Nothing that I do not know already, in truth. Forgive me. I did not mean to give offense. I was only looking beyond this journey."

"The time for that, my musical friend, is when we've done with the journey *and* are safe home with Princess Chienna! Now, instead of tempting the gods, do you want to join me in a hunt for some wine? I'll not leave with a dry throat, even if I have to wet it with that vinegar they call wine hereabouts!"

They traveled throughout the first night and lay up during the day, keeping no watches and building no fires.

"If Syzambry has put so many men on our trail that they can find three people with no smoke to guide them, the king's cause is already lost," Conan said. "I'll wager it needs us rested and fit when we reach the valley."

It was in Conan's mind that they would need more than strength when they reached the Vale of the Pougoi. They would need a wonder or two from Marr's magic or somewhere else.

Until now, the piper had been so unlike the common run of sorcerers that Conan could have doubted he was one were it not for the pipes. Yet even the most honorable intentions had not kept Lady Illyana from becoming the slave of magic, rather than its mistress.

A sharp eye and sharper steel might still be needed against Marr the Piper and all his works.

The second night and second day repeated the pattern of the first. Breaking camp in the twilight, they heard the sound of men on the march, and Conan went to scout. He returned to report that they were a band of peasants.

"They made enough noise that I could have ridden up on a dragon before they saw me," Conan said. "So I lay close and watched. They were forty or more, but wearing only their work clothes and armed only with their farming tools. Oh, a man or so had a sword that his grandfather might have carried as a free lance. But nobody had provided them arms or harness."

"That gives hope," Raihna said. "If Syzambry had called them out, surely he would not have left them a rabble."

"If he had spare arms, perhaps not," Conan said. "But they could be rallying to Syzambry of their own will. Hoping to spare their villages, likely as not."

Raihna spat. "They are fools, then. They rush to embrace a man who will be as grateful as a hungry bear."

"They do not know that," Marr said. "They are desperate, and that fogs the wits. Or have you come so far from your village that you forgot that?"

Raihna gasped and glared. Conan stared hard at the piper. The Cimmerian's look said plainly: "I have told you nothing about Raihna's birth. Have you been reading her thoughts against her will, as you said you could not do?"

Marr looked away, then lifted his pipes. Conan raised a hand, ready to snatch them. Now the Cimmerian's look said, "Earn your pardon with words, not with your magic."

"Mistress Raihna, forgive me for calling you a witling," the piper said. "You are no such thing. But I hear Bossonia in your speech, and I know something of that land."

"If you thought it bore witlings, you did not know enough," Raihna muttered, but she seemed eased.

Presently the sound of the marching peasants died away, and they resumed their own march through the silent forest as night came down.

The would-be rescuers neither heard nor met any further bands on their journey to the valley. This was not altogether by chance. Marr knew every hill, every valley, and it sometimes seemed to Conan, every tree in the forests. He knew which drew hunters and woodcutters, even in troubled times like these, and which were left to the birds and the wolves.

"There was once a good number of bears in these forests," the piper added. "But most of them were hunted out some generations back. I know of two villages where they go in fear of the beasts, so a few may still den up and live off deer and the odd sheep."

"So? We're not here to hunt animals for the royal menagerie," Raihna said.

"I do not babble without cause," the piper said. "One of those villages is close to our path."

"Then take us wide of it, for Crom's sake!" Conan snapped. It was the fifth day of their journey. Marr talked less in riddles than he formerly had, but when he did, Conan had less patience with him. He would gladly match steel against half of the warriors of the

Pougoi, or strength against the wizards' beast, simply to end this skulking about in an inhospitable land.

"I cannot lead you too wide of it," the piper said, "unless you wish to pass through the Blasted Land."

"From what I have heard of that land, I'd take my chances with the bears and the villagers both," Raihna said. Conan nodded in agreement.

"Wise," Marr said. "The Pougoi watch the farther side of the Blasted Land, and few escape their sentries, if they cross the Land at all without taking the bone-burning sickness."

"We'll fight neither beasts nor wizards with our bones turning to water within our flesh," Conan growled. "Lead as you wish."

The floor under Count Syzambry's feet was shaking. Had unfriendly magic conjured up an earthquake?

No, it was his body swaying and his legs threatening to give way under him so that he would topple like a tree overborne by a high wind. He gripped the bedpost with one hand and held out the other.

"My sword!"

Zylku, the surgeon's apprentice, stared. One of the men-at-arms lifted the count's blade from the bench at the foot of the bed.

"No. We cannot be sure that steel—"

"I am sure that steel in my hand will do much good," the count said. His voice rasped and croaked, but he still forced some authority into it. It was another gift that was returning, like being able to stand on his own feet.

"Much good," the count repeated. "Beginning with ending your babble." His hand gripped the sword. For a moment, the grip was firm. Then the weight of the sword jerked it from his fingers, nearly overbalancing him at the same time.

Syzambry's blade clattered to the floor. He did not dare meet Zylku's eyes. He would see triumph in them, and Zylku might see tears of rage in his.

"Steel in my hand will do much good when I can wield it as I once did," the count said. "It seems that the time is not now." He commanded himself to stare at Zylku. "Summon your master and bid him prepare an answer. How long will I be lame and halt, unable to lead my men against my enemies?"

"A horse litter—" Zylku murmured.

"I said *lead*!" the count thundered. The strength of his voice surprised himself as well as those in the bedchamber. "A horse litter is for women, babes, and others who must remain behind when battle is joined. A leader rides or he does not deserve the name!"

"I will obey," Zylku said. "I will also ask certain folk I know who have arts other than those of common surgeons."

"Indeed," the count said. "And what do you ask in return for this, as I doubt not you risk the wrath of your master?"

"Your silence about my asking, yours and your men's," Zylku replied. "Also, such reward as you consider fit should I learn anything that serves to restore your health. I will trust to your justice."

"You may do that," the count said. "Only remember that my justice can mean a sharp sword for those who have deceived me."

"Dead or alive, my Lord Count, I will not deceive you," Zylku said. "By anything you hold sacred, I will swear it."

The count was not sure that he held anything sacred within his heart of hearts, save well-wielded steel. Steel that, the gods willing, he would one day soon be able to hold again. If Zylku brought that day more swiftly, he could name his own reward!

It was the sixth night of the journey, and if Marr knew one rock from another, it was the last night. Conan would be glad if Marr's knowledge proved true, even if it made the man prouder than ever.

The Cimmerian did not care to tarry long here; the place was too close to the Blasted Land for comfort. Even in the darkness, he could see that the trees had unnatural shapes. The bird sounds were few and furtive, the insects altogether silent. Nothing else was to be heard, not even the sigh of a night breeze.

All three travelers were walking catfooted, trying not to dislodge a single pebble or break the smallest twig. The Pougoi did not watch this land, Marr had said. The villagers themselves drove strangers away. Yet any place so close to the Blasted Land had its watchers, who were neither wizard nor human.

That was all the piper would say. Nothing that Conan dared do would move him to speak further. He would not even say if these watchers could be dangerous, although in that matter Conan needed no advice. He would reckon on the worst and advance steel in hand.

The piper was leading. Now he was bearing to the right, past a vast twisted oak tree that seemed to be lifted half off the ground by a dozen roots thicker than a man's body. Enough moonlight crept through the clouds to show that fallen acorns lay about the base of the tree. Among the acorns lay the skeleton of what might have been a wild boar, except that no boar ever had such splayed hooves or such a bulging skull. . . .

Conan remembered the tales of the Blasted Land.

It came to be in a single night, when the Star Brothers' beast rode down from the sky in a giant stone. Fire and shards of the sky-stone cut a swathe across the land, wider than a man could ride in a single day. Within a year, the beasts and growing things returned, but they were horribly changed and misshapen.

The piper raised his hand. Raihna and the Cimmerian stopped and waited while their guide vanished into the darkness ahead. Enough time seemed to pass for Prince Urras to grow to manhood before the piper returned.

"I can see nothing," he whispered, "but I sense the thoughts of one who watches. He either cannot shield his mind or does not care to," Marr added at Conan's frown.

"Man or beast?" Raihna asked.

The piper shrugged. "I would wager that it has some of each in it. One thing is certain: it has sensed our thoughts and is tracking us by them."

"I am in ecstasy," Raihna said. She tested the draw of her sword and dagger. "Do we wait for him—it—to come, or do we go to meet it?"

Conan studied the ground. "Unless our friend can fly, here's as good as any. Better than some—no stumps or potholes that I can see."

The piper seemed about to speak when part of the darkness ahead began to move. At first it was only a small part, and without shape. It grew rapidly, however, and took on a familiar and terrible form almost as swiftly—that of a gigantic bear, brown with a ruff of silvery fur almost as thick as a lion's mane. The moonlight showed that its muzzle was grizzled as if with age, yet its coat was thick and showed no wounds or bald spots. The muzzle was shorter and the skull broader than Conan had ever seen in a bear.

Conan and Raihna unslung their bows. The piper fell back, to stand behind them. He drew his pipes but did not put them to his lips.

As Conan and Raihna nocked their arrows, the bear plunged off the trail. When it found no shadows large enough to hide itself altogether, it became a moving, difficult target. Conan tried to judge its path by the sound of its footfalls, but he heard too little. It seemed that the bear had the cunning to walk lightfooted on uncertain ground.

Had Conan and Raihna carried more arrows, they would have shot anyway, trusting to wound the beast. Decius had been able to find barely two dozen shafts apiece for them, however. Some of those had already been spent in bringing down meat for the pot.

Conan had faced enraged bears and seen what they could do. He had also seen how many arrows they could take without mortal hurt. He would shoot if the bear offered a vital spot, but not otherwise.

Now only the faintest of scrapings and the swiftest of moving shadows told Conan of the bear's progress. It seemed that it was moving around toward their rear, perhaps cutting across the trail toward the oak tree.

For a long moment the silence was complete. Then the crackle of splintering wood rent the night. Conan tried to pierce the darkness, but the moonlight refused its aid. He could only make out the oak tree shaking, as if a strong wind were blowing.

Then the moon came out, Raihna gasped, and even Conan gritted his teeth. The bear had torn a branch from the oak tree, as long as two men and as thick as Conan's arm. Now the beast rose on its hind feet, holding the branch in its forepaws.

In its *hands*. The moonlight showed unmistakable

thumbs, for all that they bore claws as long as Raihna's dagger.

Creature of magic or creature of twisted nature, the bear was still offering Conan that long-sought vital target. An arrow leaped to his string, then flew straight at the beast. It pierced deep through the shaggy brown coat and into the left shoulder.

The bear's roars filled the night as if there had been no such thing as silence since the world began. It shifted its grip on the branch to pluck the arrow from its flesh. Conan put two more arrows into the beast; then it lowered its head, shuffled its feet about like a runner seeking the best start, and lunged forward.

The bear's three human opponents scattered like chaff in a whirlwind. They had no choice. Even Conan could no more match the bear's strength than he could that of an avalanche. Against such an opponent, he had to keep his distance and wear the beast down, giving as many wounds as possible and taking none. Many slight wounds could sap the strength of any creature. There could be no such thing as a slight wound for any human, not from this monster.

Raihna was bolder. She lunged in under the bear's guard and slashed at its hind legs. The broken branch hummed and the end crashed down. Raihna leaped back and to one side, avoiding a stroke that would have shattered her skull.

She did not avoid a patch of rough ground that threw her off balance. The bear stepped forward, raised the branch high, and struck again. Raihna went down, but in going down, she landed on her rump, legs raised.

Those long legs were made for more than wrapping around a man during bedsport. They held fine,

186

hard muscle, and all that muscle now drove Raihna's boots into the pit of the bear's stomach. The beast outweighed her ten to one, but even its stout hide could not altogether cushion such a blow.

The bear grunted and the branch wavered. Raihna rolled away, cutting at the bear's left ankle as she did so. Her eye was true. Her blade caught the hamstring. The leg gave under the bear's weight, and the beast toppled onto all fours. The branch came down with it, catching Raihna across one ankle. She did not cry out, but Conan saw her wince.

He also saw that opportunity was knocking. For a moment, the bear was torn between the weapons of a thinking creature and those of a beast. Instinct overwhelmed thought. It lunged for Raihna with its jaws.

As it did, the branch lifted, freeing Raihna. She rolled and slashed again. This time her sword caught the bear across the muzzle. The creature roared to make the hills shake and turned toward Raihna as she leaped to her feet.

As she did, Conan leaped onto the bear's back. His free arm curled around the shaggy throat, squeezing like a great snake of the Vendhyan jungles gripping a particularly succulent pig. His sword slashed down. Fur and flesh gaped, and the bear's right forepaw dangled limply.

The roars the bear had uttered before seemed like silence compared to the thunder now.

It needed more than noise to disquiet the Cimmerian when he was grappling with a foe. When the bear tried to shake off the impudent nuisance clinging to its neck, it was too late. Conan had his dagger drawn, and he thrust it deep into the bear's throat. Blood flowed. He thrust again; more blood flowed, and Raihna took the opportunity Conan had given her. She ran in, thrusting hard, and her sword found the bear's heart.

The slayers barely had time to leap clear before the creature toppled. The massive paws scrabbled at the rocky ground a few times as blood pooled under the throat and chest. Then it lay still.

Before he stood up, Conan counted and flexed his limbs to be sure that all of them were still attached and fit for use. He had grazes, bruises, and sore spots all over from this briefest of grapples with the bear.

Raihna looked in much the same case, with the addition that her trousers were largely gone, and also one sleeve of her shirt. One cheek was going to be a single giant bruise by morning, and she favored one ankle.

Conan caught her by both hands, then embraced her and lifted her off her feet. "Thank the gods that it was a short fight," she said when her breath returned. "A long battle against that creature and we'd none of us been fit to fight again, or even to travel."

"Save Marr," Conan said, looking about for their companion. He was nowhere in sight, but Conan thought he heard a distant trill of pipes.

Had the piper fled after leading them into a trap? That was Conan's first thought, and an ugly one, too. Raihna seemed to read that thought on the Cimmerian's face.

"Is it worth searching for him?" she asked. She sheathed her sword with a vigorous thrust. Conan judged that it would be drawn as swiftly if she met the piper again.

"Not at night," Conan said. "We'd do better to find a place to sleep. Without a guide, we'll have to cover the last of the journey by day, or risk going astray."

"At least we can have bear meat for breakfast," Raihna said.

"That would not be wise," came a familiar voice, seemingly from the air above them. Conan whirled, sword flying clear.

"By Erlik's brass tool—!"

Marr slipped down from the oak tree and almost sauntered toward them. He might have taken a Cimmerian fist in the teeth but for Raihna. She gripped Conan's arm and pointed. Conan followed her gesture, and stared.

A youth—no, a woman hardly more than a girl—was following the piper. She wore her hair in Pougoi braids, and her face was either filthy beyond belief or smeared with dirt to make her harder to see in the dark. Even in the darkness, Conan noted her easy grace of movement and the fine figure under the tunic.

"Forgive me," Marr said. "Captain Conan, Mistress Raihna, meet Wylla. She is of the Pougoi, and a friend to us."

"Then she can share the bear meat, after you explain where you were during the fight," Raihna snapped. "We are waiting." She crossed her arms over her breasts and glared.

"To eat the flesh of that bear is not proper," the piper said. "The bear has a man's cunning. Therefore it would be as eating human flesh—"

Raihna gagged, and Conan nodded. "I see you agree with me, Captain," Marr said. "Good. As for where I was—I had to play my pipes. Otherwise, the bear's thoughts might have reached the Star Brothers. That could have been like sending a letter warning them of our coming. By the time I knew I had blocked the sending of the bear's thoughts, I sensed Wylla's approach. I had to go on playing so as to guide her safely to us and to shield her from the bear's knowledge."

Conan nodded, feigning more understanding than he actually felt. Still, it began to seem that the piper's magic might be of a kind he had never heretofore met, or even heard of. It was magic to prevent what might otherwise happen rather than to cause unnatural events such as rivers flowing backward, mountains splitting, or dead gods waking up to ravage the world of men.

No doubt such magic could in time corrupt its wielder, as with any sorcerer. But the corruption might come more slowly. Slowly enough, perhaps, for Conan and Raihna to use Marr's aid in rescuing the princess and making a safe escape.

"We had best move to a safer place, as you suggested," the piper continued. "Then, before we move on, we must consider fresh ways of rescuing the princess. Wylla has brought news that I did not expect."

"I thought that our old scheme was good enough," Conan said. "Unless your ankle will keep you from climbing the valley walls," he added, turning to Raihna.

"Climbing down, no. Climbing up—" She shrugged. "That monster on my trail may count for more than a sore ankle."

"We may need to do much less climbing than we expected," the piper said. "Wylla thinks that we have a friend among the Pougoi." The woman whispered to the piper, and he nodded. "Or at least a man who is no enemy to the princess, even if he serves Count Syzambry."

"What?" Conan would have bellowed louder than the bear had Raihna not put a hand over his mouth. More quietly, he said, "This demands even more explaining than your climbing trees to make music while we fought the bear!"

"I shall explain when we are a safe distance from here," Marr said. "The thoughts of the bear may not have reached the Star Brothers. Indeed, I believe they did not. I am less sure about the bear's kin. Do you fancy a fight against them?"

By the time Wylla and Marr finished telling of "Lord Aybas" and his curious conduct, it was too late to reach the valley before daylight. The four travelers covered some two thirds of the distance, then found a sleeping place in a stand of fir trees so dense that an army might not have discovered them.

The tale would have been longer still and much less convincing had Wylla not decided that Conan and Raihna could be trusted. So she revealed her knowledge of the lowland speech and told most of the tale herself. This, in turn, left Conan and Raihna more willing to believe it.

Not that the tale was easy to believe at best, as Raihna made plain when she and Conan were clearing a place for their blankets. "Aybas may be playing some game too deep for Wylla to understand, it seems to me," she said.

"Then it would be too deep for our musical magician, and if he's not a master of intrigue, I'm a Stygian," Conan said.

"He may know only what Wylla has told him," Raihna suggested.

"True enough," Conan replied. "But we can't turn about and run for home with our tails between our legs after coming this far. We'll go on down. If it's a trap, we can at least cut Aybas's throat in due time."

"Yes, and Wylla's." Raihna embraced him. "It does you honor that you'll not harm a woman. But I've sworn no such oath, and if Wylla betrays us, she'll go with us. I've always fancied having a serving maid, in this world or some other."

Conan returned the embrace, but he could not entirely avoid the thought that any man who made an enemy of Raihna would be lucky to live long. Did Decius know this small truth about the lady he was courting?

CHAPTER 14

Aybas awoke, at first certain that a new nightmare afflicted him. A giant loomed over him, so black that he seemed to devour light except for his eyes, which gleamed an icy blue. Others were present in the nightmare, but Aybas could make out only little of them.

Then he sensed cold steel against his skin and a sharp point at his throat. Either the demons who rode by night had new powers over the minds of men, or he was no longer asleep.

Aybas chose to think himself awake, and he asked a question that could at least do no harm: "What do you want of me, friends?"

"Hah!" the giant said. "Leave the last word off your tongue or give over pandering for a usurper."

That made it evident who the visitors were: folk loyal to King Eloikas. And that told him that they were no friends of his, and most likely why they were here.

In spite of the steel at his throat, Aybas smiled. The night had brought one surprise to him. Now it was about to bring one to his visitors.

"If you seek the freedom of Princess Chienna, I am yours to command."

The giant grunted something wordless that might have indicated surprise. Aybas could barely make out his face in the dark hut, and in any case, he was no longer looking at the giant.

Behind the giant stood a fair-haired woman of mature but still great beauty, for all her warrior's garb and appearance. Beside her—and here Aybas had to swallow—stood a man who seemed small beside the giant but who exuded a power that had little to do with his stature.

A set of silver-adorned pipes dangled at his waist. Aybas did not need a second look at those pipes for them to tell him more than he wanted to know about the man.

Marr the Piper, who had toyed with the spells of the Star Brothers like a playful cat with a mouse, had come in the service of King Eloikas.

"Then we command you to rise and guide us to the house of the princess," the giant said.

"I will do as much or more on one condition," Aybas said.

The sword point pricked harder. Another twitch of the giant's wrist and Aybas's life blood would stream over his pallet. "Wait! Hear the condition first! It may be worth the hearing."

"It may," Marr said. Aybas almost smiled. He had heard the legend that the piper of the mountains was mute save for his music. So much for the legend.

"We must rescue Captain Oyzhik," Aybas said.

The giant's sword point drew back, but the look on his face was more frightening than the sharp steel. With his eyes now fully waking, Aybas saw that the giant had the look of Cimmeria about him. Perhaps he was the new captain of the Guards of which rumor had spoken? If so, he would have no reason to love Oyzhik.

"You are here out of loyalty to King Eloikas, to save Chienna from the Star Brothers and from Count Syzambry alike. Save Oyzhik and you may do the king another service."

"How?" The Cimmerian, it seemed, was not one to waste words.

"Oyzhik is a traitor to the king, to be sure. He also knows a good many of Syzambry's secrets. He has not been rewarded for his treason, either. The Star Brothers hold him close captive, ready to sacrifice him to the beast at a whim. If saved, might he not reveal much of what he knows, out of gratitude?"

"Oyzhik has as much gratitude in him as a turnip," the woman said. "But if the king pardoned him as well—"

"Raihna!" the giant growled. "Have your wits flown after this one's?"

"No," the woman called Raihna replied. "Merely thinking that if we can win a second victory without losing our first—"

She seemed to have decided. From the look on his face, the piper was of the same mind. The Cimmerian was not, and he seemed ready to argue.

The hut door swung open, and Wylla entered as silently as smoke. "I have warned my father. He trusts no one else enough to bring them, but he will meet us at the house of the princess."

"Is anyone suspicious?" Conan asked.

"I saw none of the Star Brothers or their faction,"

Wylla said. "I think that if they suspected aught, they would be abroad."

"Likely enough," Conan agreed. He looked upward, apparently calling on the gods for patience with fools, and wisdom to tell fools from wise men. Then he looked at Aybas with a face that made the Aquilonian wish that this were a nightmare.

"We'll take your oath to aid us. Break it, or even bend it, and you'll die ten times over before the Pougoi take you."

"I expect no less."

The rescuers certainly had not expected the oath that Aybas swore. He swore at length and by many gods, partly to ease their minds, but more to ease his own. This was the first time he had used some of the sacred names since he was a child, and why not? This was likely enough the last oath he would swear as a living man, and the first in twenty years that he had no intention of breaking.

Of course, if the tales of Syzambry's being dead, or at least crippled, were false, this change of allegiance held peril. A fleet pair of heels could still take him to safety, however. The count would have ample occupation while dealing with enemies closer at hand even if he did gain the throne.

Much to Conan's disgust, Oyzhik and the princess were held as far apart as the valley allowed. The rescuers would have to divide their forces and meet at the foot of the cliff for the final scramble to safety.

Aybas and Marr had to go for Chienna. Without Aybas, she might need calming by the piper's music, as her babe surely would. Without the piper, there would be no calming either of them.

Oyzhik, however, was held so closely that a single man—even Conan—could fail. Wylla swore to find her father and bring him to the wizards' prison instead of to the princess's hut.

Conan would have cursed Aybas, Oyzhik and the Star Brothers alike had he not feared delay or noise. It might have been simpler to refuse Aybas's oath and to silence him. But they had chosen to take that oath, and now, to Conan's mind, they were bound as closely as their new friend. A world where oaths could be cast out with the chamberpots onto the middens was a world doomed to the rule of the likes of Count Syzambry and the Star Brothers.

As silent as a falling rose petal, at one with the shadows, the Cimmerian made his way down across the valley toward the Star Brother's lodge. Mist curled over the edge of the dam, and a faint breeze brought the reek of the beast to Conan. His face twisted at the foulness, and he would have known then, had he not been told before, that the creature was not of the world of men.

"Hssst!"

"Five?" Conan asked. If the reply made ten, he had met Wylla's father.

"Five," came a gruff voice. Then a shadow that Conan had taken for a bush began to move toward him. At length it turned into a man nearly as large as the Cimmerian himself. Grizzled hair and a short beard made him resemble a patriarch, but the Cimmerian's eye made out a warrior's muscles and sinews under the man's scarred skin.

"Well met, Conan of Cimmeria," the man said. "I am Thyrin, father to Wylla."

"I am Captain Conan of the Second Guards, father to none that I know of," the Cimmerian replied. "Is your daughter with you?"

"She wished to join us, but I bid her join the oth-

197

ers. She can tend the babe if no more, and with them, she will be closer to safety.

"I like not this care for Captain Oyzhik, Cimmerian. Did my daughter not say that he will do our enemies more harm alive than dead, I would spear him in a moment. It will be a chancy affair, making our way to safety with a man such as Oyzhik."

"I am of your mind. At least Marr will try to keep the alarm from being raised. Lead on, Thyrin."

Aybas was prepared to march straight up to the princess's lodgings, trusting to his standing with the guards. Raihna counseled greater caution.

"If I were the Star Brothers—"

"You could never render yourself so ugly of either body or spirit," Aybas said.

Raihna seemed to be glaring and smiling at the same time. "There is a place for the gallantries of the Aquilonian court, and this is not it. If I were the Star Brothers, I would have my most trusted men about the princess now, especially with the tales being rumored of Syzambry's troubles."

"It is the habit of the Star Brothers to have their most trusted men guarding the sacrifices," Aybas said. "Conan and Thyrin are the ones most in need of caution."

"You did not tell us that!" Raihna exclaimed.

"You did not ask it of me," Aybas replied blandly.

"If you have the wits of a louse, you should know what to tell us without being asked!" Raihna said.

"Here, now, Mistress—" Aybas began, swallowing indignation as he saw Raihna reaching for her sword.

"Peace," Marr said. "I can work against the wits of any or all of the guards as needs be. Also, no doubt the Star Brothers think that the princess needs less guarding, being a mere woman."

Raihna mimed running the piper through, and Wylla, recently rejoined with the other three, pulled a long face. Then she stuck out her tongue at both men. The unease dissolved in soft laughter.

It was good tidings that Oyzhik was lodged in a hut apart from the common lodgings for the sacrifices. No doubt the Star Brothers did not wish anyone to bear reports of his being ill-treated to Count Syzambry or the captain's friends.

No doubt, too, that the Star Brothers intended to keep Oyzhik captive until his fate was decided. His hut was backed against the cliff, and four guards stood before it. Two had bows, two had spears, all bore swords—uncommonly complete arming for the Pougoi, even among the Star Brothers' chosen warriors.

It did not help matters, either, that the hut was less than a hundred paces from the principal longhouse of the Star Brothers' guards. If the four on duty did not die silently and swiftly, they would have help from a score of their comrades before Conan and Thyrin could free Oyzhik.

"Are the sacrifices fettered?" Conan whispered.

Thyrin shook his head. "Only for punishment, and they would not dare punish Oyzhik in any way that left marks."

The underbrush and shadows could have hidden a score of men the size of Conan and Thyrin. Only guards making the rounds could have discovered them, and these guards stood before the door like temple images.

Conan's night sight, with a trifle of help from the moon, soon revealed a climbable path up the cliff. It did not offer a road out of the valley, not when they would have Oyzhik as a burden. It could take a good climber like the Cimmerian to the roof of the hut.

"I'll climb," Conan said. "When I'm nearing the hut, I'll wait for moonlight, then wave. You go forward and keep the guards busy while I reach the roof. Then you can hide so that the Star Brothers—"

Thyrin's glare would have shattered stone. "Doubt not that my honor equals yours, Cimmerian. If you must doubt my honor, at least do not doubt my wits. Wylla and I will face outlawry at best for this night's work, whether anyone sees us or not."

There seemed no more to be said, so Conan faded into the shadows until he reached the foot of the cliff, where he waited for the moonlight to give him a good view of his first few hand and footholds. Then he began to climb.

"What, ho, friends," Aybas said. "Is the princess within?"

The two spearmen at the door laughed coarsely. "Where'd she go without passing us? She knows what'd happen if she tried, too. Too fine-bred to have a taste for our kind, she is, like all the low-landers."

One of them caught sight of Raihna. "Or maybe there's some lowlanders as might fancy a hill man?"

Raihna's smile was feigned, but only her comrades knew it. "I am sent from the lowlands, indeed. I serve Count Syzambry, and I am come to examine the princess with a woman's knowledge of her fitness to bear his sons."

Aybas strangled laughter. Any woman less resembling a midwife than Raihna, he had yet to see. Before the guards could voice doubts, Raihna added, "I am also come to reward those who have served the count well."

The sway of her hips as she spoke would have made most tavern dancers jealous. The guards could not but see what reward she was promising, and Aybas doubted that they were eunuchs.

While the spearmen stared at Raihna, Aybas and Marr moved. Each stepped behind a guard, each drew a short club from his belt, and each struck their man a shrewd blow where the skull joins the neck. The guards dropped as if poleaxed.

"Lift them onto the bench here," Aybas ordered. "They often sit down while on duty. Wylla, you remain here as sentry. Make it seem that you and the guards are . . . ah, enjoying each other's company."

Wylla stuck out her tongue again, but she also drew off her tunic and pushed her trousers low on her hips. The splendid breasts and supply waist thus revealed made Aybas pray that Wylla at least would live through the night. She was not for him, that was certain, but still, she was too young to die for the folly of others.

While Marr and Raihna heaved the guards onto the bench, Aybas knocked on the door. As Wylla sat down on the bench with her arms about the two guards, Aybas heard a noise from within the hut.

"Who is there?"

"By Mitra's beard, it is Lord Aybas. I bear dire news."

A squeak like a trapped mouse was all that Aybas had of reply. He cursed softly.

"Must I tell it for all the Pougoi, and perhaps the Star Brothers, to hear? Or may I enter and speak privily?"

After a moment that seemed to pass like the melt-

·ing of a glacier, Aybas heard the bar lift. He thrust the door open and strode in, past the waiting woman. She let out another squeak, then was silent as Raihna put a hand over her mouth and showed her the dagger in the other.

The princess was still awake. The babe was sleeping, until the moment when strange folk burst into his mother's chamber, at which he awoke with a wail fit to rouse sleepers all over the valley.

The piper's music whistled softly. Then it seemed to sing with no words, but soft and soothing nevertheless. The wails diminished, and at last ceased. As the princess picked up the babe, his eyes drifted shut and he slept again.

"He has taken no harm?" Chienna said, shifting him to one arm. The other was clenched at her waist, and she seemed to wish it held steel.

"Here, Your Highness," Aybas said. He drew his second dagger from his boot and handed it to the princess. She stared at it, then at Raihna, and nearly dropped the sleeping baby.

"He will come to more harm from being dropped than from my music," Marr said. "He only sleeps, and will sleep until it is safe for him to wake."

"Safe . . . ?" Princess Chienna appeared to be mazed in her wits. Aybas gritted his teeth. Why did women of sense seem to lose that sense at precisely the worst time?

"Your Highness, I . . . we are come to take you and Prince Urras to your father. The king is alive and well, although in hiding. With you and your son by his side, the realm will rally to his banner."

The princess shook her head, making her long black hair dance about her shoulders, white and gleaming where the bedgown revealed them. The gesture seemed to end her confusion.

"Allow me to don suitable apparel, then, good people," she said with regal dignity. "It will be neither seemly nor safe to walk through the mountains in my night shift."

With an imperious gesture, she summoned her waiting woman. Raihna released the servant, and the two women vanished into the bedchamber, leaving Raihna holding the baby. As if by instinct, she began gently rocking him, and her face as she looked at the sleeping prince told Aybas a whole tale of matters that would never reach the Bossonian's lips.

The princess and her waiting woman were out of the bedchamber in less time than Aybas would have given to carving a joint of good beef. It only seemed like sufficient time for the moon to set and dawn to break across the mountains.

The princess was dressed in a Pougoi warrior's attire, with an arrangement of leather thongs and fleeces across her back for the babe. Aybas had not known that she possessed either, and his opinion of her and her house rose further.

Very surely, he had wagered on the wrong horse whilst serving Syzambry. If he gained no other reward from his change of allegiance, he would at least die with a better opinion of his own judgment.

Aybas stepped to the door. Wylla now had one of the guards' heads lolling on her breasts. The other had fallen off the bench. She had undone his trousers to give him a more convincing appearance of revelry.

"Is all well?"

Wylla shrugged, which lifted her breasts most interestingly. It also sent the guard sprawling off the bench to join his comrade.

Aybas took the shrug for "yes" and motioned the

others to come out. The princess held back. The
Aquilonian started to address her in terms unfit for
royal ears when he saw that she was pointing at her
waiting woman. The piper nodded and began to
play.

The music could not have reached even into the
bedchamber, but Aybas felt it in his bones. They
were turning soft and warm, like fresh porridge,
within him. His eyelids were vastly heavy; he
needed to grip a post of the porch to uphold himself—

The music ended abruptly. Aybas stood unaided,
opened his eyes, and saw the waiting woman
sprawled on the floor. He made a gesture of aversion.

"It was either my music or a blow," the piper
said. "Or leave her to face sacrifice to the beast."

Aybas swallowed whatever he had begun to say.
He held out a hand to Wylla, and she took it. He
realized that this was the first time he had ever
touched her.

Then such thoughts flew from his mind as he
heard the drums and trumpets of the Star Brothers
sounding the alarm to the valley.

Conan covered the last few paces of his path along
the cliff in a brief space of darkness as clouds hid the
moon. When light returned, he lay on the roof of
the hut, watching Thyrin approach the guards.

"Ho, friends. How fare you this night?" Thyrin
greeted the men.

"Well enough," one of the archers grunted. "What
of you, to be about the camp at this hour?" The
suspicion in his voice shouted to the Cimmerian.

Suspicion had not yet led to drawn weapons when
Conan struck. His first weapon was a fist-sized

stone, flung hard at the back of the archer's head. The man wore a helmet, but the force of Conan's throw would have cracked an oak plank. It pierced the helmet, shattered the skull within, and flung the archer forward against a comrade.

Thyrin's sword whirled. The second guard's chest gaped. He dropped his spear and clutched at the wound with both hands. His mouth was still open in a soundless scream when a second swordcut swept his head from his shoulders.

Conan leaped from the roof onto the remaining guards. They were standing so close that he drove them both to the ground with force enough to leave them half-stunned. He finished them with his dagger.

Conan's dagger also made quick work of the knotted thong that held the bar of the hut door in place. As he heaved the door open, it groaned. Conan wrinkled his nose at the reek from within.

"Stinks like the Aghrapur stews in here," he muttered as his eyes tried to penetrate the mephitic gloom and reach Oyzhik. When they did, the Cimmerian muttered again, and in soldier's language.

Oyzhik lay sprawled on foul straw, an empty wine cup by his outflung hand. All the smells told a plain tale of how he had been spending his captivity. At least he would give no trouble; Conan only hoped that the man had not altogether drunk away his wits.

The Cimmerian had to stoop to enter the hut, stoop further to lift the drink-sodden Oyzhik onto his massive shoulders. As he rose and turned toward the door, he saw Thyrin pointing with one hand and gesturing for silence with the other.

From the doorway, Conan saw the danger. A band of guards was marching from the longhouse, past the watchfire. Conan counted at least four of them, no doubt the relief for the guards just slain.

There was no way past the men without a fight. So best to begin it on his own terms and at his own time. Without ceremony, Conan slid Oyzhik to the ground and drew his sword.

"Hayaaaaahhhhh!"

The guards heard a war cry more dreadful than any they had ever imagined. They saw a giant figure hurling itself at them, and panic chained their limbs. Then the giant was among them, wielding a sword that seemed longer than a man was tall, at least to those who lived long enough to see it at all.

Two of the guards did not. They died at once, their skulls split from crown to eyebrows. The other two were killed as they ran. One of them screamed as he died. It was the scream, joined to Conan's war cry, that brought other guards to the longhouse door.

They did not advance into the open, however. To their sleep-muddled vision, the enemy seemed more than human. They were certain that the Hairy Man of the Mountains had come out of legend to avenge their abandoning his cult.

"The Star Brothers lied!" one man screamed.

"Forgive us, oh Great Hairy Lord!" another wailed.

Conan did not stop to correct their mistake. He lunged at the door, slammed it in the faces of the bemused guards, and wedged a long of firewood under it. Then he caught up a burning brand from the watchfire, whirled it about his head, and flung it high into the dry thatch of the longhouse.

By the time he rejoined Thyrin and Oyzhik at the hut door, the roof was well alight. The crackling of the flames mounted as Conan heaved Oyzhik onto his shoulders again.

When he straightened, the thunder of drums and the cry of trumpets had overwhelmed the crackle of flames. Thyrin cursed.

"I prayed for silence, but the gods—"

"Leave the gods well enough alone," Conan snapped. "How fast we can run matters more now."

"I am no cripple, Cimmerian," Thyrin said. "But I warn you. The paths through the village or to the way you entered the valley will be guarded now. There is another way out, and indeed an easier one for women or those carrying burdens—"

"Then lead me to it," Conan growled. He thought of handing Oyzhik to Thyrin to silence the man, then thought better of it. Conan was younger, and also less likely to drop the prisoner into a well "by mischance."

"I will, but I will also pray to the gods that Marr the Piper knows of the way and is bound for it even now."

"One more riddle—" Conan said.

"No riddle," Thyrin said. "Simply the truth. The way is easy enough once one is on it. But to reach the foot of it, one must cross the dam that holds in the beast's lake. The top of the dam is but a man's height above the water, well within the reach of the beast."

Conan's horror of sorcery made his heart leap for a moment. Then he shrugged, settling his burden into a more bearable position.

"I've been in reach of worse than your star-beast and cut my way out again," he said. "Lead where you must, my friend."

CHAPTER 15

It was not long after the alarm was raised that Aybas knew their retreat was cut off. At least the princess would not have to struggle with the cliff while carrying the babe on her back.

When he learned of the other way out of the valley, Aybas nearly lost hope altogether. Now they faced an easy climb, but to reach it, they had to pass close to the worst of all possible foes. The beast of the Star Brothers would surely be awake and hungry before they could be out of its reach.

"Perhaps," Marr said. "But think on this. If we are beyond the beast before it wakes fully, it will be a good rear guard to us. Not even the Star Brothers can altogether master the beast when it is fully awake, hungry, or enraged."

"How do we keep it from awakening before we are safely past?" the princess asked.

"I have knowledge that may help us," the piper said, touching the pipes at his waist.

The look on Chienna's face reminded Aybas of the Cimmerian's countenance when magic was mentioned. It was dawning on her just how wholly at the mercy of sorcery they were on this night. Aybas did not doubt that his own face mirrored the princess's.

For two moons he had dreamed of finding a place beyond the reach of the Star Brothers and their evil magic. Now he might be on his way to such a place. But the road to it would lead through still more magic—magic that might in the end be as unclean as the Star Brothers'. So be it. The alternative was to remain in the valley until the Pougoi killed him. Aybas believed that he had some punishment yet to come for serving Count Syzambry, but he would rather it did not come tonight.

"Very well," he told Marr. "You take the lead. Raihna, guard Marr. Wylla, guide us as needed. Princess, see to your babe before all else. I will guard the rear."

How easy it was to once again give orders instead of take them. Aybas knew that if he lived through the night, he would be fit for at least a captaincy in the hosts of the Border Kingdom.

The dam loomed against the stars, ten times Conan's height. He studied the dam's face, finding no stairs but sufficient hand and footholds for swift climbing.

"By Erlik's beard, how did the Pougoi find the hands to build this?"

"The Star Brothers found their beast," Thyrin said. "It gave them knowledge. They used that knowledge to raise the stones of the dam, and more knowledge to bind the stones together."

The near presence of so much magic made the night seem even colder. Conan rested his hand on his sword hilt for the reassurance that honest steel could give.

"It is also said that the beast itself labored on the dam," Thyrin said. "But that is a tale at best. None but the Star Brothers were close to the dam while it rose . . . or at least none who lived to tell of what they saw."

"Sorcerers like their secrets to die with them," Conan said. "Even if that's not one of the laws of magic, they all act as if it were!"

The two men fell silent in their hiding place behind a pigsty. It smelled no sweeter than any other pigsty, but that would drive away the odd passerby. The pigs were awake, grunting and squealing in unease at the alarm. Their noise would hide any small sounds that Conan and Thyrin might make as they waited.

Conan hoped that the waiting would not be long. They were in a race with the warriors, the Star Brothers, the beast, and the princess and her rescuers, all of them striving for victory—which meant life itself.

The mist over the dam swirled thickly. Conan heard the surging of mighty waters against the dam and thought he saw something rise into the mist. It might have been a trick of the vapor. It might also have been a tentacle.

If it were a tentacle, it was as long as a small ship and as thick as a man's body. It also seemed to have gaping, sucking mouths scattered all along its length.

Darkness hid Aybas's party most of the way to the dam, and they hardly needed silence. The walls of the valley caught the sounds of the drums and the trumpets, to say nothing of the cries and screams of the Pougoi. They cast the noise back and forth, raising echoes that thundered among the rocks until it seemed that they were thundering in Aybas's very head.

Aybas ceased to worry about being heard. Two-score oxen could have marched across the valley unnoticed amid this uproar.

He began, rather, to worry about the valley itself. Behind the dam, he knew, was a lake large enough to drown the whole valley if the dam ever released it. He had heard of loud sounds shattering rock and unleashing snowslides, unaided by any magic.

He hastened forward to speak to Marr, passing Chienna on the way. The princess was striding along with grim determination, for all that sweat sheened her face and matted her hair. She might not be bred to the hill life, like Wylla, but she would be no burden tonight!

As Aybas overtook Marr, he saw the man lift the pipes to his lips. Their music went unheard in the din filling the valley, but Aybas felt every hair of his head and beard prickle like the quills of a hedgehog.

They were still prickling when the piper led them up to the base of the dam. They rose even higher when two vast figures loomed out of the darkness, until Aybas recognized Conan and Thyrin.

Wylla gave a faint cry and hurled herself into her father's arms. Raihna looked as if she wanted to do the same to Conan, but the Cimmerian appeared as grim as his cold northern god Crom.

"Best save the greetings and tales until we're safe away," he said. "We've seen no warriors on our trail. What of you?"

Aybas and Raihna shook their heads. Conan seemed to ease a trifle.

"Friend Marr, if you can tame the beast, now's the time to prove it. Raihna, you stand with me and Thyrin."

Aybas began to protest against having laid upon him the burden of taking Chienna to safety if the rear guard fell to the beast. He did not think himself equal to it.

Yet he had given his oath to the Cimmerian. The Cimmerian, in turn, was giving his trust to Aybas, trust in the Aquilonian's prowess as well as his honor. Aybas had betrayed much in his life, but he would not of his own will betray that trust. The Cimmerian, Aybas decided, could have given lessons to many of those whom Aybas had served on how to be a captain in war.

Marr nodded, then looked at the sprawled figure lying beneath a bush. "Is Oyzhik fit to walk?"

"With a barrel of wine in him?" Thyrin growled. "We have no time for jests."

"As you say." The piper began to play again. This time Aybas heard the music: sharp little notes with a weird tone to them, sounding as if they came from a vast distance.

Whatever they were, they had power over Captain Oyzhik's limbs. They writhed, then lifted him to hands and knees, and finally onto his feet. His eyes were wide open but unseeing, and he lurched like an ill-constructed puppet in the hands of an ill-taught puppeteer.

The piper stopped playing, and Oyzhik sank to his knees. But it was only to spew, which he did thoroughly and foully. Aybas stepped back to save his boots and saw the Cimmerian doing the same. It was hard to judge which disgusted Conan more, the drunken Oyzhik or the piper's magic.

As Aybas heaved the pale Oyzhik to his feet, the drums and trumpets suddenly died. Then a single triumphant, brazen call rolled down the valley. Aybas heard shouts and saw Raihna pointing. His eyes followed her hand.

The longhouse of the Star Brother's guards was still blazing, and the fire lit the path leading toward the dam. On that path a score of figures ran, the light glinting on spearheads and drawn blades.

"They've rallied!" Conan exclaimed. "Marr, start Oyzhik climbing. Raihna, Thyrin, we form the rear guard."

The piper spoke sharply in Oyzhik's ear. Oyzhik almost raised a hand, then turned and all but threw himself at the face of the dam. He fell twice before he found his balance, then swarmed up the rocks and logs with the skill of an ape.

Chienna and Wylla followed. A jutting stub of branch ripped one leg of the princess's trousers from thigh to ankle, but she ignored it. Conan noted the fine limb so exposed, and also that the princess was as tall as Raihna and not much less broad across the shoulders.

A trifle thin-flanked for his taste, perhaps, but she would have been a daunting bride for a little man like Count Syzambry. Indeed, Conan wondered if the count would have survived his wedding night.

Aybas, Wylla, and the piper began their climb, Marr gripping his pipes with one hand and seeking handholds with the other. He made heavy going of the dam face that way, and Aybas and Wylla finally dropped back to help him along.

Now the vanguard was away, safe from all but the

beast. Conan nodded to Raihna. She leaped onto a boulder, an arrow already nocked. The shaft whistled toward the line of running men. Before it struck, another was in the air.

Then a huge hand gripped Raihna's shoulder. Conan glared at Thyrin and drew his sword. The other man shook his head.

"Forgive me, Mistress Raihna, Captain Conan. But these are my folk, some of them warriors I have taken into battle. If the Star Brothers have led them astray, perhaps I can lead them aright."

"And perhaps mares will give wine instead of milk," Raihna snapped. "Let go—"

"Speak, Thyrin," Conan said. "But swiftly."

Thyrin cupped his hands, and his voice made the drums and trumpets seem like a hush.

"Warriors of the Pougoi! Tonight's work means no harm to you or any of yours. We mean to end the unclean work of Count Syzambry among the tribe, and nothing more. What that demands, we shall do. More than that, we shall not do. Go from this place to your homes, guard them, and leave us to cleanse the honor of the tribe."

The line of running men slowed. Thyrin roared on, telling more of the wickedness of Count Syzambry and the shame brought on the Pougoi by their taking his gold. He did not mention Marr the Piper, the Star Brothers, or much else about what was afoot.

By now the line of running men was writhing like a broken-backed snake. Some of the men were standing still, others advancing at a walk. A few seemed to be arguing.

Conan also had his bow drawn and an arrow nocked. If Thyrin's notion of talking wits into witlings failed, he and Raihna could have ten arrows into their ranks before they moved again.

Suddenly the shouting was from the warriors, not from Thyrin. Two of them were grappling standing; others were down on the ground. Steel flashed, and someone thrust a spear down from over his head into another man's belly. A bubbling scream split the night.

Thyrin grunted, then slapped Conan and Raihna each on the shoulder. "Fare you well, if we do not meet again," he said.

Raihna's mouth opened into a silent circle. Conan understood. "Bring any men you can rally to a dead man-bear by a many-rooted oak tree hard by the Blasted Lands," he said. "We'll lead them to Eloikas."

"You'll lead them nowhere unless Her Mightiness pardons the whole tribe," Thyrin said. "It's out of dishonor that I lead them, not into Eloikas's service." Then he was running toward the brawling warriors before Conan could think of any more advice, let alone give it.

Raihna cursed Thyrin as she and the Cimmerian began their climb to rejoin their comrades. Conan said nothing. He knew more than she did of what Thyrin might think he owed his tribe, for all that they had wandered down many dark paths lit only by the false light of sorcery.

They were less than halfway up the dam when the witch-thunder rolled across the valley. Confined between the rock walls, it might have been the world cracking apart. Raihna clapped her hands over her ears, and Conan felt as if hot needles were being thrust into his ears.

They reached the top of the dam, however, just as the witch-thunder sounded again. This time it found an echo. From the water beyond the dam there began a long, low hissing.

It went on as Conan and Raihna ran along the top of the dam, which was three hundred paces long; their comrades were barely halfway across.

As they overtook the others, the hiss turned into a scream. The scream turned into a roar, and the lake seemed to catch fire, spewing out shades of crimson and sapphire, emerald and topaz. Its surface heaved and bubbled, then began to steam like a boiling cauldron.

Marr was playing his pipes through all of this, as Conan saw. But his music would have been as a child's cry against the shouting of an army when matched with the roaring of the beast.

Unheard though it might be, the piping seemed to be fulfilling some of its promise. The beast was awake, aware, and furious. That the lake was turning into a cauldron proved that.

Yet the tentacles—indeed, as long as a ship and as thick as a man's body—came nowhere near the people scurrying across the top of the dam. They reached high enough into the air to have plucked men from the top of pine trees or temple towers. They could easily have swept Conan and his little band into death in any eyeblink.

They did not, and Conan began to feel almost at ease with the presence of Marr and his spells. It was not a feeling that he expected to last. No doubt the piper would turn against them in the end, or be turned against them by his magic. Also, Conan would feel still more at ease when they were safe away from the beast, for all that the piper's magic had mastered it for now.

Conan and Raihna overtook the others fifty paces from the end of the dam. Wylla stared at them.

"Where is my father?"

"He hoped to win the Pougoi away from Count Syzambry," Conan said.

Wylla crammed one fist into her mouth to stifle a cry and struck Conan in the chest with the other. Aybas put an arm around her shoulders.

"He saw his duty and we see ours," he said. "Both see clearly, even if not alike."

Seen from close at hand, the piper appeared to be on the verge of collapse. Oyzhik looked like a walking corpse. Only the princess was bearing up well, she and her still-sleeping babe. Conan had to lay a hand across the babe's chest to be sure that he was still breathing.

Then, beneath them, the dam shuddered. Conan felt more than heard stones moving, and saw nothing at all. He had been in too many earthquakes, however, to ignore the sensation.

"Run!" he shouted, loud enough to pierce even the outcry of the beast. "Run for your lives! The dam is breaking!"

He did not need to repeat the warning. The next shuddering joined his words to give wings to everyone's feet. Even Oyzhik reached the far end of the dam at a stumbling run, and the princess might have been racing for a purse of gold.

The path up the cliff lay before them. It was indeed as easy as promised. A child of six could have found a way up it.

So could any number of Pougoi warriors if Thyrin could not keep them off of his friends' trail. Conan studied the cliff, seeking a place where he and Raihna could make a stand against greater numbers. With bows, they could even make their stand beyond reach of the beast's tentacles . . . at least until their quivers were empty, or until the Star Brothers' spells overcame the piper's and sent the

217

beast climbing up the cliff, as it did on the nights of sacrifice—

The dam shuddered for a third time, and this time the shuddering did not end. Conan not only felt but saw rocks moving, and some the size of a man tore entirely loose and crashed down the face of the dam. Dust poured up from long cracks forming amid the stones.

"What keeps you, Conan?" a voice shrieked. "Are you going to spit the beast and roast it for trail rations?"

It was Raihna, all but screaming in his ear. Conan flung her up onto the path, then leaped himself. The solid rock of the cliff was now shaking under his feet, and he nearly fell as he landed.

He did not fall, however, and both he and Raihna overtook the others in moments. None of them paused until they were halfway up the path. Then they stopped to look back.

No one would be pursuing them across the top of the dam any too easily, even should the beast die in the next moment. A gap wider than a royal road lay open in the top of the dam, and water was foaming through it. Mist seemed to rise even from the foam, and the lake itself was all but invisible.

The fires beneath the water tinted the mist in rainbow hues. Conan thought the beast seemed less fierce now, but certainly the ghostly shapes of monstrous tentacles still danced through the mist at intervals.

Conan turned to speak to Marr. He did not expect an answer, or even wish the man to cease whatever magic he was working against the beast. He did want to assure himself that the piper still heard human voice, thought. Conan opened his mouth, but before words reached his tongue, the piper staggered as if struck on the head. Then he toppled sideways. Only Conan's hand gripping his tunic kept him from falling, and had he fallen, he would have rolled off the path and down the cliff toward the lake.

Screams told Conan that others had not been so fortunate. He clutched Wylla's ankle as she sprawled face down, then held on until she dug in fingers and toes so as to keep her place.

Raihna needed no help, and Aybas had fallen sitting. He was cursing and rubbing his rump, but no man cursing so loudly could be hurt.

Oyzhik was doomed. Barely aware of the world around him, sensible only through the piper's magic, he had no hope when that magic ceased. Conan saw the traitorous captain roll down the hill toward a vertical drop, arms and legs outflung like those of a child's doll.

The captain never took the final plunge. A tentacle lunged out of the mist. Even its tip was enough to wind around Oyzhik three times. Conan saw blood spurt as the appendage crushed his chest and belly. Mouths opened in the tentacle to suck in the blood. Then tentacle and prey vanished into the mist.

As Oyzhik vanished, Conan realized that he had not seen the princess or her babe. He braced himself against a stunted tree and examined the slope. At least there was no place where falling rocks could have crushed them. The Cimmerian also saw no place where they could have fetched up safe once they began rolling—

A dark-haired head seemed to rise from the ground, and a long, shapely arm waved frantically. Conan thanked the gods that his eyes had deceived him, and he plunged down the slope.

He reached the princess only a few paces ahead of

Raihna. They were both ready, swords drawn, when another tentacle took shape out of the mist. The beast roared almost as loudly as before, sensing prey. Then it roared louder as both Conan and Raihna slashed at the tentacle. The beast was flesh and blood. It could feel pain and cry out.

Conan and Raihna gave the creature a good deal of pain in the next few moments. Conan had never swung a blade so fast or so hard in his life, for all that each blow jarred his arm from wrist to shoulder.

The tentacle was writhing now, in rhythm with the roars of the beast. Greenish ichor spurted from the wounds, and yellow foam drooled from the mouths, inundating the Cimmerian's arm, making his grip on the sharkskin hilt of his sword uncertain. The stench made the pigsty seem like a lady's perfumed dressing chamber.

Then the last rag of flesh that held the end of the tentacle to the main body gave way under a furious stroke from Raihna. The main body of the tentacle drew back, and not only mist but foam spewed up from the lake as the beast roared.

The princess was handing something up over the edge of the drop, a fleece-wrapped bundle that Conan realized carried Prince Urras, awake now that Marr's spells no longer held him asleep.

"Hold on to him and I'll pull you both up!" Conan shouted.

"Mistress Raihna! Take the babe!" The princess was adamant, and Raihna responded to her appeal. Before Conan could reach for Chienna's hands, Raihna knelt, picked up the babe, and darted up the slope.

Conan knelt in turn, gripped long-fingered hands, and heaved. The princess was no dainty court lady, and it burdened even the Cimmerian's muscles to haul her bodily onto more level ground.

It also did Chienna's attire no good. Conan had seen tavern dancers at the end of their dance wearing less than she wore now. He had also seen tavern dancers less worthy of being so clad. With the greater part of her clothes in rags, she no longer appeared so thin-flanked.

The princess seemed to want to throw herself into the Cimmerian's arms, but she only gripped his shoulders with both hands and laid her head on his chest. They were standing thus when Raihna's voice shrilled from above.

"It's coming again!"

Conan contemplated the tentacle reaching for them. He contemplated the battered sword in his hand. He contemplated the princess and gave her a firm shove on the rump with his free hand. She scrambled up the slope toward where Wylla held her babe as Raihna leaped down for a last stand beside Conan.

Then the ground upended both Conan and Raihna as if they were children tossed in a blanket. They fell and landed sprawling, but not rolling. The tentacle waved in the mist, groping, then stretched out its tip toward them. Conan lurched to his feet, shouting curses and calling on every god he thought might let him die like a warrior.

The rainbow colors in the mist and the fire in the lake died. A vast roar that made the beast's cry seem a pitiful mewling filled the night. The mist rose higher yet, but not as thickly as before. Through the base of the cloud of mist, Conan saw the dam crumble.

The water of the lake thundered into the valley in a solid white wall. It moved faster than a galloping horse, as fast as a flying hawk. Conan knew that he was seeing the death of the Pougoi.

He also saw the beast, although dimly because of the mist. A vast, carapaced shape festooned with tentacles swept into view, then washed through the remains of the dam and down into the valley.

Conan did not see the beast after that, although he knew the moment of its death ... knew it because the ground shuddered again, and a roar that was almost a scream tore at his ears and a stench like all the graves of the world opened at once filled the night.

How long the Cimmerian gazed into the mist that shrouded the dying valley, he did not know. He was recalled to knowledge of the world and work to be done by Raihna's hand on his arm.

"Conan. The rock has crumbled to within an arm's length of your feet. If any more falls, you may well fall with it."

Conan looked down and saw that Raihna was right. He shook off both her arm and his bemusement and began to climb.

"That settles the matter of pursuit, to be sure," he said when halfway up the cliff. "I only wish I knew if the Star Brothers drowned along with their tribesmen."

"Pray that they did," Raihna said. "I doubt if Marr could spellbind a stray puppy, and we've not heard the last of Syzambry's men."

The piper was at least in his right senses and sitting up when Conan and Raihna rejoined their comrades. He held Wylla close to his chest while she alternately wept and keened for the dead.

Aybas was wrapping his cloak about the princess. Above the waist, she was still more unclad than not, but below the waist, she had made herself seemly, if not regal. She was letting the babe suck on one of her fingers, and that seemed to have soothed his cries.

"Best we find a milch goat or a ewe and soak a rag in the milk," the princess said. "Urras has thrived on becoming a nurse-brother to the Pougoi. He may not do so well on the road home."

"Milch goat?" Conan echoed. He realized that he was still a trifle bemused. He hoped that it was only from being too close to such a mighty duel of magic.

"Conan," the princess said, "I could hardly ask you to carry off a wet-nurse. But every patch of hillside about here has its goats. Any who are not good for my babe's milk will surely be good for our rations, will they not?"

"Certainly, my lady—I beg your pardon, Your Highness."

"No pardon needed, Conan. You and your comrades—I would not have asked of anyone sworn to me what you have done of your own will." She looked up at the sky, where stars now shone dimly as a rising wind blew away clouds and mist alike.

"The night is half gone, I fear," she added. "Best we use what is left of it to put some distance between ourselves and any of the Pougoi who may yet live."

Conan hoped that the princess would leave the swordplay to those better fitted for it. Otherwise, he would not quarrel with her apparent wish to command on the march homeward!

He looked down into the valley. Mist still rose in random wisps, but a great sheet of water gleamed beneath it. Here and there, huts and high ground jutted above the flood, and on one patch of high ground, Conan saw tiny figures moving.

Of the beast, the Star Brothers, or Thyrin, there was no sign.

Conan rose, stretched to ease cramped muscles, then turned to Raihna.

"Raihna, which of us is the better goatherd, do you think?"

CHAPTER 16

A pallid dawn found Conan and his companions a fair march on their way home.

"The palace is no more, Your Highness," Conan said. "Your father makes shift with a tent in the wilderness. I fear it is a poor homecoming we offer you."

"Captain, anyone would think that you had spent as much time about courts as Aybas here," Chienna said. Free of the Pougoi, she smiled more readily. That smile made her face more than a trifle comely, with its high cheekbones and straight nose.

"I know how to tell the truth to princes," Conan said. "Or at least the kind of princes who care to hear it. Some don't, and those I don't speak to at all if I can avoid it."

"Our house has always kept an ear open for the truth," Chienna said. "And we have always called the whole Border Kingdom home. We will not be homeless until we set foot in another realm, and both my father and I will die before we do that."

It seemed to Conan that Count Syzambry might yet have something to say about the royal family's going or staying, let alone living or dying. But the quicker the princess and her son returned to Eloikas, the quicker the king would rally such allies as he might yet have. Had he enough, Syzambry might have nothing whatever to say about anything, including his own life or death.

Conan earnestly hoped so. Falling to Syzambry would be like being stung to death by vipers, or even being gnawed to bloody shreds by rats. 'Twas no death for a warrior, no death for anyone—man, woman, or child—who could feel shame.

Conan's band was two days on its homeward journey when they saw the traces of a fair-sized company of men.

"Pougoi," Marr said after studying the footprints. "Warriors in some number, but not all warriors. I see women and children among them."

He rose and contemplated the wooded ridges rolling away to the west. "Trying to put a good distance between themselves and their valley, I should judge. But not going toward the royal camp, unless they should stumble on it by accident."

"If they do, we can leave them to Decius," Raihna said. "What danger are they to us?"

"If they've women and children to lead to safety, they may not fight unless we force them," Conan said.

"They might also be readier to fight us than most," Chienna said. "Vengeance can make wiser folk than the Pougoi—forgive me, Mistress Wylla—forget good sense."

Wylla was so stunned at an apology from a princess of the house that had been long an enemy to her tribe that she could only stand slack-jawed. Marr put an arm around her and bowed to the princess as thanks for both of them.

"I can contrive with my magic that they do not come near us," the piper said. "But the Star Brothers may yet live, some of them, and march with their tribesmen."

"Would not their power have died with their beast?" Aybas asked. From his voice, it was clear that he most earnestly hoped so. He could not have hoped so more earnestly than Conan, but hope sharpened no swords.

"What could live Star Brothers do without their beast?" Conan asked.

"At the very least, sense that my magic was at work," Marr replied. "If they know that, they might find ways to let Pougoi scouts search for us with clear eyes and ears."

"Then let us trust to woodcraft and swift marching," the princess said decisively. "I have no more quarrel with the Pougoi, if they find none with me."

In that, she spoke for all of them. She spoke, indeed, loud enough that an unseen listener heard. He heard clearly, but they did not hear his bare feet on the forest floor as he returned swiftly to his comrades.

They met the listener and half a score of his comrades toward mid-afternoon. Prince Urras was sucking a rag dipped in the last of their goat's milk when Raihna's shriek brought them to their feet and to arms.

"Pougoi!"

Conan was the first to join Raihna at her sentry post. She was already behind a well-placed tree, bow ready, and the Cimmerian found another such from which to watch the warriors approach.

He counted ten of them, all with swords or spears in hand, the points held downward. The archers had their bows strung but over their shoulders, and at the rear of the line—

"Father!"

Wylla's shriek made Raihna's seem a whisper. The Pougoi girl dashed down the path and flung herself into the arms of the tall man at the rear of the warriors. He bent to kiss her forehead, but Conan saw that the seamed, leathery face and grizzled, shaggy beard were not quite dry.

Conan stepped from his hiding place. "Greetings, Thyrin. It's good to see you and to know that not all of your folk died along with the Star Brothers and the beast."

Thyrin gently pushed Wylla away, and his look of joy gave way to a bleaker face. "Would that the Star Brothers were dead. Two of them live, their powers yet in them, and they still have warriors at their command. Not as many as I did when I defied them, but enough so that if they find other friends—"

"Such as Count Syzambry?" came the voice of the princess.

Thyrin and Chienna stared, each trying to take the measure of the other. Neither the green eyes nor the brown ones fell, but it was the princess who spoke first.

"I do not know whether it is fit and lawful by your customs for you to have a pardon from my house. But if it is, you shall have it. Indeed, you have it now. Moreover, you shall have land to call your own, better land than you lost, if you do my house this one service."

The Pougoi were so silent that the faint breeze in

the high pines sounded to Conan like the roar of a gale. Thyrin coughed.

"Where is that land to come from?"

"When Syzambry falls, his friends will fall with him. Their lands will be the gift of the throne to our friends who have stood by us. I do not know where your new lands will be. I only say that if you stand by us, and if I live, you will have them."

This time the silence was swiftly broken by a warrior asking the question that Conan saw on all faces.

"Stand by you, Lady Princess? That means we fight your enemies? Fight the little count?"

"What greater enemy does my house have? What greater enemy can it have? If you live to see the sons of your sons' sons, you will not see a more evil man than Syzambry!"

Thyrin asked that the warriors be allowed to draw apart and take counsel with one another. This was granted. They soon returned, and most of them were smiling.

"Do we swear all together, or each man alone?" the warrior who had asked the great question wondered.

"As your laws and customs bid you," Chienna replied. "I will have no friend swearing an oath that comes strangely to his lips."

That drew cheers, which lasted until Raihna could endure them no more. "Be silent!" she cried. "Or would you let the whole realm know where we are?"

These words drew no cheers but, instead, a few sour looks and some muttered curses from those who still had breath to utter them. Conan stepped forward.

"Lady Raihna and I are both captains in the Palace Guard," he said. "By your oath to the royal house, you also swear to obey Captain-General Decius and any captain speaking for him. Yet no captain of the royal service will ever command you save through chiefs you choose yourselves." The Cimmerian ended by making suitable gestures of honor at Thyrin.

The princess beckoned Conan to her. Tall as she was, she needed to rise on tiptoe to put her mouth to his ear. "I think I have just been told how to lead the Pougoi, Captain Conan. Is that not so?"

"Forgive me if I presumed, Your Highness, but—"

"You were in haste and could not wait for my permission? My father and Decius have told me how often this excuse is given, by both good captains and bad."

Conan was silent, keeping his gaze turned toward the Pougoi. Then he heard a soft laugh.

"You are a good captain, Conan of Cimmeria," the princess said, "and therefore much may be allowed you. Bring the Pougoi forward and let us have the oath-taking. Then they can go and bring up their comrades and kin and we can all sleep at ease tonight."

The oath-taking went swiftly. Conan had expected nothing else. Nor did he doubt that the rest of the Pougoi who followed Thyrin would be as swift in declaring their new allegiance.

Some, doubtless, were of the faction Aybas had described, and always kept apart from the intrigues of Syzambry and the Star Brothers. Some might be seeing the world with fresh eyes. None could doubt that the Pougoi had little future unless they sought new allies. Homeless, their war strength shrunken, their women and children helpless prey, they could not hope to face the other tribes whom they had made into mortal enemies. The raiding for sacrifices had gone on for too long to be easily forgiven.

Conan only hoped that the Pougoi would not use

their new place as upholders of the throne as yet another weapon against their enemies. If they did, the throne would have peace with one mountain tribe and blood-feud with half a dozen others.

The Cimmerian thanked the gods that it would be Eloikas and Chienna who faced that problem, not himself or Raihna. If Aybas wanted to stay and be embroiled in it, good luck to him—and, indeed, the Aquilonian exile's experience of intrigues might make him a wise counselor to the Border throne.

First, however, came the task of being sure that there was a Border throne for Aybas to counsel!

A band of more than a hundred, with fifty fighting men, was harder to hide than Conan's handful. It also had less need to hide. Nothing save Count Syzambry's host—if he yet had one—or Decius and the Guards could meet them in open battle.

Ambushes were another matter, and the Star Brothers' magic was another still. So Conan decided that the newly united, newly sworn allies would move by day and sleep by night. Since it was near sunset by the time the last oath was taken, that meant they would begin the last part of their journey on the next day.

A cluster of huts too small to deserve the name of village offered shelter to the women and children and the princess. The huts were filthy but intact, and they had the look of having been abandoned only a few days before. Why the inhabitants had fled, and whither, Conan did not know. Nor did he care to speak of these questions where anyone less clear-headed than Raihna or Thyrin might hear.

At the end of the oath-taking, Thyrin gave chief's gifts to Conan's party. One gift was the use of a wet-nurse for Prince Urras for as long as he needed one.

The other was a tent for the use of Conan and
Raihna.

"You may share it if you wish," Raihna told Aybas. "One or the other of us will always be on watch
tonight."

Conan said nothing but considered that Raihna
might have told him first if it was her notion that
they sleep apart. They would be doing that enough
when they rejoined Decius. Raihna was too much
woman to let slip away without one final, hot tumble.

Aybas shook his head. "Thyrin has offered me the
hospitality of his tent as a peace offering." He lowered his voice and looked toward Wylla, standing
close to the piper. "Also, she is sleeping under the
stars with him, so it matters little where I sleep."

"Not so," Raihna said. "Sleep where you will wake
with a clear head. We need your wits untouched.
Aquilonia's loss has been our gain."

Aybas's face told plainly of how long it had been
since he heard such praise, but he was equal to the
occasion. He bowed, kissed Raihna's hand, and withdrew.

"Who takes first watch?" Conan asked.

"Let it be me," Raihna said. "For one night, you
should spare yourself."

"When has a woman ever made me weak, Raihna?
Even you, and I have known few women—"

She punched him lightly in the ribs. "As you say,
you have known few women if you think that none
can weaken a man for serious business. Go and sleep,
Conan."

Conan raised his hand in mock respect. "I think I
should never have named you 'Lady.' What next?
Wedding Decius, so that you have the rank in truth?"

Raihna turned away quickly, still smiling. Yet it

seemed to Conan that the smile was thinner than common for her.

Neither Raihna's smile nor anything else kept the Cimmerian from plunging into a deep sleep the moment he lay down. He had lightly oiled his blades and sworn to find the Pougoi smith at first light. The sword, at least, would not be fit to cut mutton without some skilled work.

Then he had removed his boots, wrapped himself in his bearskin, and lain down on the pine branches covering the floor of the tent. The heady smell of fresh-crushed needles was the last sensation he remembered . . . before he awoke to discover that he was no longer alone on his bed. Indeed, he was no longer alone within the furs. Someone had thrown them back and crawled under them with him.

The "someone" was a woman, and she was not asleep. She was feigning sleep, but Conan's ears were too keen to be deceived.

She was also clad only in her own skin, and *that* was not feigned. Conan ran a hand down a smooth back and gently patted firmly muscled hindquarters. It seemed that Raihna had decided against their sleeping apart after all. Having had her jest—

The woman rolled over and drew Conan firmly into her arms.

No man to refuse an invitation so plainly offered, he made quick work of his own garments and returned the embrace as heartily as it had been given. Pressing Raihna down onto the furs, he twined his fingers in her hair and kissed her soundly. Meanwhile, her own hands were at work, making Conan's roar—

Until he felt the hair, which was as fine-spun as

silk and flowed down past the woman's shoulders nearly to the small of her back.

Not Raihna's hair. Raihna's thick, fair hair ended hardly lower than the back of her neck.

Conan did not cease his kisses; nor did the woman—he could no longer call her Raihna—cease her pleasant activities. But with a free hand now here, now there, the Cimmerian quickly made himself a picture of his companion.

Beyond doubt, not Raihna. As tall and as broad across the shoulders, but not as well-fleshed. Add these discoveries to the long hair, and who was he holding in his arms?

Conan's knowledge came to him with a laugh that the woman took for a sign of pleasure. She redoubled her efforts, not that any such was needed to make her a welcome bedmate.

So he had Princess Chienna. Very well. He was a man with a fine woman in his bed, and when that was so, there was neither rank nor royalty nor anything else—except for the rites that had begun long before men and women wore crowns, or anything else.

The rites consumed much of the night and gave much mutual pleasure. The princess at last fell asleep, and Conan wondered if he should awaken her and warn her that Raihna might be returning from her watch.

Then it struck him like a thunderclap. Raihna and the princess had contrived this between them, as—a jest, to say no more.

Why? Bedding royal maidens courted death in most realms, but Chienna was no maiden and, indeed, no woman to be told where she might make her bed. Conan had no fear that the jest would turn deadly.

He still would be glad to know whence the intrigue came. Yet it seemed that the answer would need a potent spell, to let him understand the thoughts of women. A potent spell, and like a cloak of invisibility, or an invincible sword, likely to be more perilous than helpful in the end.

At least he need have no more fear of what Raihna might say should she find them together. Conan piled the furs over them again and drew the princess into his arms. She deserved to sleep warm tonight, if on no other night!

Furs and princess together so warmed Conan that his second sleep was as deep as his first. He awoke to find the princess gone and Raihna in her usual place. She looked very fair in the pale light of early dawn, but it was not in Conan to wake her.

The camp began its greetings to the day with the scrape of flint and steel kindling cook fires, the clash of pots and knives, the wails of hungry children. The night sentries came in, the day sentries went out, and Conan heard a familiar voice raised in protest.

It was Aybas, complaining to all who would hear—and some, it seemed, who would not—that he had barely slept last night. Thyrin snored.

It was then that Conan's laughter shook the tent and awoke Raihna.

CHAPTER 17

Pain still troubled Count Syzambry day and night, likewise weakness and nightmares. He was not ungrateful to Zylku the apprentice for his work with the potions he had found in the ruins of the palace. Without Zylku, both the pain and the weakness would have been impossible to conceal, and the mustering of men to his standard impossible to accomplish. So in spite of the pain, he slept well the night before the Pougoi came to his camp.

The sentries were among the best of his men-at-arms. They sent word of the coming of the Pougoi, then stood to arms instead of fleeing. Syzambry resolved to honor them for that, the more so when he learned that among the Pougoi were two of the Star Brothers.

"Star Brothers," he said as they were ushered into his tent. "I hope it is good tidings that you bring me here, on the eve of final victory."

"The tidings could be better, and likewise worse," the elder of the two Star Brothers said. He had a beard bound with brass wire into three plaits and a fluent command of the lowland tongue.

"We have come without our beast, which cannot live away from the lake we made for it. We have also come with only part of the warriors of the tribe. The remainder were needed to guard our women and children from those tribes that would use a time of weakness to avenge themselves for our service to you."

Syzambry had a sense of being told both less and more than the truth. The courtly manner of the Star Brother did not ease his mind. The wizard seemed to have spent much of his life winning allies by telling them what they wished to hear.

"How many warriors have you brought, and what chiefs?" Syzambry asked. That should smoke out some of the fleas at least—

"Fifty warriors, among the best of the tribe, but no chiefs whose names you would know."

"Then who will lead the warriors in the final battle?"

"We shall stand close to the forefront of the battle," the younger Star Brother said. "As we shall also be among the warriors, what we say, they will hear easily."

"I am sure they will," Syzambry said. Pain throbbed in his head, not from any wound but from the old sick headache that came from rage at fools. "But will they hear the commands of men wise in war? I doubt not your intent, but have you ever fought in such a battle as this will be?"

The two Star Brothers could do no more than shake their heads.

"I thought as much. Will you grant that I may

place one of my own captains over your warriors?
It will be prudent for you as well as for them."

"You doubt our courage?" the elder asked, bristling.

"I doubt that the greatest sorcerer in the world
can cast a useful spell when he is trying to keep steel
from entering his guts," Syzambry said. He tried to
keep his voice level. From the look of the Star Brothers, he had not succeeded, but they recognized his
authority.

"Good. Then I will chose a captain within days,
and you may come to know him before we march. Is
there more?"

The wizards shook their heads and withdrew. Syzambry waited for a decent interval, then summoned
Zylku and told him of the meeting with the Star
Brothers.

The man listened in silence, but his face grew pale.
"You want me to spy on these ragged-arse hill men?"

"I want you to sit down with them and some good
wine first. Drink lightly, see that they drink deep,
and listen. Listen, and what you hear, tell me. You
are no soldier, but you are something at times worth
more—a man with keen eyes and ears, and a mouth
he can keep shut. Also, I think you understand more
of magic than you admit."

Zylku's face said nothing to these last words, but
he nodded. "Ah. You smell something, too, about the
Pougoi coming in like this?"

"You presume greatly to hint that I am a witling."

"Forgive me, my Lord Count."

"Earn your forgiveness, by learning what the Star
Brothers are hiding."

It might be risking much for little to offend the
Star Brothers, and doing so for no more than satisfying curiosity. Yet Syzambry was certain that more

was amiss with the Pougoi than the Star Brothers had told him.

He was almost certain that Eloikas and his minions had a hand in it. And if it was something that might give new strength to the flagging royal cause and make it more formidable on the day of battle—

Syzambry cursed and smote the tent pole with his open palm. The shock awakened pain in several places; he stifled a cry.

When he was crowned king, the count decided, his first command would be that all who wished the royal favor would wait on him in his bedchamber. Especially Princess Chienna, and she would wait on him in very particular ways.

When Conan returned leading a host of Pougoi, Decius would have sympathized with Count Syzambry. The captain-general did not doubt Conan's tale, marvelous though it was. He did doubt the Pougoi's change of allegiance. Doubted it aloud and often, until at last Princess Chienna summoned him and bid him hold his tongue.

"These folk have no home and no retreat," she said sharply. "They can go forward only to doom at the hands of the tribes they have fought, or to some safety in friendship with us. Safety for those warriors who survive a battle that you yourself tell me will be a slaughterhouse. Safety, also, for their women and babes."

"You almost persuade me," Decius said. "Yet this matter is so grave that if King Eloikas—"

For a moment, Decius was sure that Chienna was about to strike him with an open hand. Then her fingers closed on the hilt of her dagger. When she spoke, her voice would have curdled milk.

"Decius, I am neither queen nor regent as yet. But

239

if you trouble my father with this, I will find some way to repay you, outside the law if I find none within it. Go and make sheep's eyes at Mistress Raihna, or grant Lord Aybas his captain's warrant, or do anything that is of use! But do not trouble my father, or I will do more than trouble you!"

Decius bowed and took his leave. In truth, the princess had the right of it. King Eloikas's heart was weakening. It would be a marvel if he lived to see the day of victory.

If it came. The ruin of the Pougoi, their beast, and the Star Brothers had dealt a shrewd blow against Count Syzambry. It had by no means ended the war.

Men were coming in from towns and villages the count had looted to support his host. But few were well-armed, and fewer still knew their way about a battlefield. Aybas would have his captaincy and more if he wished it, not because Decius altogether trusted him, but because beggars could not choose. A dozen captains and three hundred harnesses would have been more to Decius's liking.

There were tales as well that some of the tribes who no longer feared the Pougoi might take a hand in the war. But on which side? If they did come to the royal camp, would they keep the peace with their enemies for generations? Perhaps it would be better for the royal cause if the tribes remained in their hills.

A score and more such questions marched and countermarched through Decius's mind as he walked from Chienna's tent. By the time he reached the edge of the camp, he decided that he would indeed visit Raihna. Not to "make sheep's eyes at her"—in his dreams, he was doing far more—but to take counsel from her. Also from her Cimmerian, and even from

Lord Aybas and Marr, if they could be brought to speak—

A drum began to beat somewhere behind him. Decius turned and saw Conan himself striding down the slope. His face was hard, and only the icy-blue eyes seemed to live.

"My lord captain-general. You are summoned to Her Highness."

A cold hand gripped Decius's heart. Foreknowledge came, so he felt no surprise when Conan added:

"King Eloikas has just died. As chief among the nobles present, you—"

"I know the laws and customs of the realm, Cimmerian. Believe me, I do."

Decius's voice nearly broke on the last words. He wanted to cry "Father!" so that the stars and the moon would hear him.

The Cimmerian had the grace to look away until the captain-general regained command of himself. When he had done so, the two warriors began retracing their steps up the hill toward the royal tent.

Count Syzambry shifted restlessly in his padded chair. He had spent the whole day not merely out of bed, but at work, save for the short sleep that his surgeon urged upon him in the afternoon. An afternoon nap, as if he were a child still in smallclothes!

Perhaps he no longer needed that nap. Perhaps it was that which kept him awake now, growing more restless and uneasy as the sun slipped below the mountain peaks. The sunset gilded some of the snowcaps on the highest peaks, turned others crimson. The breeze had died with the coming of twilight, and the count felt as if the world were holding its breath in anticipation.

Anticipation of what? He knew what he awaited,

at least. Tonight Zylku should return from among the Pougoi. Perhaps he would even return with the truth about the state of the tribe.

From the scouts who watched the royal camp, Syzambry had learned that at least some of the Pougoi had turned their colors. They were led by a man who might be Aybas—and if Aybas had turned traitor, Syzambry could not think of a death hard enough for him!

At least the turncoat Pougoi had no beasts or Star Brothers with them as far as the scouts could judge. There was no approaching the royal camp closely, by night or by day. The scouts who tried to had never been seen again, save for one who was found gelded, disemboweled, and otherwise turned into a direful warning.

After that, the scouts kept their distance, and much of what they brought back was rumors or, at best, tales. One tale ran so far as to say that King Eloikas was dead. If so, should Syzambry offer peace on terms of being named regent for Prince Urras?

Syzambry looked at that notion now from one side, now from another, as color left the world and night swallowed the camp save where watchfires sparked with saffron flames or crimson coals. It was full dark by the time he judged it best to hold his tongue for now. When he knew his own strength, as well as his foe's weakness, the time might be right for making nimble tongues do the work of sharp steel.

Where was Zylku? The count would not know his own strength until he knew the state of the Pougoi, and he would not know that until the man returned.

Boots scraped rocky ground. Swords and spears clattered and clanged. The count's guards were alert. The count himself drew his sword and laid it across his knees as his servant opened the tent flaps.

A dark shape emerged into the circle of the watch-fire: Zylku, looking much the same as he had three days ago, save for an unshaven countenance and a dark cloak thrown over his garments. He stepped lightly toward the watchfire.

The count leaped from his chair, raising his sword to the guard position. In the fire's light he saw that the agent's feet were bare. Bare—and bloody, as if he had run barefoot for days over sharp stones.

Syzambry's breath hissed out in alarm. Otherwise, he would have called the sentries. They needed no calling, though. They had seen the same as their lord, and they stepped forward to do their duty.

The first two guards to reach the agent gripped him gently by the arms, as they would have done with a harmless madman. With the strength of ten men, Zylku gripped the guards' throats. With the strength of twenty, he slammed their heads together. The crack of shattered skulls was loud enough to raise echoes. Then, for good measure, Zylku's fingers closed on the men's throats and crushed their windpipes. They were dead twice over when he flung them violently away from him, to crash into their comrades.

The guards' oath to their lord, and perhaps fear of his wrath, held them at their posts. They did not, however, again advance upon Zylku. As what had been a man ambled toward the fire, they ran hastily to form a wall of flesh and steel before their lord.

"Life me up, you fools!" the count stormed. He hated any order that would remind others of his lack of stature, but he had no choice. All he could see before him was a line of jerkined backs and helmeted heads.

Two of his servants lifted the chair. They staggered under its weight. Two guards ran back to join the servants. They were eager to be as far as they could contrive from Zylku.

The four men together bore chair and count out of the tent and raised Syzambry until he could see over the heads of his guards. He swallowed a cry of horror when he saw clearly, and his limbs responded to an urge to leap in panic from his chair. The chair swayed, the men struggled to uphold it, the count clung desperately to both his dignity and the arms of the chair, and the guards tried to look in all directions at once.

Chaos threatened, but it did not quite prevail. The count settled back on the cushions and forced himself to stare at the sight before him.

Zylku stood in the fire, whose flames leaped as high as his knees. They had already burned the boots from his feet, and now they were turning the flesh on his bones to charcoal. He seemed to feel no pain, though, but stood as if his feet had been in a warm bath, scented with healing herbs—

The man's mouth opened and he spoke. Or at least words came forth. Count Syzambry did not care to think about who in truth had put the words in Zylku's mouth.

"Count Syzambry. This time it is not you who pays the price for seeking unlawful knowledge of our secrets. Nor will it be you unless you further fail to heed such lessons. There will be a lesson each time you seek what you may not know. Each time that lesson will cost the life of a man under you. Think. How many such lessons will the courage of your men endure?"

Then, at last, the spell that had bound Zylku broke. All the pain of being burned alive struck him in a single moment. Count Syzambry would have sworn that no such scream could issue from a human throat.

"Kill him!" the count howled, nearly as shrill as the wretched man himself. The order was not needed. Half a dozen spears were in Zylku's breast before he could scream a second time. There would have been more had several guards not dropped their weapons to clap their hands over their ears. One fell to his knees, spewing.

As Zylku died, so did the fire. The count thanked the gods for the darkness, which hid his own pallid and fear-twisted countenance from his men. He hoped that the gods were still present in this land to be thanked.

At least his guards and servants were present and in command of their limbs and senses. They did their duty so that when the count's wit returned, he was wrapped in furs and in his bed, with a leech attending him.

Syzambry listened with but half an ear to the leech's earnest mutterings about bleeding and purging, green bile and wind. His thoughts were elsewhere, pursuing the mystery of who had ensorceled Zylku and sent him to his dreadful death.

No one but the Star Brothers and the royal house could have secrets they would kill to guard. The royal house had no magic at its command, unless the piper still served them. The Star Brothers had magic more than great enough for this dreadful work, even without their beast.

Yet the Star Brothers were his allies! The count almost choked on the word. Was this a way to treat an ally, one who had promised to raise them and their folk high in the Border Kingdom? Slaughtering a trusted man, sowing fear among the soldiers, and unsettling the count's own mind?

Roland Green

The Star Brothers had done it, though. Perhaps they were like their hill folk after all, with no sense of honor outside the tribes. Perhaps they did not care what they did, because the secret they wished to protect was that they could prevail without Count Syzambry's aid.

With the fire gone, the night could not have been darker. It seemed colder, though, and the count drew the furs more tightly about himself as the chill seemed to strike at his wounds. Amidst the throbbing pain, the thought of offering peace to the royal house came again.

"Tell your master that peace shall come only when he offers his sword to Our service without conditions," Queen Chienna said.

Decius smiled at the look on the faces of the handful of surviving court officials. The royal "We" was the prerogative of a reigning monarch, not of a regent for an underage king. Nor had it escaped their attention that Urras was still called "Prince."

It seemed that the matter of a regency would not arise for some time, mostly likely not until after the decisive battle against Count Syzambry. This did not displease Decius in the least.

To be sure, as captain-general, he would have been a leading member of any Council of Regency. But there would have been others, more each day as nobles with more loyalty than strength rallied to the royal standard.

Some of these nobles considered themselves well-versed in war. They would not seek Decius's office, but neither would they cease to advise him how to conduct it. As for what they would say to Conan being captain of the Guard, or to Raihna and Aybas being captains at all, or Marr the Piper's very pres-

246

ence in the camp—Decius was happy that he would not have to listen to any of it.

All he would have to listen to was Chienna saying, "We wish it done," or "We do not wish this done," and then obey. It was enough to make a man not merely believe in the gods, but to be convinced that they had some concern for justice and decency among men.

"May my master not even expect a pardon?" Count Syzambry's messenger queried.

The queen's eyebrows drew together in a way that Decius had seen a hundred times, ever since she was a child. No furious words followed, however. Her dignity was indeed regal as she merely said: "Our words were simple. 'Without conditions.' Are you or your master deaf, that you cannot understand?"

The messenger seemed to at least understand that he would gain no more by staying, and perhaps lose the chance to make a dignified withdrawal. He made it, and shortly afterward the clatter of hooves told of his departure.

Decius made the rounds of the sentries, told them to keep a watch for the return of Conan's picked men from their training march, then had a brief audience with the queen. She was trimming her toenails with a soldier's knife as they spoke, but it seemed to Decius that she was more graceful than ever.

"We did not ask your advice before refusing the count's offer," she said. "For this, We ask your forgiveness. Do you think it was worth more of a hearing than We gave it?"

Decius's laughter was a harsh bark. "Count Syzambry is trying to enlist your aid to save a lost cause."

"Or the tales may be true, that he has Pougoi allies

as well and fears them as much as he does Us," Chienna pointed out.

Decius's dignity would not allow him to gape, but his face revealed enough to make the queen laugh. "Decius, I should be angry at your thinking I am not old enough to hear such things. Remember, I am Queen of the Border, a poor queen, perhaps, but all the realm has—unless you think that Count Syzambry really should rule?"

Try as he would, Decius could not laugh at that jest. "Captain Conan would be ten times fitter for the crown than Syzambry."

"At least," the queen said. She put the knife away and drew her stained robe down over her bare feet. "We are well pleased with your service and value your counsel. May We always be able to trust them as We do today."

Decius bowed himself out, thinking that wishes, even royal wishes, could not bind the gods. He was twice Chienna's age and would be fortunate indeed if he lived to teach Prince Urras the art of war.

Perhaps he should marry again. After burying a wife and three sons, it might be tempting fate, but his children and Urras might grow together. The prince would need friends and playmates, certainly, and—

"My lord Decius. Do you wish to be alone?"

It was Raihna, who had come out of the darkness beside the path as silently as a cat. Decius started to nod, then knew that in his heart he did *not* wish to be alone.

"Mistress Raihna, in truth I would enjoy your company."

They walked side by side to the captain-general's tent. They were a sword's length apart, and Raihna's garb was no more revealing than usual, yet Decius had never been so aware of her as a woman.

They sat on furs just inside the mouth of Decius's tent. The captain-general sent away his bodyservant and drew a skin of wine from under the furs.

"Poor hospitality, I fear."

"No hospitality is poor when the host is a treasure."

Decius hoped that the firelight did not reveal him flushing like a boy. He sensed that there was more than Raihna's nimble tongue in that praise.

Raihna drank deeply, then handed the skin to Decius. In doing so, she let some drops fall on his wrist.

"Forgive me, my lord. Here, let me . . ."

She put her mouth to his wrist and began licking off the wine.

That Decius had been long a widower did not make him a fool. He put both hands under Raihna's chin and lifted her face to receive his kiss. Her mouth bloomed under his, and her arms went around him.

It was amazing how swiftly the lacings of armor could be undone by skilled fingers. There was nothing amazing about what followed, unless it was that Raihna was even fairer to look at than Decius had suspected.

It was not until Raihna was sleeping in his arms that Decius realized they had not closed the tent flaps. They had been tumbling in the furs, clad only in the firelight, in full sight of anyone who wished to wander by. Had Conan chosen to pass along this path—

No. Decius would take the word of both Conan and Raihna that the woman was her own mistress. After that, he would take her into his arms again, if she was willing.

He dared not think about taking her to wife, not

until the battle was won. That would be tempting the gods, and for now, they had given him enough and to spare. His thought on leaving the queen had been a true one: the gods did have some care for humans.

Conan returned to the camp at dawn. The men he was taking against Count Syzambry had needed little more training, save at setting ambushes by night. This he had given them, and they now knew as much as he thought necessary.

The Pougoi was masters of them all in the art of night fighting, he knew. But the queen did not care to send the tribesmen far afield and out of reach of her loyal men. Thyrin had borne this with more grace than Conan expected, although no one could call the man pleased. The gods willing, he should even be able to keep the peace among his warriors—

It was no great surprise for Conan to find that Raihna was not in his tent. It was somewhat more of a surprise to see that her clothing and weapons had likewise departed. It was a considerable surprise indeed to find Wylla asleep in the furs.

At least the hair spread out over the furs was the color of Wylla's, and the shapely bare arm that trailed off onto the floor of the tent was that of a woman as young and comely. Conan removed his boots and crept on hands and knees to the furs. Kneeling, he gripped the furs with one hand and poised the other over the arm.

Then he snatched the furs away. The morning light proved what he had suspected. Wylla lay there, as bare as a newborn babe and much more pleasing to look at. She also lay so deeply asleep that Conan realized other measures than removing the furs might be called for.

He bent over, ready to kiss her.

Her arms took on a life of their own, leaping up to twine round his neck. She embraced him so tightly that she lifted herself clear of the furs, pressing her whole length against him. Conan felt every curve, and the heat of her blood flowed into his.

Wylla began to croon softly as Conan returned her embrace. Conan knew a moment's unease at the singing, but he soon passed beyond caring about such matters. Wylla saw to that.

The song ended as Wylla curled against him, taking and giving warmth, one hand still twined in the Cimmerian's black hair. The silence lasted until Conan's laughter broke forth.

"What is the jest, Conan?"

"I hope it ends as a jest, you being here."

"You fear Marr?"

"I fear offending any man who had that power."

"It shames both him and me to say that you need fear anything from this—" she patted the furs.

"You and Raihna."

"Eh? Oh, that we are both our own mistresses?"

"Yes. Although I do not think that Mistress Raihna will be so free for long. Not if Decius lives—"

Conan's laugh was louder this time. "I won't ask where Raihna spent the night, because I think I know. But I will ask this. Did she—?"

"Send me? Of course. She said that Decius was not made by the gods to be as alone as he was. You were, but no man should be without a woman on the eve of what might be his last battle. So I came, and you were not."

"Suppose I turn you over my knee for speaking ill-omened words about last battles?"

"Oh, if that is your pleasure—" She wriggled, raising herself so that he could pull her over his knee if he wished. At the same time, her hands danced along

251

Conan's limbs in a way that could have only one conclusion. This time Wylla fell asleep when they were done.

Conan did not sleep. Quietly he slipped from under the furs, garbed and armed himself, and went to find his rest under a pine tree just inside the sentry line.

He would not ask the gods to let him understand women, even if they could give him that power. But would it be too much to ask that women should not understand him as easily as Raihna seemed to?

CHAPTER 18

The scout was looking over his shoulder when his time came, not ahead as he should have been. Small shame to him, however. He was an honest trapper's almost equally honest son, who had taken service with Count Syzambry many years ago.

He had not imagined then that he would end as the scout for a host led only in name by the count. He had not imagined that the Pougoi wizards, the Star Brothers, were even real, let alone that they would come forth from their valley.

As for believing that they could put fear into the count and all his host—a thousand men or more—the scout would have called it madness. He would have suggested that the speaker needed physicking, to restore his wits.

And if by some chance he had believed that he would end serving the Star Brothers, he would have fled the Border Kingdom as fast as his feet would carry him. Indeed, he would have crawled, if need be, to put distance between himself and those monster-worshipers.

Not having fled, or even left the count's service, the scout was now bound to his master and his duty. Bound as with bands of iron by loyalty to his comrades, oaths to the count—and by stark terror of the Star Brothers.

It was that terror that made the scout look back over his shoulder at the wrong moment. He had just decided that no spy for the wizards followed close on his heels when a hand like steel closed on his sword arm.

The scout tried to whirl around, cry out, and draw his sword with his left hand. He accomplished none of these. Another hand clamped itself over his mouth, both hands jerked, and he soared through the air into the bushes as his sword flew out of his hand.

Conan tapped the scout's head gently against a fir trunk, and the man went limp. The Cimmerian listened to the man's breathing, judged him fit to travel, and slung him over his broad shoulders.

Carrying his prisoner as he would the carcase of a deer, Conan loped away from the trail and deep into the woods. Only when he was beyond any human senses did he turn west, toward the royal vanguard that awaited him.

Count Syzambry was short of stature, not of sight. He was also a warrior of great experience and proven courage.

So he rode forward when a messenger from his scouts came to tell of the missing man. He sent the messenger ahead again, with orders for the scouts to hold where they were. Then he rode swiftly with a small escort to join them.

After joining the scouts, Syzambry dismounted. He needed help to do so, which his men gave willingly, but he no longer had to stifle gasps of pain. After he had examined the ground closely, he needed no help in climbing back on his mount.

Some of the aches and pains had to be stiffness from being too long in the saddle. He had not ridden for so long that he had almost forgotten something he learned as a boy!

He laughed, which seemed to hearten his men. Those who served him out of loyalty rather than greed or fear had felt for their lord's pain and weakness. They were glad to see him leading as he had done before.

It gave them more hope of victory and less fear of the Pougoi wizards. They had no fears of the royal host. What could a ragged band of fugitives half their strength, fighting on behalf of a woman, really hope to do?

The count's laughter ended quickly as another messenger cantered up. This one was of the Pougoi, and the Star Brothers spoke through his mouth. They also heard through his ears but did not, to the best of Syzambry's knowledge, see through his eyes.

"Hail, Brothers. I wish I had better news," the count said.

"What is it?" The Star Brothers had learned enough of war in recent days to know the value of time.

Syzambry explained what the disappearance of the scout might mean. "Of course, he may simply have fled in fear," the count ended. "If so, I give you leave to hunt him down as you wish."

That was an invitation for the Star Brothers to use their magic to bring the scout to heel. The count had offered such invitations several times since his host marched. Each time, the Star Brothers had refused. They either had less magic than they claimed, or they feared the spells of Marr the Piper more than they admitted.

It hardly mattered. If the Star Brothers could remove Marr from the balance of the coming battle, the count was sure of victory. Then, before the wizards could become suspicious, it would be time to settle with them.

"We do not wish to spend our strength against a single common man," the messenger replied. "His death would prove nothing, except our presence with this host."

At last, something like a reason for the silence of the Star Brothers! Syzambry doubted that the royal captains were ignorant of the Star Brother's presence. If they had been, the scout would tell them soon enough, and it would need no magic to loose his tongue. Hot irons would serve as well.

Still, if the Star Brothers wished their presence concealed to the last, it did Syzambry no harm to humor them. The more they thought he did their bidding, the less they would be on their guard after the battle.

"Very well," Syzambry said. "I judge that we should slow our advance, however. The scouts must walk two, even four, in company, with archers close at hand. Also, I think I shall send more scouts out to either flank. A royal captain has thought to snatch a man of our vanguard. His next scheme may be to ambush it. If we can find the rear of those ambushers before they find our flank—"

"Such matters of war we leave to you," the messenger said.

That was exactly where they belonged, the count considered. If the Star Brothers ever tried to take the command of his host from him, he might have to fight a battle to his rear as well as to his front.

Conan had seen councils of war meet in better heart. Most of those, however, were composed of fools who did not know the chances of the forthcoming battle. A few had met before battles where the odds were so much in their favor that only a fool could waste strength in worrying.

None of the men and women here in the royal tent were fools. All of them knew that tomorrow's battle was one against long odds, and that it could go either way.

They also knew that, win or lose, it would bring a decision in the war in the Border Kingdom. The land would not be harried for years by the contending hosts, until no babe could be born or crop harvested in safety.

"Rather than bring that fate to the land, I would flee to the Black Coast," Chienna said. "I would even drive my dagger into my own breast and dash Prince Urras's brains out on the nearest rock."

Decius flinched at hearing such words from Chienna, and he shot an anguished look at the woman he might have loved. Would have loved, save for the whim of the gods that made her his half-sister.

Conan hoped for Decius's sake that he would soon grow used to plain-spoken women of iron will. The captain-general seemed resolved to wed one, and she would not change to please him or any man.

"Let's not be burying our cause before it has stopped breathing," Conan said. "With all due respect, Your Majesty."

"How much respect do you think is due a queen, Captain Conan?" Chienna asked. Her face was hard, but Conan thought he saw a hint of a smile at one corner of her mouth and more than a hint of laughter in her wide eyes.

"As much as she earns," Conan said, and this time not only Chienna but the rest of the council laughed aloud.

Talk turned swiftly to the morrow's battle. Knowing that the Star Brothers were among the count's host somewhat confined the scope of their plans now.

Marr the Piper had to be protected. He was confident that he could hold back the Star Brothers' spells; he was not sure that he could leave the Star Brothers helpless against a well-wielded sword.

As for striking down them or anyone else with his magical piping—

"The gods did not make me fit to do that," Marr said firmly.

"Fit, or willing?" Decius asked.

"Peace, my lord Decius," the queen said. "Thyrin, you seem eager to speak."

"Marr is telling no more than the truth," the Pougoi chief said. "His spells are not to be wielded as a sword, like those of the Star Brothers. They are more kin to a shield, or to a good leather helm."

Conan hoped that Marr's piping would be more like iron than leather. Leather helms had a way of letting the skull within them shatter at a shrewd blow. If he was going to fight with magic as a friend as well as a foe, Conan wanted the friends to overmatch the foes.

He also wanted to know if Thyrin was telling the truth or merely favoring Marr in the hope that he would finally declare for Wylla. Having his daughter wed to the legendary Marr the Piper could make Thyrin mighty in the land, not just among the Pougoi.

He would certainly be undisputed chief among any Pougoi who lived to see tomorrow's sunset.

As to how they would array the royal host—if five hundred men deserved that title—much would have to wait on the morrow. They could resolve to march in such order that the arraying would be swift. It would also be as well if Queen Chienna were in a safe place, or at least in a well-guarded one.

"Give the queen first claim on any men we can spare from the fighting line," Marr said. Wylla threw him a stricken look, and he patted her hand.

"No, this is not folly. I am no great warrior, but I am fleet of foot. What my spells cannot turn aside, I wager I can outrun."

This was wagering the fate of the Border Kingdom on Marr's feet, but little save a dry throat would come of stating what all knew. Conan was silent.

As if she had read the Cimmerian's thoughts, Chienna rose. "Good people, We judge this council to have done all it can. Mistress Raihna, will you do Us the favor of pouring the wine?"

Count Syzambry would not have fought on this day, or on this ground, had he been free to choose.

He was not. His scouts had advanced unmolested until they came up against the royal vanguard. That it was the Palace Guard was no surprise. That the giant Cimmerian was captain over it was. That giant would be shorter by a head by sunset, Syzambry resolved.

First, though, he had to win the battle, and to win, he had to fight. He could not fight on ground that would let him array his whole host, not without retreating. That would dishearten some of the weaklings, and perhaps provoke the Star Brothers. Their silence since dawn was a blessing from the gods; Syzambry would not cast it aside now.

So it would be here—in this vale—where, at best, half of his men could form line at once. This was not altogether to his disadvantage, as his foes would also suffer. The ground would slow any attack, trees protect the count's archers, and a few level patches give his mounted men room to charge.

Syzambry summoned his messengers and watched them ride out. They did not have far to go before they vanished, not only among the trees, but into the mist. Syzambry had cursed the mist without effect, except that it now seemed to lie in patches rather than equally everywhere.

At least the Pougoi and their Star Brothers were safely in the rear. In the middle of a circle of baggage carts defended by their tribesmen, the wizards could conjure as they pleased with what effect they might contrive. They could not distract a man trying to win a realm.

One of the messengers was riding back, faster than he had ridden out. He reined in his lathered horse and gave a salutation that was all but a wave.

"The royal host is upon the field!"

"Where?"

"There!" At first the count saw nothing save a patch of mist, thicker than most. Then he saw that at the heart of the mist were marching men. The Palace Guards were taking the field, the giant at their head. Syzambry recognized the flowing black hair, for the man was bold enough to face him bareheaded!

Well, it would hardly matter whether the head was bare or helmeted once the count had it on a lance outside his tent.

CHAPTER 19

This was the kind of battle that Conan liked less than most.

The two hosts were simply flinging themselves upon one another, with less art than pit-wrestlers for all that the combat was deadlier. Perhaps there was no blame to the captains on either side, for the ground was broken and the mist made seeing what one was about no easy matter.

That was certainly true enough for Conan. He saw the veterans of the Palace Guard with their spears and the newer men with their swords holding their place against Syzambry's levies. He saw Raihna dashing back and forth, encouraging both her men and some of Decius's.

Every man with a bow had brought it to the field, but Conan was allowing only the best of his archers to shoot. Arrows were too few to be flung wildly into patches of mist that might hide enemies.

The Cimmerian thought he saw blue fire dancing from the treetops and in the heart of patches of mist, as Marr and the Star Brothers dueled. He also thought he saw Thyrin and the Pougoi to the right of the Guards instead of to the left, where they belonged. Perhaps they had only lost their way in the mist, not being accustomed to fighting in orderly array.

Thyrin stepped into view from a mist-shrouded clump of fir, but Conan did not ask the man about his tribesmen. How many men were fighting here today, Conan did not know; he only knew how much noise they made. The host of Turan at the charge could hardly have outshouted them. Any question to Thyrin and any answer from the man would be lost in the din.

"Steel Hand! Steel Hand!"

This time the levies shouted the count's war cry as they advanced, not their own lord's. Conan sought for the count's standard in the misty woods beyond the levies and found nothing. A pity, because putting an end to the count would put an end to the war.

No. The Star Brothers had to meet the same fate as the count, their Brothers, and their beast. They could not be allowed to wreak more havoc.

Their deaths would leave Marr the Piper the only sorcerer in the Border Kingdom, to be sure. That was one sorcerer too many, and a good reason for Conan's being on the way south once the battle was won. But at least Marr was not one to run wild and wreak havoc, unless provoked. Chienna and Decius would have the task of not provoking the piper.

Conan's own task suddenly presented itself as meeting four of Syzambry's levies. All had swords, two bore shields, and one carried a long dagger that he wielded in combination with his sword. Conan judged him the most dangerous and moved first against him.

The two-blade fighter was a small man who, until his last day, had won as much by swiftness as by skill. He had never faced Conan's combination of speed and length of reach.

The Cimmerian's blade struck his opponent's dagger out of the hand holding it and went on to gash the arm. The man had the courage to close and the speed to make that a wise move.

Conan took the swordcut on his chest and felt mail links drive through his arming doublet into his skin. His reply crashed through the small man's guard and laid open one whole side of his face.

That would have to do for the man, with three other opponents to face. Conan saw one back away from the fight at the sight of his leader wearing a bloody mask, but the other two came on. They seemed to have fought together before, and both fought well enough that the Cimmerian had a moment's need for caution.

Then his blade crashed through the guard of the man to the right, and he kicked upward at the man to the left. His boot caught the man in the groin and lifted him clear of the ground. At the same time, Conan's steel chopped through the other man's arm just below the elbow.

Screaming, the one-armed man fled into the mist, seeking to spend his last moments among his comrades. Conan faced the small man again just as pain and bleeding drove the other to his knees. The sword stroke that clove his cap and skull together was a mercy.

Conan saw the last of the four men writhing on the ground and a Guard recruit with a spear standing over him. As the Cimmerian watched, the spearhead dipped, then thrust in deep. The man's breath bubbled in his throat, he clutched at the spear shaft and writhed, then his limbs went limp and the life went out of his eyes.

"Back to your place!" Conan shouted at the recruit. "And where did you find that spear?"

"The man who held it before me is dead," the recruit shouted back, eyes wide with battle-rage and defiance. "I will be dead, too, before I put it down."

Conan cursed under his breath. If the line of spears was falling into the hands of the recruits, the Guards might not hold much longer. When they ceased to hold, so would the right flank of the royal army.

It seemed time for a messenger to seek out Decius. This butting of heads like two rams had gone on for a good while, with no great harm to the royal cause. It had drawn the whole royal host into the battle, though, and Conan doubted that Syzambry was in the same case. He might have men to spare with which to seek a flank. Best that the royal army find his flank before he found theirs.

"I will take your place," Conan shouted to the recruit with the spear. "You run to the captain-general and say to him—"

Conan's message died on his lips. Wylla ran out of the mist and the witch-fire clad only in her skin belt and ivory dagger. Her face silenced Conan's impulse to fling her over his shoulder and carry her to safety.

"Conan! Marr says that the count has the Star Brothers and their Pougoi to his rear. He wants my father and his warriors to strike them. With his pipes warding off the star-magic—"

"Crom!"

The Pougoi advance would uncover the right flank of the Guard, already at full stretch. It might sow havoc in the count's rear. It might also slay all of Thyrin's Pougoi, and even Marr.

There was only one way to stave off this disaster. The Palace Guard must charge with the Pougoi. Struck in front as well as in flank, Syzambry's wing might falter and fail. Certainly it would be launching few attacks of its own until the fate of the royal charge was decided.

Conan said no prayers. This was a moment when only one god existed for a Cimmerian, and cold, grim Crom was not one to listen to mortal mewlings. He called a warrior to do his best and to accept his fate if that best was not good enough.

Which was at least as much justice as Conan expected he would receive from Decius. Captains whose battle plans were cast to the four winds by footloose underlings were not often even-tempered.

Conan sheathed his sword, cupped his hands, and ran along the line of the Guards, shouting the rally.

Count Syzambry had no idea of what might be happening on his left. The mist and the ground hid it. What noise he could hear hinted of a royal attack. Perhaps even one in some strength, for a messenger he had sent to learn what might be happening had not returned.

Yet the attack could not have the strength to drive far into his rear. Even if it did, the Star Brothers and Pougoi together would be a tough nut for any royal handful to crack.

The count's gaze returned to his front, where he could see more clearly. What he saw there was heart-lifting. The royal host was spread thinner than he would have dared believe possible. Decius was no fool; he knew the need to keep a flank strong.

Nor were the royal men—the Palace Guard, it

seemed—dead at their posts. There were too many bodies of Syzambry's men lying among the rocks and bushes, but far fewer of the Guards. In dying, had Syzambry's men broken the Guards?

The count's breath came quickly, for all that it made his ribs ache beneath his blued-steel armor. He had few men in hand save his mounted men-at-arms, and none too many of them. Also, they were scattered and would need summoning were they to charge in a mass behind him.

But if they charged as he knew they could, the battle was won. Won, moreover, with little owing to the Star Brothers.

The count raised the mace topped with the steel hand that was his mark of captaincy. Messengers sitting at the head of their horses leaped up and began to mount.

Now Queen Chienna would see who had the skill in war to rule this land.

Aybas had no particular place in the battle line, being a captain without a company of his own. He had no doubt that he was not yet altogether trusted.

He had made friends with a village head man who led the peasant levies, however. Decius had planned to keep them in the rear of the line, but when the Pougoi ended on the far right flank, the captain-general had to devise a new array. This brought the levies forward into the line, and it was with the levies that Aybas stood when Count Syzambry charged.

It was like no charge that Aybas had ever seen, or even imagined. The fifty or more armored horsemen seemed to trickle forward, like drops of water flowing down the silver face of a mirror. They formed no line, and few seemed to have proper lances to make such a line deadly even if they formed it.

Yet they were coming on swiftly, and if they had few lances, they had swords and maces in abundance. If they reached level ground in the midst of the royal line, they would pierce it like an arrow through silk.

They could also be stopped short of the line and level ground if one could deny them a little hillock a hundred paces ahead. Aybas looked along the line of peasants, saw the fear already in their faces, and knew that he must command a charge.

Whirling his sword over his head, he gave the war cry of the house into which he had been born.

"Wine of Victory!"

Then he charged, one man against fifty. He did not expect to reach the hillock alive, but somehow he did. He did not expect the levies to follow him, nor did he dare to look back, but somehow he was not alone when he started climbing.

Before he could draw breath, he found himself among the boulders with fifty men around him, all of them cheering as if the battle was already won. Two were beating on the helmet of a fallen horsemen with their felling axes.

"Leave be!" Aybas shouted. It was unknightly to abuse a fallen foe, as he had learned in boyhood. It was also foolish to give attention to a harmless foe when there were many still fighting. That Aybas had learned in manhood, from many rough teachers.

His shouting brought the levies around to face their front just in time. A bold horseman was spurring up the hillock. Aybas knew that his reprieve was about to end as he dashed forward.

The man whirled his mace in a fine gesture, then brought it down. He would have been better advised to forgo the gesture.

Aybas leaped up with a speed he had hardly known

he had in him and caught the shaft of the descending mace. At the same time, he slashed hard at the man's leg and heaved himself backward.

His blade only clanged on armor, but the rest of Aybas's attack carried through. The man flew out of his saddle, too surprised to even cry. He struck the ground headfirst, sprawling beside Aybas with his helmet flattened and his head at an impossible angle to his neck.

Aybas leaped again and caught the reins of the dead man's horse. The stirrups danced wildly, almost defeating his efforts to mount. At last he succeeded, and the levies greeted him with a wild cheer.

Syzambry's horsemen did not cheer. Indeed, it seemed to Aybas that they were no longer charging and were even looking to their rear. It was hard to make out what they might be looking at between the forest and the mist.

It seemed, however, as if someone had flung himself against Syzambry's rear and was giving it a fight for its life. A moment later, Aybas's ears told him more than his eyes did as a peal of Marr's witch-thunder rolled from the forest.

Within the forest, the witch-thunder made Conan deaf for a moment. He did not care. For now, he needed only his sword, and his eyes to guide the blade. Also, perhaps, his legs to bring him to close quarters with the Star Brothers.

Not that there were no foes ready to hand. As the Guards and the Pougoi hacked their way into Syzambry's rear, they met every sort of soldier the count had not put into his battle line. They also met men who could not be called soldiers by any conceit. Most of these fled, and this was as well. Conan had no love for killing men as helpless as babes. There were enough foes worth a man's steel already, and the day was not yet won.

Conan cast a look behind him. Marr the Piper was running with the soldiers, playing as he ran. His eyes were wide but unseeing, and Conan would have sworn any oath asked of him that those eyes glowed blue.

Magic, surely. But without magic, how could the man both play and run, and without the piper close, how could Conan face the Star Brothers?

The Star Brothers were also close, more so than Conan realized. He burst through a line of dwarfish ash trees to face a circle of baggage wagons swarming with Pougoi warriors. In the middle of the circle stood two Star Brothers, chanting so loudly that Conan heard them even over the piping.

A roaring Cimmerian battle cry eclipsed both piping and chanting. Guards and Pougoi swarmed through the trees to join Conan.

"Archers!" Conan thundered.

Every one of his men who had a bow seemed to nock and draw in a moment. Arrows skewered twenty Pougoi and as many baggage animals. The shooting would have won no prizes in Turan, but this was not Turan. Conan's archers had all the skill they needed against the target before them.

Before the Pougoi could recover, Conan was leaping forward. Also, those of his men who bore crossbows had time to nock and shoot. Some of their bolts pierced dead men or baggage animals.

One bolt, unheralded, pierced a Star Brother's thigh. He broke his chanting to scream and lurched against his comrade.

The star-spells did not break, but their masters no longer commanded them. Some of the Pougoi closest to the Star Brothers grew old in an instant, their faces as wizened as babes and their heads either white or bald.

Their comrades stared at them, then stared at one another. The berserk spells were striking wildly and doing worse than aging those within reach.

Conan saw a man with all of his guts, and his heart and lungs as well, on the outside of his body. He saw a man suddenly grow purple scales with green spots, and claws on both hands and feet. He retained his thumbs, however, and came at the Cimmerian with a battle ax.

Conan leaped back before the lizard-man's rush. He wanted space between himself and the spells. He also wanted to give his archers another clear shot. He would ask no man to face these abominations hand-to-hand.

Now some of the baggage animals were also developing scales. Others grew batlike wings, which beat frantically and knocked down most of the Pougoi not ensorceled into something other than human.

The few left human and on their feet leaped from the circle of baggage wagons and ran screaming in mortal terror. Blind with fear, most of them ran straight into the ranks of their fellow tribesmen. Thyrin's men laid on with a berserk fury, as if every servant of the Star Brothers they killed was one more cleansing of the tribe's honor.

The sound of a cracking and crashing rose above the din of magic and fighting men. A huge pine beyond the ring of wagons swayed, jerked roots loose from the rocky soil, then toppled. It came down with a crash that made every other sound before seem like a mother cooing to a babe. It smashed wagons, beasts, men and not-men with blind impartiality.

As the echoes of the forest giant's fall died away, so did the piping. Conan felt a sharp pang of doubt that he would not yet call fear. Then Marr the Piper thudded down at the Cimmerian's feet as if he'd leaped from a high wall. In one outflung hand he gripped the shattered pipes.

Conan had one moment of seeing his death waiting; then he saw his duty just as clearly. He leaped onto the trunk of the fallen tree, bare for most of its hundred paces. Running as fast as on level ground, he leaped down beside the Star Brothers.

The one with the bolt in his thigh lay twitching feebly in a pool of blood. His comrade was still upright, though ashen-faced and chanting softly.

Conan's sword leaped at the wizard's bearded head. Leaped, then rebounded as if it had struck a castle wall. Five times Conan struck, with the same futile results.

The sixth time, the chanting grew louder and his sword not only rebounded, but flew from his hand. Conan stooped to retrieve it, but as he gripped the hilt, the blade began to smoke. A moment later the whole weapon was too hot to touch, and the sharkskin binding of the hilt was on fire.

Conan did not wait for the sword to turn into a puddle of molten steel. The last Star Brother was building a new spell, and there was no Marr the Piper to content with him ... only a Cimmerian ready to trade his life for the lives of those he led.

His sword useless, Conan snatched up the first weapon that came to hand, the shattered tongue of an ox-wagon. Wielding it as he would a quarterstaff, he lunged at the Star Brother. The weapon passed through the spell's barrier and drove hard against the Star Brother's ribs. All the breath *hfffed* out of him, and he flew backward to lie sprawled and writhing.

Whatever power the spell had against iron, it had

none against wood. Conan lunged again. This time the splintered end of the wagon tongue drove deep into the Star Brother's chest. His last spell died unuttered on his lips as he coughed blood onto the three plaits of his beard, looked for one last time at the sky, and lay still.

Conan had to lean on his weapon for a moment to keep from falling to his knees. He used that moment to look about him.

Pougoi and Guards were swarming all over the wagon circle, making sure that dead men and notmen stayed dead. A few were binding prisoners. Conan was glad to see that the discipline of the Guards was holding. Even the newest recruit could call himself a veteran and a soldier after this day.

Thyrin leaped onto a wagon next to Conan, then jumped down beside the Cimmerian. Cleansing his tribe's honor seemed to have taken twenty years from Wylla's father.

"Marr lives!" he shouted. "He will not pipe again, but he lives!"

"Good," Conan said. The word did not come strangely to his lips, even though he was speaking of a sorcerer who was living instead of dying.

"See Marr to safety," Conan said. "When Syzambry learns that we are in his rear, he will be desperate. I want us ready to meet him before then."

Though the new recruits might call themselves veterans and soldiers now, there would be more fighting before they could call themselves victors.

Count Syzambry was bearing more and more to his left. The ground helped him. So did the fight the royal host was making directly to his front. Most of all, the one messenger who had returned from the left had said that the royal flank was open.

But what was he seeing to his rear? The mist and the trees as before, but also running men. Men garbed like Pougoi warriors, and others like his own levies.

He saw a warrior leap from a stump onto the back of a dismounted man-at-arms. Mail was no proof against strong arms that jerked a head back or a sharp dagger drawn swiftly across a bare throat.

"Treachery!" the count screamed. "The Pougoi are turning against us! Kill the Pougoi!"

He hoped that enough of the loyal men in his rear yet lived to hear him and obey. Otherwise, he had the tribesmen and—gods deliver him!—the Star Brothers squarely behind him.

Syzambry spurred his horse. He was a light burden so that even after a long fight, the roan bore him forward rapidly.

His swift movement drew the eye of a tall, black-haired man who had stepped unseen from the shelter of the trees.

Aybas needed the boulder at his back that he might stand. Soon he would be unable to stand even with its aid. He had two sword wounds to match against the five men he'd slain this day, and one of those wounds would ere long send him to join the slain.

A bear reared itself before Aybas. Had the magic of the piper or the Star Brothers sent the animals of the forest into the battle on one side or another?

Aybas sat down. He could not run from the bear even if it were a foe. Sitting gave him a moment's clear vision. He saw that the bear was Captain-General Decius's banner and that Mistress Raihna held it.

"Lord Aybas!" Decius called. "Be at ease. We have

brought up men to join yours. The flank is safe. You bought us the time to make it so. Lord Aybas!''

Decius's voice took on a questioning note as he called the name several times more. The man so addressed did not hear him. He heard instead his mother, calling him by his birth name.

"Peace, Mother," he said. "Peace. I am coming."

Conan measured the space of open ground between himself and Syzambry. He also counted the archers in sight.

The sum of both was good. Conan flung his sword-belt aside but wasted no time removing his mail. It would not slow him enough to matter.

Then he hurled himself out of the trees, his long legs devouring the ground. He drove into the rear of Syzambry's guards before any of them knew that an enemy was at hand.

Then he leaped. He leaped onto the rump of the count's horse, and one hand snatched at the reins. The other arm went around the little count's throat.

"Ride toward the Silver Bear or I'll have your wind here and now!" he commanded.

Syzambry raised both hands, but one of them held a dagger. Conan dropped the reins and gripped the count's mail-sleeved arm, twisting fiercely. The count gasped and the dagger fell.

But the Cimmerian was alone in the midst of enemies. The disarmed count might be a shield against archery, but the sheer weight of numbers—

It was the sheer weight of numbers that prevailed as the Silver Bear rolled forward. Conan saw Raihna striding beside Decius and holding the banner high above a head as fair as ever, if filthy and drawn from the battle. Behind the banner streamed fifty-odd of

Chienna's best fighting men, horse and foot all charging together.

Count Syzambry had no more than twenty men around him. A moment after Decius struck, he had ten. Then those ten were throwing down their weapons and raising their hands, crying for mercy.

"You may have it, but that's for the queen to say," Decius snapped. "For now, off of your mounts and down on your knees. Conan, need you fear that we would give you no trophy of your valor, that you needed to snatch this one?"

"I've a taste for gifts that will please queens," the Cimmerian said, grinning. "Think you that this will please Chienna?"

Syzambry said something more than rude. Conan tightened his grip, and the count returned to silence.

"More than likely," Decius said. "What else have you done since you and our whole flank vanished into the woods?"

Conan waited to speak, because he saw Queen Chienna riding up with her handful of Guards. She wore armor and leather breeches, and it seemed to Conan that perhaps the Border Kingdom had found its warrior-ruler after all.

Then he told of his day's work, and as he finished speaking, Thyrin came up to say that Syzambry's men were yielding. By the time the work of disarming them was done, it had begun to rain.

The rain did not silence the cries of the wounded and dying. It did hide the *chunnnkkk*! as an ax took Count Syzambry's head from his shoulders and toppled it into the mud.

It was not Conan's hand wielding the ax. He thought headsman's work beneath him but did not say so. Instead, he said that Syzambry should die at the hand of one of those he had offended and of his own land.

The head man of the peasant levies, who had lost half of his family when Syzambry burned his village, did the work well enough.

It was not beneath Conan, however, to lift Aybas's body onto the bier for the dead of the royal host. What sort of name Aybas had left behind on his travels, Conan did not know. The man would leave behind a honorable name in the land where his travels ended.

CHAPTER 20

It was just past dawn on the eleventh day after the battle, with the promise of a day perfect for traveling fast and far. Conan's own restlessness had touched his roan stallion, once Count Syzambry's mount. It was pawing the ground gently, but persistently. From time to time it raised its head and snorted at the Cimmerian as if to say, "Will you never be done with your nattering?"

Conan threw a baleful glance at his mount. He would say a proper farewell to Decius and Raihna or the beast could start the journey south without him!

"The queen spoke well of you again lat night," Decius told him.

"Indeed," Conan said. He wondered how much Decius knew of the reasons Chienna had to speak well of the Cimmerian. "I hope she's not still after having me as chief of the Guard?"

"No," Decius replied. "The gods be praised, she understands that after your ... disobedience, that would be impossible. She suggested that you share the post of royal huntsman with Marr. That will give you quarters in the palace—"

"What palace?" Conan said. All three laughed, and even the horse nickered softly. The Border Kingdom might be at peace after Syzambry's death, but peace would rebuild no ruined palaces nor pay any royal servants' wages.

That was first among the reasons Conan was departing to resume his journey to Nemedia. It was likewise the reason why he was taking little save the horse, a new sword, enough armor to discourage bandits from thinking him easy prey, and enough silver to purchase food for man and beast.

"Marr seemed willing to share the work," Raihna added. "After the betrothal ceremony, we both swore to carry the queen's offer to you. What answer shall we carry back?" She smiled as she had so often done before when she already knew what Conan would say.

"Tell her that you last saw me spurring desperately—no, I'll not insult her. Say that I cherish the honor of having served her well, which is enough reward for one like me." To lighten everyone's spirits, Conan changed the matter of their talk. "I trust that the betrothal went well enough. Thyrin held his peace?"

"He did," Raihna said. "I know not if he is truly happy with his daughter marrying merely the royal huntsman, not Marr the Piper. I do know that Wylla had words with her father two nights ago. She said, 'Marr has lost his pipes and with them, their magic. He still has what he needs to make the magic between men and women.' I do not think Thyrin has been speechless for so long since his manhood ordeal!"

"Trust Wylla to see to the heart of things," Conan said. A retired sorcerer and a wild girl from the hills were an odd match, but Conan had seen odder. Such as a warrior noble of the Border Kingdom and the daughter of a Bossonian yeoman who would now be the first lady of the realm next to Queen Chienna . . .

"You will not even stay for our betrothal?" Decius asked.

"Could you swear that Queen Chienna would not use the time to scheme some new way of keeping me here?"

"I would rather swear to fly to Dembi Castle by waving my arms," Decius replied.

"Wise of you," Conan said. "I will return for the queen's betrothal if I hear of it in time to make the journey. That I swear. I also advise you to start hunting a suitable husband for her."

"Indeed," Decius said. "We will need a man of proven valor and keen wits to stand beside Chienna. It will also be best if he is tall of stature and black-haired."

Conan's mouth opened. Decius's face was a mask, the mask of a man holding within himself so much laughter that if he let it out, he would laugh himself into a fit. Raihna looked at her betrothed and her face twisted and turned red.

Then the three of them let out all the laughter inside until it echoed from the rocks. By the time the echoes had died, Conan was spurring his horse downhill. On level ground, he let the mettlesome beast out to a full gallop, and by the time he turned to look behind him, Decius and Raihna were gone.